The Golden Isles

To Joey
Enjoy meeting
these
lovely
ladies

Carol

A Postcard to Fear

A Postcard Mystery by

Carol Tonnesen

www.postcardmysteries.com

Available on www.Amazon.com

Though based on the events occurring in and around the Georgia Coast during World War II, this mystery, the shipyard, the industrial accidents, and the characters are works of fiction. Any resemblance to actual events, people, or places is coincidental.

Have you ever wondered what it would be like to step into a postcard?

Imagine an adventure that begins when a postcard arrives in the heroine's mailbox inviting her to change her life. Each Postcard Mystery, like the postcards they are based on, weaves a tale of romance and mystery about places and history. In every Postcard Mystery, postcards serve as a catalyst that catapults ordinary people into unforeseen adventures. Written to appeal to individuals who believe they can change their lives, these entertaining mysteries feature true-to-life characters, who, when faced with unexpected challenges, throw caution to the wind in order to try something different, opening themselves up to mystery, adventure, and finally, love.

The Postcard Mysteries:

Rumrunner's Reef: A Postcard to a Smuggler

The Highlands: A Postcard to Deception

The Zephyr: A Postcard to a Hostage (short story)

The Fishing Bridge: A Postcard to a Traitor

The Red Bus: A Postcard to an Assassin

To Karl
You will always be my Hero

To Phyllis Heck and Ginnie Whalen
You are the two women I admire most
Thank you for being my mentors and friends

To my beloved ACS,
who after 75 years still loves Ray

Carol Tonnesen

ACKNOWLEDGMENTS

Each of us can often see a real life person in fictional characters. The young women in this book are no exception. I would like to extend my heartfelt thanks to the women of St. Patrick's Episcopal Church for sharing their memories of World War II with me. Ruth, June, Betty, Orma, Erna, and Jackie, you are truly an inspiration to us all. This is your book, your story. It is my hope that the young women in this book capture your infectious joy and curiosity in life. May you always be surrounded in abundant love.

Thank you Margaret for encouraging me with so many helpful insights. Your friendship and support speaks volumes of your love.

Barbara, thank you so much for being my lifelong friend.

My deepest thanks to Nancy for listening to me read aloud for hours on end. You are a patient and wonderful friend.

And Vestal—where would I be without your love and support? You are a most amazing woman, so gracious and loving. You have truly blessed my life. Thank you.

A special thanks goes to the wonderful staff at the Brunswick Library for allowing me access to their archives.

Prologue

Spring 1948

"*I* should have married Ray!"

After making her startling announcement, Helen gathered the full skirts of her wedding gown and fled the bridal salon. She ran until she reached the base of the Lover's Oak. Hampered by her voluminous dress, Helen struggled to climb into the comforting embrace of its broad low branches. There, hidden by thick tendrils of Spanish moss, she gave herself up to long ago memories, still sharp and clear despite the passing of time.

"I'm so sorry, Momma. I just can't go through with this wedding," Helen whispered when her mother touched her hand a little while later. Helen's voice came out flat and colorless. "I thought I could move on. I thought I could leave Ray behind in the past. But no matter how much time passes and pulls me along with it, I love Ray. I will always love him."

Chapter 1

Ray

April 1942

*C*aptain Ray Birkett stood on the beach watching the ship burning in the distance. Angered by such wanton destruction, he clenched and unclenched his fists in frustration. How he longed to strike back at the German U-boats that preyed on the vessels plying the Atlantic Ocean. He scanned the faces of the people nearby to ascertain their reactions. The unexpectedly bright light from the moon made them clearly visible. Expecting to see horror and anxiety, their expressions of outrage and fury galvanized him. These people would not stand idly by when attacked, they would strike back.

As a wounded veteran of the Battle of the Atlantic, Ray had already had his fill of war. He knew first-hand the devastation and chaos war brought to a nation, a city, a life. He'd served on several different vessels that took part in the British naval blockade of Germany. Mounting casualties of war spurred his rise to captain in the British Royal Navy. His life at sea came to an abrupt end when an enemy torpedo struck the bow of his battle cruiser, sinking it. Even now, nearly a year later, his memories of that moment remained as vivid as the scars on his leg. Though he had graduated from crutches to a cane, Ray was well aware that his limp would remain with him the rest of his life.

The Americans lining the shore on this warm April night were another story. Safely an ocean away from the raging conflict in Europe, they had not experienced the terrors of war. Standing on the beach beside the well-lighted pier in Saint Simons Island, Georgia, these people had yet to comprehend that a German submarine had just brought the war to within a few nautical miles of the United States mainland. Ray swiveled his head to take in the street lights, auto headlights, and illuminated store fronts of Saint Simons Island's main business district just beyond the pier. He wondered when it would dawn on them that any ship passing by at night would be silhouetted against the bright lights of the coastal town and therefore easy prey for a U-boat.

An explosion rocked the stricken tanker and suddenly Ray was back aboard his ship. The sound of the surf breaking on the beach sand mimicked the sound of water lapping against the hull. The night wind brought with it the smell of burning fuel oil. Wave after wave of memory crashed into him bringing the metallic taste of fear to his mouth. Ray swallowed hard, his breathing shallow. Locked in the past, he could hear the shouts of dying and injured men, sense the ship's deck listing beneath him, feel the heat of the flames licking his skin. He could scarcely breathe as remembered panic enveloped him.

Just as his peripheral vision began to narrow, someone moved into his line of vision. Ray fought hard to focus and his eyes came to rest on a young woman. Beneath a shiny mass of black hair, her angelic face was a mask of fear. She stood so still, he wondered if she was breathing. A deep felt need to protect her caused his own fear to recede into the past where it belonged.

Mesmerized, Ray couldn't tear his eyes away from her face. One look, one moment, and he knew. With knowledge as old as time, Ray understood that the sight of her changed the very course of his life. An incredible and highly inappropriate feeling of joy crept upward from his toes. Another explosion boomed across the water, taking his attention away from the lovely young woman. When he looked again, she was gone.

2

Chapter 2

Helen

*A*pril 8, 1942. Helen knew she would never forget the date. Until that day, the war had seemed far away and indistinct. Following the tragic and unprecedented sneak attack on Pearl Harbor, her life had changed very little. Certainly, she found completing her final year of high school odd since nearly all of the boys in her senior class had enlisted or been transferred to the state colleges to begin their programs of study early. The halls and classrooms echoed emptily without their energetic masculine voices laughing and joking with each other. But, otherwise, her day-to-day routine had not really been affected. Since he hadn't left Brunswick, even her brother, Richard's, enlistment had so far failed to make an impact. Although they read the front page news with detached interest, Helen and her girlfriends didn't really talk about the war. Their biggest concern and what they spent most of their time discussing what they were going to do about graduation parties and the upcoming senior dance this year. Naturally, they would be subdued affairs, without the usual long dresses and all night dancing. Helen supposed it really wouldn't matter. She and her friends would have few dancing partners.

Helen's understanding of war changed completely the instant the first explosion rocked the night. The blast jolted her awake, filling her family's modest beach house on Saint Simons Island with the sound of shattering glass. Though unsure of its cause, an unwelcome feeling of dread settled in her stomach. She heard her parents running downstairs to investigate. Her mother's voice high and shrill with

3

concern. Her father must have opened the front door because she heard people shouting in the street.

"U-boat!" yelled a man as he raced by the house on his way to the beach. "I heard the ship's distress call on my short-wave radio." He ran on before anyone could ask him any questions.

Throwing back their covers, Helen and her sister, Lilly, hurriedly pulled on clothes. Rushing downstairs, they joined their parents and brothers in the front hall. Confused and excited, they all spoke at once, not really expecting answers to their questions.

"Afton, whatever could have made such a horrible noise?" asked Helen's mother fearfully.

"Daddy, do you think it's true—what the man shouted about the U-boat—I mean?" asked Helen.

"U-boat? U-boat? Afton, do think the Germans are making a landing?" her mother asked, her voice shaking with fright. She clung to her husband's arm and swayed alarmingly.

"Now, Enid, calm down. We don't know what is happening. There's no sense you jumping to conclusions." Afton Stevens comforted his wife, holding her close, patting her back. She pressed herself against his tall form in search of protection.

"Germans! I want to see the Germans!" shouted Helen's younger brother Mickey. Heedless of the glass strewn on the floor, in his slippers, he ran to the window in hopes of spotting the enemy.

"Mind the glass, Mickey," said his mother automatically. "Afton, are the Germans making a landing on Saint Simons?" Enid Steven's voice quaked with fright.

"No Enid—we're much too far away for a German submarine to be in the area. They'd have to cross the entire Atlantic Ocean," soothed her husband.

"But the man shouted the word 'U-boat'."

"It's all right, Enid. I'll go and find out what is happening." He gripped her hands in an attempt to move away from her.

Home on leave and excited at the prospect of seeing a U-boat, Helen's older brother, Richard, could hardly contain his eagerness. Oblivious to his mother's distress, he asked, "Can I go with you to the beach to investigate, Dad? Can I?"

Afton glared at his son when his wife began wailing anew.

"Oh Afton! If it is a German submarine, it's not safe to go to the beach!" she cried. "Who knows, the explosion we heard might be Germans shelling the island! Listen! I think I hear gunfire!"

"Enid, calm down. There's no gunfire outside," Afton urged, his voice calm, steady, and reassuring. "And Richard, think about what you're saying. Even if they could get close enough, why would the Germans want to come ashore on Saint Simons Island? They'd go for some place more important like New York City, Washington D.C., Charleston, or even Jacksonville."

"But what about the explosions? What could cause that? They must be shelling the beach! Look at our beachfront windows. All the glass has been blown out of them." With the confidence of the young and newly enlisted, Richard announced, "I'm going down to the pier to find out what's happening."

"Afton! Don't let him go alone!" cried his mother.

"Don't fuss, Enid. I'll go with him."

"Daddy, can I go too? *Pleeeeease*, can I go?" begged Helen's younger brother, Mickey.

"We should all go with you, Afton. We need to stay together and not get separated." Surprising them all and with visible effort, Enid Stevens straightened her dress and opened the front door.

Less than fifteen minutes later, Helen and her family stood speechless on the beach near the Saint Simons pier, staring at the flames that outlined a ship against the night sky. War had come to the Golden Isles in spectacular fashion.

Nauseous with fear, Helen listened to scraps of conversation as it floated around her.

"It's the *Oklahoma*," someone said. "She's been hit just below her waterline."

"Why is the ship surrounded by a halo of flames?"

"It's an oil tanker. That's oil seeping onto the ocean that you see burning."

"Those poor men. If they live, they'll be horribly burned."

"The Coast Guard's going out to see if they can rescue any survivors."

"What was that shooting I heard earlier? It sounded too big to be small arms gunfire," asked someone else.

"The U-boat must have surfaced and fired at the tanker to sink her."

"Why not launch another torpedo?"

"The U-boat wouldn't want to waste torpedoes if they can sink her with cannon fire. Submarines can only carry so many torpedoes."

"Do you think they'll shoot at us here on the beach?" At this question, everyone in the vicinity of the speaker took an involuntary step backward and looked around for shelter.

"How close to shore do you think that U-boat can come?" asked someone, suddenly aware of their vulnerability on the beach.

"Well, there's that sand bar protecting us. 'Course it depends on how big the sub is."

"Do you think it's still out there?"

"Do you think there is just one U-boat working alone? Could more German ships be nearby?"

"Do you think they'll attack and land?"

Terrified by the prospect of a German landing, Helen could hear her own heart beating wildly in her ears. Her chest constricted to the point that she could barely take a breath. Unconsciously, she reached for her mother's hand. She gripped it so tightly, Helen was sure the bones would break.

Out to sea, another explosion rocked the night. Thunderstruck, the onlookers on the beach took a moment to process that only a few miles to the south, a second ship had been sighted and torpedoed less than an hour after the first. Unimaginable—not one, but two tankers burned off the Georgia coast—both torpedoed by a single German submarine. The night sky glowed an eerie red as the flames consumed the ships. Afraid to as much as blink, Helen stared out to sea at the two beacons of firelight burning brightly in the near distance. Two ships in one night! The lightly armed Coast Guard boats would be powerless against such firepower. How could the men aboard the two ships be saved?

An explosion ripped through the dying tanker and rolled through the night air. Stunned, Helen realized that war had arrived in her hometown in breathtaking fashion. Helen had always thought that this war, like the last one, would take place somewhere else—over there—certainly not off the coast of Georgia. She hadn't even known that a German submarine could travel the great distance separating Europe and the United States. And if a submarine did, could battleships and bombers be far behind?

Chapter 3

Ray

*A*s an emissary for the Great Britain's Royal Navy, Ray's duties included visiting a number of army and naval stations in the United States to give informational lectures on conditions in Great Britain. Ray was glad of the work; his wounds would never allow him to rejoin his unit. At least he could help by preparing the Yanks for the time when they would join the battle.

On Saturday evening, April 11th, Ray entered the high school auditorium. As part of their bond drive, earlier in the week, Brunswick's town council had asked him to speak about his experiences in London during the Blitz. A war bond fundraising dance, held in the gymnasium, would follow his presentation.

Ray fidgeted on the stage, waiting for things to get started. He never liked speaking to an audience. He was a man of action, now side-lined by his injuries. The chairs in the auditorium were nearly full and the large crowd maintained a steady hum of conversation. Restlessly, he watched people entering the main door of the auditorium. Ray sat bolt upright in his seat when a raven-haired young woman paused on the threshold of the room. Seeing her standing there looking so apart from the others caused his heart to catch in his throat. The young woman from the beach hadn't left his life after all. Ray stared at her, transfixed. He had not expected to see her again. Yet here she was.

His glimpse of her at the beach had only given him a taste of her beauty. Now, under the muted auditorium lights, he drank in the sight of her. If there were any service men in the audience tonight, she would leave no doubt in their mind about why they were fighting this war. Thick, shiny, black hair tumbled in waves over her shoulders and down her back. She was taller than he remembered. A frisson passed through him at the thought of how neatly she would fit in his arms, her height complimenting his six-foot two-inch frame. Her emerald green sleeveless frock accentuated her narrow waist and statuesque figure. Her sparkling dark eyes stood out against her creamy, nearly white, complexion. She had a hint of pink flush on her cheeks. Even standing still, she exuded vitality and intelligence.

The loud tap, tap, tap of a finger against a microphone brought Ray back to the present. He moved mechanically to the podium and following a smattering of applause, he found her face in the audience. Their eyes met and held. In hers, Ray could see hope. Hope for a brighter future. Hope for those fighting this war. Hope for him.

Suddenly Ray realized that his prepared speech didn't say what needed to be said. He cleared his throat and set his notes aside, allowing his words to come from his heart. After the first few hesitant sentences, the audience melted away and Ray spoke only to the girl with the deep brown eyes and raven hair. As if mesmerized, their gaze remained locked during his entire speech.

"Edmund Burke once said; 'for evil to triumph all that is necessary is for good men to do nothing.' Many good men are now engaged in an epic battle against evil. There are those who speak of the virtues of war— courage and hope for the future. What is courage but ordinary people doing extraordinary things. When people call me a hero and say I showed great courage during the Battle of the Atlantic, I tell them that I was just doing my job. Most heroes don't have a choice; they just do the best they can under the circumstances.

Me, I was lucky enough to get through it. That's the way I look at it. People ask me if I was afraid. My answer is yes. Fear was a constant companion out on the water. Like dozens of my fellow seamen, I kept it at bay by doing what I had to do. At the time, all I asked was that when I was put to the test, I would acquit myself well.

Hope for the future is what all of us need at times like these. We all need the courage to do the best we can. If we have hope for the future, we can all find the hero in ourselves. We must never allow ourselves to do nothing. We must never allow evil to triumph. We must hold on to hope..."

Later, Ray couldn't recall a word he said. He could, however, describe every feature of the dark-haired, dark-eyed girl.

After what seemed to Ray to be much too long a time, his host signaled to him to wrap up his question and answer session that followed his brief presentation. Abruptly, he finished his sentence and relinquished the microphone. Lecture over, duty done, Ray ignored the questions coming at him from all sides and walked as quickly as his game leg allowed straight toward the raven-haired beauty. She stood near the doorway where he had first seen her as if waiting for him. When he reached her, she smiled a shy, disarming smile.

"Hello," Ray began with a shaky breath. "My name is Captain Ray Birkett."

She laughed delightedly and pointed at the poster announcing his name and presentation title. "Yes, I'm well aware of who you are, Captain Birkett. How do you do? I'm Helen Stevens."

Helen extended her gloved hand and he grasped it like a lifeline. Now that he was in her presence, Ray couldn't seem to speak. He swallowed hard. She stared at him quizzically. Above the noise of the congested hallway, he heard the sound of the band playing in the distant gymnasium. Though they were nowhere near the dance floor, Ray stammered, "Miss Stevens, may I have this dance?"

Again, her laughter sparkled in the air. He liked the sound of her laugh, the way it wrapped him in its comfortable warmth. Above a perfect smile, her eyes twinkled delightfully. Before she could respond, an ensign approached and saluted.

"Captain Birkett, Admiral Jarabek requests your presence, sir."

"In a moment ensign—" Ray snapped. He could hardly tear his eyes away from Helen to answer the man.

"I'm supposed to take you to him immediately, sir. It's a matter of great importance."

"So is this ensign, so is this." Ray smiled at Helen.

"Sir, Admiral Jarabek requests your presence now," the ensign repeated.

The ensign's grave expression left no doubt in Ray's mind that this statement was true. His soldier's training rose to the surface and he unconsciously straightened his posture in response to the command.

"But Captain Birkett, what about our dance?" asked Helen softly, her eyes holding his.

Yes, thought Ray, what about their dance? Never had he wanted to dance with anyone as much as he wanted to dance with Miss Helen Stevens. He stared into her eyes picking up the threads of his hopes and dreams, weaving them into his future. Ray reached for her hand.

"I said in a moment, ensign," Ray said in a voice brooking no argument.

In one fluid movement, Ray handed his cane to the surprised ensign and took Helen into his arms. It was as he thought it would be; she fit perfectly. Stars shining in their eyes, they began to sway to the strains of *I'll Be Seeing You* right there in the hallway. People smiled encouragingly at them and gave them room. It didn't matter that they could barely hear the distant music. It didn't matter that his steps were hampered by his injuries. It was enough just to be in each other's arms. He pulled Helen close against his body and savored her. For the first time since the sinking of his battle cruiser, Ray felt strong, whole, and hopeful. Her eyes dared him to believe in forever.

At the end of the song, the ensign cleared his throat loudly. Helen lifted her head off Ray's shoulder and gazed into his eyes.

"Are you trying to memorize my face, Captain Birkett?" she asked, a smile playing on her lips.

For a moment, Ray was tempted to say something flippant but the look on Helen's face told him that how he answered her question would be very important to her. Instead of making a glib comment, he told her the truth. "I already have."

Chapter 4

Helen

$\mathcal{C}$aptain Birkett squeezed her hand, released it, and followed the ensign down the hallway. Abruptly, he turned, his head visible above the people separating them. He caught her eye and shouted, "Miss Stevens, what are you doing for the rest of your life?"

Before she could answer, the crowd swallowed him up. "Spending it with you," Helen whispered to herself.

"What was that all about?" asked Helen's closest friend, Hazel Ann, her pretty face alive with curiosity.

"I don't really know," responded Helen. She felt slightly dazed, as if she had just woken up from a nap. Suddenly, the sights and sounds of the people around her threatened to overwhelm her. Would she be seeing Captain Ray Birkett in all the old familiar places like the song said?

"Well, you better come up with an explanation. Your momma's going to have a hizzy fit when she hears that you've been dancing with a complete stranger in the hallway of the high school."

"Like Momma'd be any happier if you danced in the hallway of the high school with someone you know," said Helen's younger sister, Lilly.

"And it won't matter that you were dancing with a man who looks just like Gregory Peck in the movies," added Avis Lou, another of Helen's friends.

"Tall, dark, and handsome," sighed Hazel Ann.

"Oh, Helen, you're so lucky!" exclaimed Lilly, her voice tinged with envy.

"She won't think she's so lucky when her momma gets ahold of her," laughed Hazel Ann.

"Oh, will y'all quit talking about my momma!" Helen didn't want anything to disturb the pleasant sensation that lingered on her skin after having been held by Captain Birkett. Without realizing it, she began to move slowly in a circle, mimicking the steps from their dance.

"Well will you look at her," snickered her sister. "She's still dancing with the dashing captain."

Helen stopped dancing and put her hands on her hips. She glared at her younger sister.

"Helen, don't you go and get upset with Lilly. We all saw you making eyes at Captain Birkett all during his presentation. I declare, he never looked at anyone else," said Hazel Ann.

"Helen, is that you?" said a masculine voice behind her.

"Richard!" Helen was relieved to see her older brother. She knew the instant he appeared that at least Hazel Ann would switch her focus away from Captain Birkett.

"Why, hello Hazel Ann," said Richard. He flushed deeply when Hazel Ann flashed him a tiny smile.

It startled Helen to realize that her brother was actually blushing.

"Hello Richard. You look very handsome in your uniform," Hazel Ann said shyly. She stared at her feet and twisted her handkerchief in her hands.

Richard had left college at the end of the fall term and volunteered for the army. Having completed basic training, he was now assigned to radar training school at the Navy Air Station on Saint Simons Island.

Helen had to admit that his uniform flattered his athletic physique. No wonder Hazel Ann was tongue-tied.

"Richard, what did you think of Captain Birkett's speech?" asked Avis Lou. She and Helen were used to dealing with Hazel Ann's shyness around Richard.

"I found it very interesting. He's given us all a fine example to look up to. I only hope that when I face danger like he did that I can respond in kind," Richard responded gravely.

Helen thought that Hazel Ann would swoon right there in the hallway. She half-hoped she would. A good swoon would make sure no one would think anything of her dance with the handsome Captain Birkett. Helen crossed her fingers and watched Hazel Ann sway slightly. But, it was not to be. Her brother put a steadying hand under her friend's elbow.

Suddenly Helen realized the difference between Captain Birkett and the boys she'd known so far in her brief life. Like her older brother, Captain Birkett exuded a quiet power. Each of them had taken and passed some crucial test. Where other men had to trumpet what they knew or bluster or posture, they didn't have to prove a thing to anyone.

"May I escort you to the dance, Miss Hazel Ann?" Richard asked politely.

Hazel Ann gazed adoringly at Richard and nodded.

"What's she going to do when he gets shipped overseas?" whispered Avis Lou when the couple moved away.

"I don't know. It's not like they've declared their intentions or anything," said Helen.

"Your brother has been sweet on Hazel Ann for years. Everybody in town knows their intentions. How could they not, whenever those two get together, it's like the rest of us don't exist."

Chapter 5

Ray

*R*ay stared out the window of the car as it rolled through the thick, humid darkness. If he concentrated hard enough, he could still feel the warmth of Helen's breath on his cheek. Why had fate torn her from him so abruptly?

"If you don't mind my saying so Captain, the way you were dancing right there in the hallway and all, you seem pretty hung up on that girl," ventured the ensign after they had driven a dozen or so miles in silence.

"I'm going to marry her," Ray announced with conviction.

"Marry her?" the ensign responded incredulously. "Didn't you just get here from England? Gee whiz! You, Brits, sure do work fast. You just met her and now you want to marry her! Are you sure you have got the right timing? The right place? Hell, begging your pardon sir, are you sure you've got the right woman?"

The right woman. Yes, Ray was sure Helen Stevens was the right woman for him. He remembered how she fitted so comfortably in his arms. He remembered how strong, whole, and hopeful he had felt. Yes, he knew he definitely had the right woman. He couldn't do anything about the time and the place. In the meantime, he had to report to Admiral Jarabek in Jacksonville.

"She's a woman worth falling in love with," said Ray more to himself than to the man beside him in the car. "Say ensign—I'm sorry—I don't remember your name."

"Ensign Wayne Donaldson, sir."

"Ensign Donaldson, would you mind doing me a big favor?"

"What's that, sir?"

"Can you get a note to my girl? I don't know when I'll return to Brunswick."

"Sure."

"I don't know her address, just her name; Helen Stevens."

"You don't know—" exclaimed Ensign Donaldson. Something in Ray's face told him he'd gone far enough. He amended his sentence. "That's okay, sir. If she lives in Brunswick, I'll find her. It's a small town."

"Thanks. Do you have anything to write on?"

"Look in the glove compartment, there might be something in there, sir."

Ray used a small flashlight to search the glove compartment. He finally unearthed the stub of a pencil and an unused postcard. He grimaced at the sight of the postcard. It wasn't one he would have chosen. He couldn't imagine any woman being thrilled to receive a postcard of men loading cargo on a ship. However, given the events of April 8th and 9th, perhaps a ship was appropriate. He held the flashlight under his arm while he wrote his note to Helen.

Chapter 6

Helen

"*H*elen, please come in here," called her mother from the kitchen. "We need to talk about last night, young lady."

Helen braced herself for her mother's lecture. Past experience told her that her mother would be more than a little perturbed about Helen's dance at the fundraiser. Reluctantly, she walked into the kitchen. In the background, on the radio, static crackled and hissed. The announcer's voice faded in and out as he reported the war news. "*We switch you now to our correspondent in London...Go ahead London...London here. News is scarce for military reasons. Unofficial sources report heavy fighting taking place. The Axis counterattack has been repulsed...*"

To Helen, the man always sounded distorted and far off. Or perhaps the swishing sound accompanying broadcasts from London seemed to mimic ocean waves lapping on the beach and brought to mind the image of someone speaking under water. Whenever she heard it, Helen thought about the mighty Atlantic that once was enough to separate a warring Europe from her peaceful life in the United States. And then she would remember the night the U-boat attacked. Now, she understood that an enemy invasion presented a real threat.

These days, the radio in her home was never silent. Helen couldn't help but think that listening to the war news made her high-strung mother even more nervous and fretful than usual. So much tension! As the gruff-voiced announcer relayed more and more bad news, Helen felt a wave of sympathy and understanding toward her mother. What must it be like for a mother to worry about the safety of her son in battle? Helen remembered how secure she had felt in Captain Birkett's arms. Would she ever feel that safe again?

"Momma, why do you listen to the war news all the time? It upsets you so." Helen moved to turn off the radio.

"Don't switch that off! I have to know—I know each broadcast is a mix of evil and information—but, I have to know. You never know when Mr. Churchill might speak. He always makes me feel like we will win this thing." Her mother stared into space and Helen tried to tiptoe out of the room. "Where do you think you're going, young lady? And don't you try to change the subject again either. I declare I don't know what's gotten into you! I didn't bring you up to dance in the hallway of the high school with a perfect stranger! An Englishman at that! The whole town is talking about it today so don't even think of denying it!"

Since Helen had been teased unceasingly by her friends about her dance with Captain Birkett, she didn't need her mother to tell her she was the talk of the town. "Momma—how can I deny it? Last night I met *someone*, someone very special." Helen placed extra emphasis on the word 'someone', giving it a much deeper meaning. Her expression took on a dreamy quality as she danced around the room to music only she could hear.

"Helen!" snapped her mother sharply. "Stop your silly sashaying all around the kitchen and pay attention!"

"I am paying attention. I'm so happy, I just can't stop dancing." Helen hugged herself, completely oblivious to the look of displeasure on her mother's face. Helen continued to spin around slowly, wondering how on earth she could explain what happened last night to her mother. How could she possibly describe to anyone how she felt about Captain Ray Birkett? He was more than just a man she met for a few brief moments, not even the length of a dance, so much more. One chance meeting and now everything was different. She was different.

In the face of Helen's silence, her mother decided to continue. "I'm told that that young captain drew quite a crowd. But Helen, why did you dance with him? You know better than to dance with a man you haven't been properly introduced to! Young lady, you know better than to dance with a *man* at all!"

Helen knew her Momma was right; she shouldn't have danced with Captain Birkett. But she did and now everything was different. Even though she was only eighteen and an inexperienced eighteen at that, Helen knew in her heart that something momentous had taken place during the brief time Ray had held her in his arms. She sighed. Helen could hardly explain how she felt to herself, let alone to her mother. She tried again. "I'm serious, Momma. Something happened last night when I danced with Ray. It was like my heart recognized him."

Before responding, Helen's mother studied her daughter's face carefully. As if to give herself time, she rinsed her hands and dried them on a dish cloth. Finally, she could control her temper no longer. "Ray? You just met him! You haven't been properly introduced and already you're calling him Ray," cried her mother, turning her full fury on Helen. "I will not have my daughter gallivanting around with a stranger!" She gave the countertop a furious swipe with the dishcloth as if she could wipe away Helen's hopes and dreams.

Warmed by memories of Ray, Helen held her ground. She refused to let her mother's ideas about what was right and proper spoil the magic of her time with the young captain. "Momma, I've never experienced anything like it. When I walked into the auditorium last night, the first thing I saw was his face. It was as if everyone else in the room didn't exist. I couldn't take my eyes off him. During his presentation, I felt like he was speaking to me alone. All that talk about hope and courage made me want to become involved in the war effort. When he finished

I waited for him by the door. And then we danced. Momma—we danced right there in the hallway!"

"Don't worry, the whole town's made sure I know that you danced right there in the hallway. What on earth did you do that for? I thought you had better sense than that! How could you embarrass your father and me?"

"There wasn't time—he had to leave—we only had that one dance—" Tears filled Helen's eyes at the thought of her one dance. Would she see Ray again? All she knew about him was his name. How would she find him? How would she get past her mother's watchful gaze?

"Helen, it's not like you to act so rashly! What on earth has gotten into you? Are you feverish? Did you come down with something when your father allowed you to go down to the beach the other night? I swear— that man! Wait 'til I give him a piece of my mind." Helen's mother brushed her hand across her daughter's forehead.

Batting her mother's hand away, Helen cried, "Momma—you've just got to understand! Ray is different! I feel like I've known him all my life. He's the one, Momma. I know he is."

"You cannot possibly be serious! You're barely past eighteen. You're just infatuated," responded her mother, dismissing the notion. "It's not unusual for young girls to become infatuated with young men in uniform. Just look at Hazel Ann and the way she tags along after Richard. I declare, what is the world coming too?"

"Momma, you don't understand. You couldn't possibly understand," wailed Helen with all the emotion and misunderstanding that accompanies a generation gap.

For a moment, her mother's face softened and her eyes took on a dreamy faraway look. "Actually, honey, I do. I remember how your father looked in his uniform in 1918."

"Momma!"

"Don't 'momma' me," said her mother, coming back to herself. "I've seen this sort of thing before. I'm sure all you young girls thought that handsome British captain looked just like a movie star. Your aunts told me that he looked just like Gregory Peck."

Helen opened her mouth to protest, when the sound of something being slid through the mail slot in the door caught her attention. Curious and wanting to end the argument with her mother, Helen went over to pick up the postcard that lay on the floor. It was addressed to her. Her hands shook with foreboding when she read the message.

Helen

I must go.

More U-boats sighted.

Leave Brunswick Now!

Don't plan on coming back until the danger is over!

Capt. Ray Birkett

Gone. Ray was gone.

Chapter 7

Ray

"*C*aptain Birkett, thank you for joining me on such short notice."

Near dawn, Ray met Admiral Jarabek on the beach in Jacksonville, Florida. Together they watched the disturbing sight of a ship in its death throes sinking in the water off the coast. Ray worked hard to suppress the memories that welled up in him. Instead of staring at the sinking tanker, Ray studied the man in uniform standing beside him. Admiral Jarabek had the look of a man used to keeping himself fighting trim. His stern face, set in a frown, also showed he would tolerate no nonsense.

"Yes, sir, Admiral Jarabek, sir, what can I do for you?"

"Let me start by saying that I've asked for and received permission from your superiors in London to borrow you and your expertise in naval intelligence for a while," began Admiral Jarabek, his voice sharp and authoritative. "It's hard to admit, but the U.S. coastal defenses are woefully unprepared for war."

Ray wasn't sure how to respond to this admission, so he stood at attention and waited for the admiral to continue.

"At ease Captain," said Admiral Jarabek before returning to the topic foremost on his mind. "I'm sure you're well aware of the ships that sunk off of the coast of Brunswick, Georgia on April 8th with significant loss of life."

"Yes sir. I had the misfortune of standing on Saint Simons Island beach and watching the *SS Oklahoma* and the *ESSO Baton Rouge* burn off-shore," responded Ray quietly. The memory of the evening still distressed him. Ray kept his eyes focused on the admiral and away from the burning ship.

"Did you hear any of the details about the two tankers?" asked the admiral.

"According to the dispatch I read, the *Oklahoma* and the *ESSO Baton Rouge* were medium-sized oil tankers."

"Yes. Of course, unlike the military dispatches, the news media knows them only as ship No. 1 and No. 2. A single torpedo struck the starboard side near the *Oklahoma's* engine room and sunk it in about forty feet of water. The captain reported that after firing the torpedo, the sub surfaced and shelled the ship at least fifteen times. Of the thirty-eight man crew, exactly half survived. They never even knew what hit them until it was all over. The Coast Guard and some men from Brunswick and nearby Saint Simons Island rescued the seamen from the *Oklahoma* who managed to board three lifeboats. When they towed them in, I went down to the dock. The survivors looked pretty roughed up. They were covered with oil, burned, and soaking wet. The generous people of Saint Simons Island and Brunswick provided the seamen with food, clothes, and shoes."

Ray stiffened perceptibly at the words oil and soaking wet. He could remember all too well the slimy sensation caused by the mixture of oil and sea water on his skin. It would be forever inscribed on his nerve endings. He had passed a miserable cold night on a life raft in the North Atlantic with pain racking his body and the smell of oil and sea water assaulting his senses. With effort, he concentrated on what the admiral was saying.

"An hour after the attack on the *Oklahoma*, the U-boat launched a torpedo at the *Baton Rouge*, striking it on the starboard side. The two boats were only three miles apart! Even though the submariner did not fire on the ship when it surfaced, it had to be the same submarine. Losses weren't so high on the *Baton Rouge*, only three seamen died; thirty-five others made it to the lifeboats."

"Didn't I hear that the *Oklahoma* carried over four million gallons of oil destined for Britain?" asked Ray. The loss of life and precious fuel made Ray furious. Every ounce of fuel, every pound of material made a difference between life and death on the tiny island of Britain.

"Yes, it did. The *ESSO Baton Rouge* carried nearly as many gallons of oil. When the torpedo struck, the blast shattered glass in buildings as far as eighteen miles inland." The admiral shook his head in amazement. "The U-boat attacks didn't stop there. Late on April 9th, the Germans attacked again, successfully sinking another medium-sized U.S. tanker, the *Esparta*, about fourteen miles south of Brunswick. Brazen attacks by an audacious U-boat captain. Even after the first two attacks, no one—I repeat—no one thought a U-boat would be cruising these waters. We know all about the wolf-packs operating in the North Atlantic, but here—on our coast—unthinkable!"

"From what I understand, sir, a German submarine has a range of operation of over 10,000 miles. The larger U-boats operate out of the French port of Lorient." Part of Ray's job in naval intelligence involved studying the habits and attack strategies of German U-boats.

"Even so, we never expected them to venture this far west. We've always been complacent about our coastline, preferring to believe that the mighty Atlantic will safeguard us."

"That will change with these great losses," responded Ray. He understood the threat U-boats posed. Only the narrow width of the English Channel protected his own homeland.

"You're right about great losses. The *Oklahoma* carried four point four million gallons of oil. Sunk in forty foot of water. The *Baton Rouge* held three point eight million gallons of oil. Twenty-two sailors dead, dozens more injured." The admiral intoned the words like a litany, stressing each syllable. Then he roused himself. "In each case, that sub couldn't have been more than five hundred yards away! How did it manage to get so close? Those ships didn't stand a chance!" The admiral took a deep breath and a look of disgust crossed his face. He gestured at the burning ship sinking in the water off Jacksonville Beach. "Tonight, as you can see, that blasted U-boat scored another hit, the *Gulf America*. You're not going to believe this. The U-boat commander had the audacity to surface between the shoreline and the stricken vessel. He gave those on the beach quite a show while he shelled the tanker and sank it. What a spectacle that was! One of our destroyers took chase but lost the sub in deeper water."

Admiral Jarabek looked around at the people on the beach watching the last remnants of the debris flame out. He snorted in disbelief. "Don't these people realize we're at war? Black-out curtains should have gone up right after Pearl Harbor! And if not then, the events of April 8th and 9th should have convinced them of the need for one. Instead, this place is lit up like a carnival! One day, when this is all over, they'll probably want to give the U-boat commander a medal for not shooting toward the beach."

"I seriously doubt that, sir. As for the black-out, tomorrow night, things will be different."

"Captain, the East coast is sitting on pins and needles waiting for the next attack. Topographically, this entire coastline is vulnerable to attack. As of yet, no civil defense patrols have been established. Rumors are rampant. I've heard everything. Landings by German troops. U-boats being sunk. Enemy destroyers sighted. I've even heard that a U-boat was captured and bread wrappers and theater ticket stubs from Brunswick were found onboard! Next we'll be hearing that U-boats are fueling at the docks in Brunswick and Jacksonville." The admiral shook his head in vexation before continuing. "Unfortunately, one rumor is true. The enemy will attack again."

"Do you think that the U-boat will strike again soon, sir? Do you think it is the same U-boat?" Ray hadn't expected that. How had the U-boat managed to carry enough fuel and armament for multiple attacks over several weeks? Lorient and fresh supplies were thousands of miles away. The German U-boats must be refueling somewhere in the Atlantic in order to stay so long on the U.S. coast.

"Young man, though it hasn't been announced in the news, German U-boats are sinking ships all up and down the coast. I'm going to share with you some facts that most of our citizens are completely unaware of. Since January of this year, we've lost nearly eighty ships. Eighty! Add up the crewmen who perished and it's more men than the 2,400 killed or injured at Pearl Harbor. Thousands more!"

"I hadn't realized the losses were so heavy, sir," said Ray, truly amazed.

"Neither, it appears, does anyone else." Admiral Jarabek gestured at the lighted shops and homes behind them on either side. "Jacksonville Beach. The Germans sunk one of our ships right at the water's edge. Can you believe it? I'll say it again. Why didn't blackout curtains go up when the Germans declared war on us? It's as bright as day out here! Doesn't anybody realize that all an enemy submarine has to do is lay in wait beyond the shipping lanes? These lights back-light the ships and silhouette them against the night sky. Sinking the cargo ships along the coastal shipping lanes is easy as shooting ducks at a Coney Island shooting gallery!"

"Hasn't the need for a full black-out dawned on anyone? Why wasn't one declared for the entire East coast months ago?"

"The powers that be don't want to frighten the population. Moreover, local merchants know a black-out will hurt their business. Jacksonville isn't the only place lit up like a Christmas tree. It's like this up and down the coast." The admiral snorted with disgust again. "I'm glad you're here. We can really use a man like you right now."

Ray thought angrily of his leg injuries and his need for a cane. The admiral must have sensed where Ray's thoughts had taken him because he said, "Never mind your war wounds, Captain. It's your brains and experience we need. You're probably the only person in the coastal Georgia and northern Florida area with anything remotely resembling recent combat experience. For the next few months, I've arranged for you to work with my staff to set up a training and reconnaissance program to coordinate our fliers with our patrol ships. Something must be done to stop the wholesale slaughter of our merchant shipping."

Admiral Jarabek went on to describe the need for planes in the air and ships at sea as soon as possible. A talented military strategist, he understood how to use their combined power to protect America's southern coastline. In the shallow waters off the coasts of Georgia and Florida, a submarine would not be able to submerge to any great depth, in some cases only deep enough to cover its conning tower. The clarity of the shallow water off-shore left the U-boat vulnerable to being spotted from the air. Effectively coordinated, planes could easily transmit the submarine's location to nearby warships. The Navy hoped the combined presence of planes and warships would deter further submarine attacks.

Over the next few weeks, Ray worked hard to share as much information about aerial bombing and the vulnerability of German U-boats as he could to the pilots who would be serving as sub-chasers. Time was of the essence. Two more freighters, the *Leslie* and the *Korsholm*, were sunk off Cape Canaveral on the 13th. Six days, six ships, one U-boat. Ray found the numbers discouraging. He knew Hitler's fleet would refuel the submarine somewhere in the open ocean just out of reach of the U.S. air and naval forces. The question now was: when would the U-boats be back and where would they strike next?

Chapter 8

Helen

May 1943

*"W*elcome home honey!"

Upon seeing her father, Helen squealed with delight and leapt into his arms.

"Daddy! I didn't expect you to be at the train station to meet me today! Shouldn't you be at work?"

"Hello Doll. I couldn't let my favorite daughter get off the train by herself, now could I?" Afton Stevens gave his oldest daughter, who looked like a feminine version of himself, a tight hug. Helen liked that he still called her by his pet name, Doll, despite her having grown up.

"Daddy, I know I'm not your only favorite daughter!" Helen chided. She reached over and squeezed Lilly's hand. "It looks to me as if the whole Stevens clan showed up to greet me."

Besides Helen's mother and sister, gathered around her were all of her aunts, uncles, and brothers. Helen ran from person to person, hugging and greeting each one.

"Richard!" Helen laughed with delight when he stepped out from behind her uncle, Eugene Clay. Her brother looked so much like her father, she nearly gasped. "I declare, Rickard, you look just like Daddy!

I can't believe you're here too! Shouldn't you be at camp or something?"

"I asked my commanding officer for a couple of hours away from base so that I could be here to greet you. It's been a year after all."

"That's wonderful." Helen gave her brother a huge hug. "I'm so happy to see you!" She was too. With the country at war, she never knew from one moment to the next when she would see him again. Tears sprang to her eyes at the thought of not seeing him for a long, long time. She hugged him tighter and noticed her mother plucking at the sleeve of his uniform. Helen felt her heart constrict. What must it be like for her mother to see her oldest son in uniform?

"My two favorite men," breathed Helen, her eyes moving from her father's face to that of her older brother's.

"Hey! What about me?" asked her younger brother, Mickey. Blond like his mother, his eyes were full of mischief.

Helen gathered him into her arms and said, "You're my favoritist."

"That's not even a word," sulked Mickey. He pulled away, not wanting to appear pleased to see his sister.

"It is to me," answered Helen. She ruffled his hair.

"Here, let me take your bags," offered Richard. He picked them up and placed them in a small red wagon.

"What's this? Why is Mickey pulling his wagon?" Helen asked.

"We walked into town and we'll be walking back," answered her aunt, Elva Clay.

"I can't believe we've sunk this low," complained Helen's mother. She linked her arm with Richard and rearranged her face into a watery smile.

"Saves on gasoline and rubber," said Aunt Elva succinctly. "The walk will give us a nice long time to catch up on the news."

"I'll leave you to it. I've got to get back to the shipyard," said Afton. He kissed his petite blond wife on her lips before she could protest. She bit back a smile and waved him away.

"Bye Daddy. See you at dinner." Helen kissed her father's cheek.

"Don't go eating all the peach preserves before I get home, darlin'."

Helen followed her family out of the railroad station. She didn't look back. The sight of all those young soldiers and sailors made her want to cry. Once on the train, they would leave behind girlfriends, wives, children, families, parents, brothers, and sisters. She didn't want to think about what that meant.

"Well, now, tell us all about Atlanta. We haven't seen you since last year at this time," said Helen's Aunt Ora. Knowing her Aunt Ora's tendency to prattle on, Helen waited before responding. "That postcard you received, with its frightening message, certainly sent you in an unexpected direction. You fled the Golden Isles like your hair was on fire. How was your stay at Uncle Roger and Aunt Ulanalee's?"

Helen fingered the postcard from Ray that she kept in her pocket. It was never far from her heart, a reminder of their magical moment together. *'Don't plan on coming back until the danger is over!'* She could still remember the devastating effect the message had had on her. Ray gone. More ships sunk off the Georgia Coast. The unending bad news reported on the radio. Helen had felt surrounded by evil. Even now, touching the postcard brought alive the cold kernel of fear that she carried deep inside her. Like the heart-stopping moment when President Roosevelt announced that the country was at war, the sinking of the ships off the coast of her home had changed her view of life forever.

'Don't plan on coming back until the danger is over!' Well, Helen thought, she hadn't, at least not for over a year. Just before they parted, Captain Birkett had asked her what she was doing with the rest of her life. Now she knew, at least for the time being. A few weeks ago, she decided to leave Atlanta and return to Brunswick to become more involved in the war effort.

"Helen?"

Seeing her aunt's expectant expression, Helen abandoned her musing and replied enthusiastically, "Aunt Ulanalee and Uncle Roger were absolutely wonderful! I enjoyed living with them very much. They have a lovely home."

"You'll have to get used to sharing a bedroom with your sister again. After that big house and a room of your own in Atlanta, you're not going to enjoy having just half a closet and two dresser drawers," said her mother.

"Oh, Momma! I'm sure Lilly and I will get along just fine. We did before. I haven't been gone all that long," laughed Helen, glad to be home with her family.

"What did you do while you were in Atlanta?" asked Lilly, tugging on Helen's arm as they walked.

"Didn't you read my letters?" Helen shook her finger at her younger sister, a pretty blond version of herself. "Since you didn't, I've got a mind to keep my news to myself. Don't you remember, in them I told you how Aunt Ulanalee and Uncle Roger encouraged me to take courses at the university!"

"Courses normally reserved for men," added her mother disdainfully. 'In all my born days, I never heard of such a thing!"

"But Momma, the young men have all left for the war. The university has lots of classrooms to fill. I managed to complete twelve courses while working for Uncle Roger. Isn't that wonderful?"

Her mother sniffed derisively, denying Helen the affirmation she sought.

"Don't you go launching into one of your hizzy fits, Enid," interrupted Aunt Elva. "You know Roger willingly paid the tuition fees. Why he even encouraged Helen to take management courses in cost accounting, purchasing, and industrial safety.

"It's not right for a woman to be learning man's work," said Helen's mother.

"But Momma, I helped out in Uncle Roger's construction business when I wasn't in school. He's so short-handed with all the men gone. There was so much for me to learn." To avoid the inevitable confrontation with her mother, Helen searched her mind for a topic to divert the conversation away from her Atlanta experiences. "Richard, I declare you look so handsome in your uniform. How is your training progressing? Please, tell me what is going on here in Brunswick."

Richard, who enjoyed being the center of attention, spoke up right away. "We haven't seen them, but we know U-boats continue to patrol the coastal waters off Georgia and Florida. The Civil Air Patrol and the Navy work together to keep them at bay. I'll take you down to the beach, if you'd like," offered Richard. "You can still see the ships off the shores of Saint Simons Island. Plans are underway to refloat the *Baton Rouge* and the *Oklahoma* despite the gaping holes in their sides!"

"You think those ships sitting out there would serve to remind everyone here about the merchant marine's high losses. Eighty-two ships in the first five months of 1942 alone!" Helen's Aunt Elva shook her head in despair. "People didn't begin to pay attention to the need for coastal blackouts until late last summer! Merchants still grouse about how the blackout decreases their evening business. You think they'd realize there is a war on."

"I declare all this talk of war gets on my nerves. That's all that is on the radio and I won't even think about going to the moving pictures. I just can't sit through those newsreels. They're so graphic! It's enough to give a body nightmares. Helen, I don't know why you've taken a job at Brunswick's new shipyard," complained Helen's mother, returning to Helen's reason for coming home.

"Momma, I want to help with the war effort. It's important to me. Based on my coursework at the university, the shipyard hired me on the strength of my application alone. Uncle Roger's letter of recommendation described how I applied my classroom learning to improve his business practices. When the personnel director contacted me, he stressed that I am exactly the type of person they need for the Industrial Efficiency department." To herself, Helen thought, so this was where the postcard has lead, away from Ray and toward a career in a man's field. Why did it have to be one or the other?

"I don't understand why we have to have such a shipyard here in Brunswick," said Helen's mother.

"We should be proud that Brunswick was chosen because of its natural harbor," answered Richard. "Our shipyard is one of sixteen nationwide created to build cargo vessels called Liberty ships."

"Give me Liberty or give me death!" shouted Mickey with the enthusiasm of an eight year old.

"Mickey, must you keep shouting about like Patrick Henry?" asked his mother. "If we're forced to walk home from the train station, the least you can do is show a little decorum." Enid flapped her handkerchief in front of her lightly perspiring face.

"But Momma, that's why they're called Liberty ships," said Mickey, unfazed by his mother's displeasure. Enid swatted ineffectually at her youngest son. He skipped lightly out of reach before running ahead shouting, "Give me Liberty or give me death!"

Ignoring his brother's antics, Richard said, "Our shipyard is crucial to the war effort. Liberty ships are the workhorses that will keep the overseas supply lines open between the U.S. and Great Britain. The vessels need to be constructed at a feverish rate in order to replace the millions of tons of ships and cargo lost to enemy U-boat encounters."

"But why does Helen have to work there?" asked her mother.

"Momma, that's the point," stated Helen. "I am finally going to get my chance to help in the war effort doing something else besides organizing bond drives and collecting scrap metal. As important as those two activities are, they don't feed the desire to help that has burned in me ever since I watched the *SS Oklahoma* and the *ESSO Baton Rouge* blaze on that warm April night."

Chapter 9

Ray

*O*ver a year had passed since his first visit to Brunswick. Though his work as an emissary for the British government had taken him all over the United States in the last twelve months, he would soon be back in Georgia's Golden Isles. Ray couldn't believe his good fortune. After over a year's separation, over a year spent in silence, he would soon be near Helen Stevens.

Ray had never forgotten the raven-haired beauty he had danced with for a few heart-breakingly brief minutes on that April night. She lingered in his thoughts and haunted his dreams. Whenever he thought he caught a glimpse of her in the crowd, he would hum a few bars of the song they danced together. *I'll be seeing you in all the old familiar places. That this heart of mine embraces...* Ray tried to imagine what it would be like to meet her again after such a long time. Would she even remember the wounded naval captain she danced with in a crowded hallway?

He often wondered how Helen had responded to his postcard—if she had even received it. He hoped the ensign had been true to his promise. Ray was grateful that the looming threat of German attacks on the U.S. mainland had proved unfounded. Whether or not Helen had left coastal Georgia, she had been safe enough. Still, he couldn't help but wonder if his postcard—and his brief dance with her—had changed her life in any significant way.

Ray wasn't worried about finding Helen. Brunswick wasn't a large town and he knew her last name. No, finding her was the least of his worries. Finding time for her, now that would be an issue. At Admiral Jarabek's insistence, Ray had been assigned to liaise with American ship builders. Since the original design for the Liberty ships originated in Britain, apparently the admiral felt Ray would be of some use to the project. Ray greatly doubted he would add a single useful idea, but he jumped at the chance to return to Brunswick.

"Welcome, Captain Birkett. It's good to see you again after so long."

Admiral Jarabek's greeting included a warm handclasp and a clap on the back. The back slap was so forceful that Ray had to use his cane to steady himself. He couldn't help but wonder about all this bonhomie and goodwill. He was a naval officer with a bum leg for heaven's sake, not a ship builder. Ray forced a smile to his lips and said, "Yes sir, it has been a while."

"Captain, you need to develop a better poker face. Your eyes give you away. I can tell that you're wondering why I've insisted that you join me in this backwater coastal town."

"Well, Admiral, to tell you the truth, yes sir, I am wondering why you've chosen me for your project," admitted Ray. "I may know a lot about submarine strategy, but, with all due respect sir, I don't know anything about ship construction."

"I can understand you might question your purpose, but I feel certain you are the right man for the job. With your experience at sea and your training in naval intelligence, you understand ships as well as submarines. You know the lingo. I watched you during those training sessions we held last year. Men like you. They gravitate to you. You have a knack of winning people's confidence. I've also noticed how quick thinking you are. The job I have in mind for you involves putting those traits to good use."

"You certainly have aroused my curiosity, sir."

"Captain, do you remember our discussion about the need for black-outs along the coast?"

"Yes sir."

"They are in place now. We've also begun to protect our shipping along the coast through the use of convoys. The oil companies whose ships had been sunk initiated that effort. The ships also put into port at night if possible. German submarine sightings and the sinking of ships have been greatly reduced. Unfortunately, our nation is facing another threat, one that also threatens the future of your country, too."

"Sir?"

"Espionage. Spies. Sabotage." The admiral let the words hang in the air for a moment before continuing. "I'm sure you've read the news about the most publicized attempt. On June 12th 1942, a German U-boat landed spies at Amagansett, New York. On June 16th, their accomplices came ashore at Ponte Vedra Beach. In case you didn't know, that's just south of Jacksonville Beach where you and I first met. The teams of saboteurs brought with them enough explosives and incendiary bombs to wage a two-year terrorism campaign. Their mission included the destruction of hydroelectric plants, key railroad bridges and stations, and important manufacturing facilities. We're lucky to have caught them."

"Yes, sir." Ray remembered reading about the ongoing saga in newspapers nationwide. Two of the men were still in prison; the other six had been executed in August of 1942.

"These are dangerous times we live in," continued Admiral Jarabek. "We have to ask ourselves whether or not other spies have landed on our coast. And if so, where are they operating? For all we know, the Germans are planning a raid similar to the Canadian's raid on the German-occupied port of Dieppe."

Charles grimaced at the mention of the Dieppe raid. The invasion, intended to determine whether or not the Allies could seize and hold a major port in France, had ended in disaster. Without Allied artillery support, sixty percent of all the troops had been killed, wounded, or captured by the Germans. Ultimately, Dieppe had been a bloody fiasco.

"That brings me to your job," continued Admiral Jarabek, unaware of the direction of Ray's thoughts. "We have reason to believe that saboteurs are at work at our Brunswick shipyard. Recently, a number of accidents have occurred there that have delayed ship construction."

"But, Admiral, what could I possibly do to help?" Ray protested.

"Captain, like many of us taking on new assignments, you'll learn." Admiral Jarabek gave Ray the full force of his penetrating gaze. "I'm a member of the U.S. Maritime Commission. My job is to ensure that America gets the ships she needs as quickly as possible. That means preventing sabotage. And Captain, you're exactly what we need, an outsider who can observe the happenings at the shipyard with new eyes. Fortunately for us, the shipyard is building ships for both the U.S. merchant marine and the British Navy. No one will question your presence at the shipyard."

Admiral Jarabek shuffled some papers on his desk. Finding the one he was looking for, he added, "You'll be able to recognize the British ships because all the ship's names begin with SAM, which stands for Superstructure Aft of Midships. Let's see, there is the *Samdee*, the *Samalness*, the *Samfairy*—where do they come up with these names? However, I digress. We've set you up in a supervisory position as an on-site representative overseeing the construction of the ships bound for the British fleet. That way, you will have complete run of the facility. The position gives you the right to study any and all aspects of ship construction. You'll report directly to me and liaise with General Dirner. Your primary contact at the shipyard is the head of the Industrial Efficiency department, Burton Dixon. With your quick mind, you'll be able to flush out any saboteurs. With your military training, you'll be able to handle them effectively."

Ray found himself speechless. He couldn't imagine knowing enough about ship building to spot an act of sabotage if it appeared right in front of him.

"Like I said before, Captain, you had better work on that poker face of yours," said Admiral Jarabek, with a grim smile. "That will be all, Captain Birkett."

Chapter 10

Helen

"*H*elen, dear, why do you want to work so hard?" her mother demanded when Helen returned home from a long day at the shipyard. "More importantly, why do you want to do a man's job? Why don't you work for the Red Cross or participate in War Bond drives? The Red Cross needs people to roll bandages and make up care packages. Of course, you can always knit scarves, hats, and mittens for the troops, or you could become a USO volunteer hostess."

Helen found her mother's suggestions limiting to say the least. Until she went to college, Helen couldn't help feeling out-of-place and out-of-step with the other women who wanted a home and a family at a young age. She wanted—no craved—so much more. She had found it too, in the topics covered in her classes. Her mind had come alive with possibilities. She felt as if she'd found herself, found the best use of her talents. Each day, at work in the shipyard, Helen achieved a sense of clarity and purpose. Her metamorphous from confused high school student to competent professional had begun. Her life seemed both strange and familiar at the same time.

Helen rarely shared these sorts of thoughts with her mother. Many an argument had ended in one or the other of them leaving the room greatly upset. Helen reined in her emotions and responded evenly.

"But, Momma, I like my job and I'm a USO hostess too. A lot of the women work all day at the shipyard and then change from their coveralls to their party dresses to go to Camp Stewart to serve as USO hostesses in the evening."

In response, her mother gave one of her characteristic sniffs of disdain. "I don't know why you'd want to be a USO hostess and dance with all those Yankee boys, anyway."

"Now, Enid, leave the girl be. I declare, sometimes I think you won't be happy no matter what Helen does," interrupted Helen's Aunt Ida, who had been sitting quietly nearby. Since her aunt normally kept her thoughts to herself, her statement startled both women into silence. Having their full attention, she continued, "Young people nowadays all want to do their part and perform essential war work. Helen's got quite a bit of education to help her. Let her use it. At least she's here in Brunswick unlike so many of the other young women. Just think, she could have run off and left Brunswick for good. I declare, Enid, the way you go on, sometimes I think it would make you happier if she joined the WAVES or the WACS and went overseas."

"Certainly not! But, surely Helen can find a job with a little more glamour. Good heavens, she wears coveralls at work! Imagine, a Stevens walking around with grease-blackened hands! I've heard about the long hours the women at the shipyard work. Why any woman would want to do a man's job requiring so much physical effort, I don't know. And they work out-of-doors! Think of the heat and humidity! The shipyard's been built on the edge of a marsh, for heaven's sake! I shudder to think of the millions of black gnats ready to eat you alive!"

"Momma, my job is important! Liberty ships transport tanks, guns, supplies, and even planes to our fighting men. Unless they have the supplies provided by our merchant marines on the Liberty ships we build, they can't fight the war."

"But, you're working in the Industrial Efficiency department," countered Helen's mother. "How could that possibly help?"

"Momma, that's where my university education can be most effective."

"There you go again with your university education speech. I declare, you think you were the only woman in Brunswick who ever went to college," retorted her mother. "Why I ever let your Uncle Roger talk me into letting you go to Atlanta, I'll never know."

Helen bit her tongue and didn't rise to the bait her mother was so adept at throwing out. "The shipyard must build ships quickly to replace the ones lost at sea in enemy action. My job is to make sure our employees are working as quickly and effectively as we can without sacrificing safety or quality."

"You sound as if you're repeating a mantra," complained her mother.

"Well, it is sort of a mantra—an important mantra. Do you realize that if things go along as they are now; it will take us nearly 300 days from the laying of the keel to launch to build a Liberty ship? Ships are being sunk by the dozen every week! We can't replace them at a rate of one per year! That's ridiculous! Using innovative methods copied from mass production, our department hopes to make improvements so that we can build a ship in as little as two months! Imagine 60 days instead of 300! We can't do that unless we find ways of doing the work better. I'm part of the team that is going to make it happen. Don't you understand that I want to be useful?"

"I still don't see why—" Helen's mother's voice faltered here and her face took on an intolerant look. She changed tactics again. "Keep in mind, Helen, men don't want intelligent and clever wives, they want charming ones."

"But Helen is charming," protested Ida to no avail.

"I didn't say she wasn't. Helen's just a bit too clever for her own good," snapped Enid.

Helen knew her mother well enough to know that further argument would accomplish little. She sighed and turned to her Aunt Ida for support.

"Now Enid, you know we Southern women need to do something! We like to feel useful. It's how we show the world we care," said Aunt Ida. "Helen needs to work at something she enjoys, something that is worthy of her talent and time. Helen is old enough to choose for herself, especially now that she's earning a salary. She's smart enough to do something that will make us all proud."

"When I was her age, I was more concerned about meeting a nice boy," said her mother, taking yet another tack.

"Enid, I seem to recall that you signed up to take nursing courses in hopes of joining the men overseas."

"That was a different time, a different war," sniffed Enid.

"Oh, Enid, was it really all that different?" sighed Aunt Ida. "Don't we all want to make a difference? To do our part?"

"Our war was supposed to be the war to end all wars! And now, here I sit waiting for my baby boy to be called up. Isn't that bad enough? Do I have to watch my beautiful little girl dress in coveralls and work at a shipyard too?" Helen's mother brought a trembling hand to her lips and stifled a sob.

"Enid, why don't you go upstairs and lie down a while? You've got yourself all worked up," Aunt Ida suggested gently.

Enid dabbed her face daintily. "I think I'll do just that."

After Enid left the room, Ida said, "Helen, honey, you've got a zest for life and it's time you went out and lived it. You've got to believe in yourself and what you want to accomplish with your skills. The route you've chosen will have many ups and downs and twists and turns. There will be times that will test your belief in your choice. Try not to take it personally; remember to enjoy the life you've chosen."

Chapter 11

Ray

"*W*elcome Captain Birkett. My name is Burton Dixon. Folks around here call me Burt. I hope you will too." The head of the Industrial Efficiency department greeted Ray with a warm handshake. Ray had to tilt his head back slightly to look up at the big man with curly jet black hair shot through with silver. It was rare that anyone topped his own six-foot-two inches.

"Thank you, sir. I'm happy to be here."

"No need to 'sir' me unless we're around the men. Remember, it's Burt." Burt smiled widely at Ray. "At Brunswick Shipyard, we believe that modern war is an industry. Everyone has an assigned and vital role to play. Our department's duty is to make sure they do their job efficiently and safely. Since you're new here, why don't we take a tour of the facility?"

Dixon handed Ray a yellow hardhat and put on his own. Emerging into the shipyard, Ray was nearly overcome by the noise and commotion. Whirring, hammering, grinding, buzzing, banging, clanging, and clanking sounds battered his ears painfully. The noises were so loud and overpowering; they blotted out all coherent thought. Ray jumped when a thunderous boom split the air. Unperturbed, Burt grinned at Ray.

"Rattles your teeth, doesn't it?" asked Burt with a broad, confident smile. "You'll get used to the sound of a large, heavy piece of metal being dropped either on the pier or on a ship."

Ray tried his best to smile back at the man, though he felt like the new kid on the block going through ritualistic hazing. They walked deeper into the cacophony of noise, eventually entering a small building that turned out to be a classroom. Ray noticed that the walls were covered with photographs.

"I see you're studying our training photos. We use these photo boards to show step-by-step the work that needs to be done," explained Burt. "For instance, these pictures show how to lay a weld. Notice this group of photos depicts what good welds look like versus this group of photos that show bad or unacceptable welds. The same photos are also posted at the job site. Everyone who sees them will know what good work looks like."

Ray studied the photographs with care. He could learn a lot from them. The information would be useful in his search for a saboteur.

"Let's start over here with this scale model of a Liberty ship." Burt led Ray away from the photographs to a large model ship. "From the one side you can see what the exterior of the ship looks like when it's complete. The other side is cut-away so you can see what they look like inside. We use this model for training our employees."

Ray and Burt considered the model from all angles. The Liberty ship had long slab sides with a pointed bow and a slightly rounded stern. To Ray, it looked like a big bathtub with a lid. This was supposed to be the ship that would supply the war? It didn't look like it would stay afloat in the rough Atlantic seas. Based on his next statement, Burt must have read his mind.

"They're not very elegant are they?" admitted Burt. "What they lack in elegance, they make up for in cargo space. Liberty ships are the workhorses of this war. They'll carry supplies to the men who need them. Each ship can carry about nine thousand tons of cargo. That's the equivalent of five hundred railroad box cars."

Ray whistled at this enormous amount of cargo. He studied the model more closely, this time registering the two huge cranes attached fore and aft of the mid-ship pilot house. The cut-away side of the model revealed five large cubic holds with a center engine room with a single smoke stack. The ship positively bristled with guy wires that held up everything from the communications nest fore of the pilot house to the flag pole on the stern. "Nine thousand tons? She'll really hold all that?"

"That's just what the ships are designed for, but believe it or not, they often carry more."

"Very impressive."

Burt studied his face for a moment as if to reassure himself that Ray truly did find the big, bulky ship impressive. Satisfied, he shared more details about the ship.

"We hope to be up to speed soon and constructing four ships every month. Our Industrial Efficiency department tries hard to simplify the work by breaking it down into steps. It helps that each Liberty ship is built to the same specifications. They measure 441 feet in length and nearly fifty-seven feet across the beam. A Liberty ship drafts twenty-seven feet nine inches and displaces about 10,500 tons.

"That's truly a lot of tonnage. How are they powered?" Ray figured that if he understood the workings of the ship, he'd be better able to pin-point weak spots for potential sabotage. Burt was turning out to be a fount of information. Ray knew his best course of action would be to listen, watch, and learn.

"For easy operation, the engine design is relatively simple. Two oil-fired boilers generate the steam required to operate the single screw that propels the ship forward."

"How many men aboard?" asked Ray, noting on the model key areas for sabotage.

"Liberty ships are manned by civilian merchant marine seamen. A crew numbers between thirty-eight and sixty-two men."

"Are they armed?"

"From twenty-one to forty naval personnel are also onboard to operate the stern-mounted four-inch anti-submarine deck gun and the anti-aircraft guns." Burt pointed at them on the model. "Liberty ships are not well-armed and they aren't very fast, only eleven knots as a top speed. It's essential that these big crates travel in convoys."

"You said you've seen some pretty heavily loaded," said Ray.

"Yes, I've seen several Liberty ships so loaded down that they need wheels on their bottoms and someone to push them across the Atlantic," Burt said, only half joking.

"Are the ships loaded here in Brunswick?" asked Ray.

"Not usually. Sometimes a ship will dock here in Brunswick to take on things like rice and cotton, but mostly, after a Liberty ship passes her sea trials, she travels north to join convoys that are loaded in New York or New Jersey." Burt used the common language that named all floating vessels 'she'.

Outside, a siren shrieked an alarm, causing Ray to jump.

"Accident," said Burt succinctly. "Wait here. I'll be back."

Chapter 12

Helen

"*H*elen, I've got a special assignment for you," said Helen's boss, Burt Dixon, said when the injured lathe operator had been taken away. "You've heard about the safety pennant that Admiral Jarabek will award to the shipyard with the best safety record, haven't you?"

"The pennant is awarded every six months, isn't it?" she answered his question with a question.

"Yes and I want our shipyard to win it each and every time. That's where you come in. You did a fine job with those training photographs. I'm sure you'll do a great job with this next assignment."

Helen flushed with pleasure at his compliment. She knew her amazingly competent supervisor appreciated talent in members of his staff. He recognized that their abilities made him look good. He staffed the department with meticulous, quick-thinking, efficient, and discrete individuals with poise. Burt didn't seem to mind her being female. Helen worked hard to live up to his standards.

Members of the Industrial Efficiency department labored night and day to create work methods that would increase productivity, improve quality, and minimize unsafe incidents. Helen was particularly proud of the series of training photographs she had created for several of the more difficult operations. The eight by ten photos, suspended on large boards in the appropriate work area, showed each step in the process. Additional photographs, complete with arrows and text, described acceptable and unacceptable output.

"Your records show that you took safety courses in college." Burt paused waiting for her to tell him what he already knew.

"Yes, sir. I received high marks in two safety courses."

"Well, it's time that we put that knowledge to work. Our shipyard workers complete their training so quickly that a lot of times they don't absorb information critical to safety. This lack of knowledge causes our employees to make bad decisions."

"I think I understand what you mean, sir. You're referring to the man who was grinding on a piece of metal last week without wearing safety glasses, aren't you? Metal chips got into his eyes."

"Yes I am," Burt answered gravely. "There are lots of people who say it didn't amount to much. He'll be fine. All our doctor had to do was flush out the man's eyes. He'll have some inflammation for a few days but no permanent damage. They say the same thing about flash burns from the welders. What bothers me is how people overlook the other costs of these incidents."

"You mean the lost work time while the man was off the job."

"Yes and the disruption of work while others helped him to the aid station. We lost a valuable employee for several days and if it had been more serious, we could have lost him forever. He's not the only one. Remember last week when we had our first truly hot day of summer? One of our welders failed to wear his regulation equipment. A welding spark got under his collar and burned him." Burt gestured to the accident reports in his hand.

"No permanent damage, but a disruption of work and lost time while his burns were treated," responded Helen.

"Exactly. And look at what happened with this lathe operator—another avoidable launch-delaying accident. We've got to improve safety by averting even the most minor incident. We've got to prevent operator error from occurring. I'm going to appoint you safety officer for the shipyard. It will be your job to institute on the job training to stop accidents and injuries. You'll also investigate all accidents and incidents and develop methods to prevent their reoccurrence. You're smart and observant. I want your thoughts and impressions on the causes of accidents. It's a tall order I know, Helen, but you're up to the challenge."

Prevent, prevent, prevent. Burt was right. They needed to institute methods that would prevent accidents. Helen decided she'd begin her new job by inspecting the facility. As she walked around, she kept her eye open for unsafe behavior. She didn't have to look far. In the first building, Helen observed a group of men creating a makeshift ladder from a forklift and a pallet. Before she could stop them, a man climbed aboard the pallet and his companion in the driver's seat of the forklift operated the controls to elevate the forks. The pallet and the man riding on it reached a height of about four feet before he fell off. Over the noise of the forklift's engine, Helen heard the sickening scrunch when the man landed hard on his ankle.

As she helped the injured man to the first aid station, Helen couldn't help but think that her new job hadn't gotten off to an auspicious beginning.

Chapter 13

Ray

*B*urt returned to the training room and invited Ray to tour a Liberty ship. Turning away from the model, the two men walked out into the blazing summer heat. They paused for a moment to allow their eyes to adjust to the glare of the mid-day sun.

"Whew! This heat's enough to give a man the sun-grins," said Burt, mopping his brow with his sleeve.

"Sun-grins?" asked Ray.

"That's what we say around here when a person gets too much sun. The sun makes them so addle-brained that they sit around grinning like fools."

"I can see how that can happen," said Ray, searching around for some welcome shade.

From where they stood, the shipyard spread out before them, a jumble of gray and orange-painted steel. Ray looked toward the skeletons of the unfinished ships in their berths. Workers swarmed everywhere. High above, tall gantry cranes stood poised, their operators ready for the signal to dive down and pick up the required piece of steel and insert it into its appropriate place. Constructing a ship must be like building a puzzle. To Ray it seemed like all the puzzle pieces were of a variety of shapes but all the same color of gray. How would he ever sort it all out?

Over the noise of the shipyard, Burt shouted, "Brunswick shipyard has six shipways or cradles on which to lay the hulls and construct the ship from bottom up. All six shipways, ways for short, allow the ships to be launched directly into the Brunswick River at high tide. From there they are moved to the wet basin dockage for their final fittings and preparation for sea trials. The shipways are never empty. Once a ship is launched, a new keel will be laid the very next day. We've got over ten thousand workers working three shifts around the clock, seven days a week. About two thousand of our workers are female."

Ray raised his eyebrows.

"Yep, two thousand women work as welders, fitters, joiners, riggers, machinists, inspectors, and tool room attendants. They do a pretty good job. They don't know much about building ships, but they sure learn fast and work hard."

Burt walked briskly toward a group of welders working on what resembled a large tree stump. "Let's start over here in this platen." Seeing Ray's perplexed face, he added, "A platen is a sub-assembly area. To save time, we do most of the construction on the ground, creating prefabricated parts that are fitted onto the ships as required. It's one of the methods we picked up from mass production. We use a gantry crane on railroad tracks to move pieces from the sub-assembly areas to the ships."

Walking closer, Burt gestured to a hollow, stump-like object. "It's hard to recognize the parts when they're not attached to a ship, isn't it?" Burt asked good-naturedly. "This is the anchor mount, one of those holes you see on the bow of a ship. The anchor chain passes through the hole as the anchor is raised and lowered. It takes eight yards of triple welding to create."

Shielding his eyes from the spray of fiery sparks with the welding mask provided, Ray watched the woman skillfully weld the large piece. White hot welding sparks flew about like fireworks. The welder certainly knew her job; at least it looked that way to him. Ray wondered if he would ever understand ship building enough to do his own job. He held few hopes that he would be able to differentiate between work well-done and sabotage.

"I noticed the myriad of colored hard hats being worn by the workers. Why?" asked Ray.

"The helmet colors are important. Each color represents a different department. You'll need to memorize them. Riggers wear red hats; shipwrights wear school-bus yellow with a black rim. Ship fitter's are light blue. Tank-testers are tan with a black rim. Ventilator's hats are medium green. Plumbers are yellow. Marine electrician's hats are apple green," Burt rattled them off in rapid succession. Seeing Ray's confusion, he added, "There are others. I'll get you a list."

Burt led the way to a nearly completed ship. Together, they moved quickly up the gang plank and onto the Liberty ship's deck. To Ray, it felt good to be onboard a ship again, even if the ship was in dry dock. He followed Burt, trying to hear the man's on-going commentary above the noise. Once deep in the bowels of the ship, Ray was glad he had studied the cutaway model. Anyone on their first trip inside the ship could easily get lost. Burt waved at a man who was about to go up a ladder.

"William," shouted Burt. "There's someone I'd like you to meet."

The man in a yellow hardhat walked toward them.

"Captain Birkett, I'd like you to meet William Browning. William works in the Industrial Efficiency office. William, this is Captain Ray Birkett. Captain Birkett is here to observe the production of Liberty ships bound for Britain."

"Nice to meet you, Mr. Browning," said Ray as he shook the man's hand.

"Nice to meet you too. What does your job entail?"

"I'll be monitoring the ships while they are being constructed, keeping track of their progress, and filling out a lot of reports," answered Ray disarmingly.

"Sounds like a government job to me," joked Browning.

"Me too."

"I'll be seeing you around. Don't hesitate to look me up if you have questions." Browning gave a half-salute and continued on his way.

As they made their way through the different compartments, Ray couldn't help feeling as if they were being watched. Occasionally he heard sounds of footsteps starting and stopping when they did. There were other little furtive noises that didn't seem normal for a ship. Several times Ray turned around and studied the shadows behind them. Once he pointed a man out to Burt, but Burt merely said that, based on his hat, the man was a rigger and had every right to be on the ship. Since Burt seemed unaware of anything amiss, Ray tried to ignore his intuition and put the feelings down to his unfamiliarity with the vessel.

In the engine room, Ray pointed to a cartoon of a man's head peeking over a wall. Beneath the figure were the words "Kilroy was here."

"What's with the cartoon?" Ray asked Burt.

"You've never seen Kilroy before? I figured you being a Navy man, you'd know," answered Burt. "From what I heard, a guy named James Kilroy at the Fore River Shipyard in Quincy, Massachusetts came up with this doodle to mark where he finished riveting at the end of his shift."

"Why didn't he just put a simple chalk mark like most riveters do?"

"Well, since each riveter gets paid for the number of rivets he completes per shift, some sneaky workers on the later shift moved the chalk marks."

"That's an easy way to increase your pay," commented Ray.

"Didn't make some of the riveters very happy, especially this Kilroy guy. So anyway, he comes up with this funny looking little drawing of a guy peeking over a wall to mark where he finished riveting for the shift. Next thing you know, seamen are putting this cartoon on walls at every port they visit around the world. It's kind of like a race to see who can write 'Kilroy was here' first."

After his tour with Burt, Ray sat in his make-shift office and studied the copies of the accident reports that Admiral Jarabek made available. At first glance, he couldn't see much to indicate that a saboteur was at work. On paper, the accidents certainly were plausible. Anytime unskilled individuals are trained to do complex tasks, the opportunity for mistakes arises. Burns from welding equipment, falls from ladders or other high places, cuts and bruises, they could all easily happen.

For the second time that day, the hair on the back of Ray's neck stood up. He looked up quickly to find a pretty dark-haired woman standing in the doorway. For a moment, he thought it was Helen Stevens. He stood up quickly.

"Hel—" Realizing he'd been mistaken, Ray slowly slid back down in his seat. He willed his heart back into a normal rhythm.

"Hello to you too," said the woman. "By the look on your face you were expecting someone else. I wouldn't mind being that someone." She smiled wistfully. "Are you Captain Birkett?"

"Yes," answered Ray, more calmly. He stood up and walked toward her. "How can I help you?"

"I have a delivery from Admiral Jarabek."

"Thank you, Miss—"

"Dorothy. Dot. Carson. Let me start again. I'm Dorothy Carson. My friends call me Dot. It's nice to meet you, Captain Birkett." She smiled a flirty smile at Ray.

"It's nice to meet you too, Dorothy Dot Carson," Ray answered good-naturedly.

"Say, that's funny," responded Dot. "You're new here, aren't you?"

"Yes, though I visited Brunswick briefly last year."

"Well, if you need someone to show you around, don't hesitate to ask for me. I'm in the secretarial pool." Dot smiled at him again.

Ray accepted the heavy package and returned to his desk. He opened the thick envelope and found a large stack of photographs inside. Taken in order to keep track of the progress of each ship, dozens of pictures showed nearly every stage of the building process. Since he wasn't getting anywhere studying individual accidents, Ray decided to approach the problem from a different angle. Namely, where would sabotage be most effective? Ray searched the stack of sketches and photographs of Liberty ships until he found several that interested him.

The first drawing showed a Liberty ship broadside. Someone had helpfully labeled key aspects of the ship. Ray noted the five huge holds, three fore of the engine room, two aft. The oil-fueled steam engine sat mid-ship beneath a squat building housing crew quarters, the mess hall, and storerooms. At its top, in front of the single funnel, perched the command center—the flying bridge. A mainmast stood just fore of the bridge. Two cranes one between holds two and three, the other between holds four and five enabled cargo of any size to be shifted from the dock to the ship.

Ray briefly allowed himself the luxury of remembering what it had been like to be at sea. He had served as naval intelligence officer on several ships. His voyages had been uneventful until the last one. Recognizing that those days were over, he turned his attention to an interesting photograph. The cargo deck on this particular ship was stacked with tanks, trucks, disassembled aircraft, and even two locomotive engines. Despite the squat ugliness of the design, Ray couldn't help but marvel at the enormous carrying capacity of a Liberty ship. Designed as freight haulers, they were like a rectangular box with a pointed bow.

Another photograph showed ten Liberty ships, bow first against a pier, lined up side-to-side like cars in a parking lot. According to the caption, they were being loaded with goods bound for Britain. He studied the photograph and considered a variety of scenarios all related to timing the destruction of one Liberty ship in a way that would destroy the other ships moored alongside. Ray's stomach turned when he realized it could be another Pearl Harbor. The same thing could happen here in Brunswick where the six shipways were built close together. But time-bombs and destruction while being loaded didn't appear to be Admiral Jarabek's chief concern.

The next photograph gave Ray reason to pause. It showed a Liberty ship that had literally broken in half—snapped neatly in two—crosswise, right through the middle. A note on the back cited weld failure as responsible for this catastrophic failure. Ray knew he would have to investigate the welders to determine how easy it would be for them to weld in such a way as to pass inspection but cause weld failure on the high seas.

The next few photographs were of specific facets of the ship. Funnels, cranes, ventilation shafts, clamping plates, engine pistons, the pictures captured the endless array of fixtures necessary for the operating of a ship of this size. Ray couldn't help but be a bit daunted by the enormous number of opportunities for sabotage. How would he ever ferret out a saboteur in all this complexity? He didn't even know where to begin.

Ray decided to have lunch in order to clear his mind. On his walk across the shipyard, Ray tilted his face to study the sky. Above him, the seagulls darted and swooped, reminding him that the facility had been built on a marsh. A blimp floating silently overhead, startling him. He had forgotten that blimps had been deployed to keep a lookout for enemy activity along the coast. Ray wondered what it would be like to be looking down on the scene from above. The shipyard would surely resemble a hill of ants, furiously moving here and there engaged in some purposeful activity. Would it appear like chaos or would the viewer be able to sort out the method in the madness?

Chapter 14

Helen

"*H*elen, you were such a whiz at setting up tables and booths for bake sale at the church on Saturday," exclaimed Dot while they sat eating lunch together in the cafeteria.

"It was nothing, really," responded Helen. "I just sorted out things that needed sorting out."

"Nothing? Nothing? No one else could have handled Mrs. Wilson so cleverly. I couldn't believe it when she pulled a fabric measuring tape from her pocket and began checking the size of her booth," said Hazel Ann.

"I thought we were all in deep trouble when that old biddy figured out that her booth was six inches narrower than specified in the agreement she had signed. I mean, what is six inches either way?" asked Avis Lou.

"Well six inches turned out to be important to her! Furious! The woman was furious! And the way she kept hollering about being entitled to her entire booth! You'd have thought the world turned on her! She started pushing and shoving the nearby tables around just to make sure her booth was the right size!" added Winona.

Helen giggled. "You're right. It was something to see her pushing and shoving and re-measuring all the tables."

"Mrs. Wilson is always looking out for her own self-interest. My mouth dropped open when she demanded that all the booths be moved! After all the work we went to!" cried Avis Lou. "It's a good thing you managed to rearrange the booths and smooth ruffled feathers just in time for the event to open."

"Well—I couldn't have old Mrs. Newcastle sitting on the front steps, now could I? I'd much rather keep my eye on the goal. We sold one hundred and ten war bonds. At eighteen dollars and seventy-five cents each, that's over two thousand dollars!" Helen smiled happily.

"That will really help the boys at the front, including my Bill," said Avis Lou.

Helen noticed the tightness around her friend's eyes. She couldn't imagine what it would be like to have a husband or a lover overseas. She admired Avis Lou's ability to cover her fear with smiles and laughter. Only a close friend would recognize the effort it took.

"Helen, I can't believe that when you're not working at the shipyard, you're directing bond drives and bake sales too!" exclaimed Dot.

"She's the consummate organizer," said Hazel Ann. "We noticed that it didn't take long for the head of the Industrial Efficiency department to recognize your organizational skills. No wonder they whisked you out of the secretarial pool and into a real job."

"It wasn't so bad being a file clerk," protested Helen. Though it wasn't a glamorous job, she knew her friend liked working in the secretarial pool.

"It's an easier job than being a welder," said Hazel Ann philosophically.

"But it doesn't pay as well," added Winona.

"I'm not in it for the pay. I'm doing my part to help win this war and bring my husband and all the other boys home as soon as possible," announced Avis Lou.

"Helen, you're just like your Aunt Elva. Now there's a tireless woman. Just look at her fundraising parties! They're fun and helpful at the same time. I can't wait until the next one." Winona rarely missed a good party.

"Winona, you sound as if you're bored," commented Hazel Ann.

"You must admit that there isn't much going on here. All the men are under sixteen or over forty. Either that or 4F or worse—married," complained Winona. "What's a girl going to do for a good time?"

"She's got a point. What else can a girl do besides work?" asked Dot.

"You said it, honey," answered Winona. She took a drag on her cigarette. "At least here at the shipyard, men out-number women eight-to-one."

Helen's attitude toward work couldn't be more different from Winona's and Dot's. She loved her job. It gave her purpose. Brunswick had always had a small shipyard, however after Pearl Harbor, the contractors for the U.S. government built a large shipbuilding facility. Helen and thousands of employees worked around the clock to build ships to ferry men and material across the Atlantic Ocean to the war zone. Now that she had settled into her job, she loved the pressure-filled, workaday aspect of getting ships ready to launch. She was proud to be a part of such an important war effort. She was about to say so when Dot changed the subject.

"Hey, did you see the new guy tagging along after Burt this morning?" asked Dot. "I delivered some papers to his office today. He's cute and he's funny. I can tell by the laugh lines around his eyes. He's also very British."

Helen's heart constricted at the words. Even now, a year after their dance and his urgent postcard, she still dreamed of one particular British captain—Captain Ray Birkett. Truth be told, though she dated other men, she longed for Ray. She waited for the pain in her heart to lessen before replying flippantly, "Dot, you say that about most of the men here. Unfortunately, they're usually neither cute nor funny."

"Oh, don't get all huffy. You'll get your chance to meet him. He's asking for an assistant. Maybe he'll pick you." Dot made a quick jab at Helen.

"Yeah, Helen, you don't know what you're missing. I saw him. What a looker!" Winona whistled appreciatively. "If you're going after him, Dot, I'll have to hope he has a twin."

Sighing at her friend's flirtatious nature, Helen knew it was time to go back to work. She got up to leave and something made her hesitate. She looked back at her friends and noticed nothing out of the ordinary. For a moment, she wondered what caused her to stop, and then she shrugged her shoulders and made her way out the rear door of the cafeteria.

Chapter 15

Ray

*R*ay stood on the threshold of the cafeteria. He felt a stirring in the air and the hair on his arms stood on end. Breathlessly, he scanned the room searching for a head covered with a glorious fall of raven hair. To his dismay, all the women wore kerchiefs or snoods which hid their hair from view. To make matters worse, most of the men and women wore overhauls that made the sexes nearly indistinguishable. Sighing at his own folly, Ray picked up a lunch tray, went through the line to select his meal, and joined Burt at a table near the window.

"Have you found a place to stay?" Burt asked conversationally.

"Right now, I have temporary quarters at the hotel. I have to move out the day after tomorrow," answered Ray.

"You had better get on your way then. It will take you the rest of today and the better part of the week to find a place to live."

"What do you mean?"

"Look around you, son." Burt gestured out the window at the men scurrying from here to there around the shipyard. "A hive of bees couldn't be busier. When shift changes, for about two hours, you won't be able to walk down the street; it will be so thick with men going and coming. You'll learn that smart folks stay off the street during shift change. Anyway, back to your problem. Where do you reckon all these people live?"

"To tell you the truth, I hadn't really thought about it. Temporary housing I suppose. Didn't I see some on the road into town?"

"The temporary housing built by the government doesn't begin to cover the need for homes! Besides the people who've moved here to work at the shipyard or the Hercules Plant or the pulp mill, we've got the wives and family members of the servicemen stationed at Camp Stewart. That's a lot of people needing a place to rest their heads. No doubt about it, just finding a place to stay is an enormous challenge. People find rooms just about everywhere imaginable."

"What do you suggest?" asked Ray, a bit overwhelmed.

"Go knocking door to door. See if anyone's got a room available. A new hire recently told me he found half a living room to rent. Says it's real convenient, just a couple of blocks away."

"Half a living room?"

"Yep. The enterprising people who own it rented the other half to another desperate couple. To make it work, they hung some blankets on a clothesline to separate one half from the other. The guy who told me about it says that he and his wife don't mind sharing the space with another couple. They're glad of the room."

"Sharing a living room? There would be no privacy. How are they managing?"

"He says it's not too bad. Tough part is that there is only one bathroom for eight people. Seems they've got a schedule posted on the door to make sure everyone gets their time. 'Course it's better than the folks living where they don't have indoor plumbing."

Ray shook his head in amazement.

"Having half a room beats hot bedding or sleeping in a car," said Burt philosophically. "I've even heard that some people go to the movies at night just to have a place to sleep."

"Hot bedding?"

"That's where one person gets the bed while the other person is working. Sure is efficient."

"Efficient yes, comfortable no," Ray responded.

"Reckon you've seen that sort of thing back home in England when people evacuated London and the Channel coast and needed to find housing. I've seen it on the newsreels."

"Well, yes, but not to this extent."

"Good luck hunting for a place to rest your head. Like I said, try knocking on doors. Best you find a place to stay before coming back to the shipyard."

"Thank you for your advice. I'll start right now. Hey Burt, if I wanted to find a navy guy I met the last time I was in Brunswick, where should I look?" asked Ray.

"Try the USO. Somebody there should be able to help."

"Thanks."

Standing in the late afternoon sun, Ray had to admit Burt had been right. He'd been looking for a place to stay for hours now and had had no luck at all.

Ever since April 8th and 9th 1942 when 54 survivors of the two torpedoed tankers were brought ashore and twenty-two of the drowned seamen had been laid to rest in the town's cemetery, the citizens of Brunswick had put their backs into the war effort. The city had changed dramatically in the past twelve months. Ray couldn't imagine where all the people had come from. According to the hotel clerk, sixteen thousand workers had migrated to the Golden Isles in search of employment, either in the shipyard or the services supporting it. When the shipyard workers arrived with their families, Brunswick's population soared to 65,000. Finding Helen Stevens in a town of 15,000 people would have been a challenge. Finding her now that 50,000 more people had invaded the town would require a lot of hard work and more than just a little luck.

Ray heard the whistle blow at the shipyard announcing the shift change. He mopped his perspiring face with his handkerchief. As he uncovered his eyes, Ray caught sight of a solid wall of workers coming toward him. His eyes opened wide in alarm. He had only one thought as the wave of people engulfed him like an ocean wave crashes against a beach during a storm: how would he possibly find Helen in this sea of coveralls?

Rumpled and tired from walking around Brunswick in the sweltering heat, Ray returned to his hotel room and thanked his lucky stars he had somewhere to stay for the night. He kicked off his shoes and collapsed on the bed. The shoes thumped on the floor, reminding Ray that he'd need to handle them with care. Shoes were rationed to just two pairs a year. He'd seen a number of people going barefoot to save the shoe leather. No shoes, no place to rent, no Helen. His assignment wasn't starting off very well.

He'd knocked on door after door in search of a place to stay. Boarding houses, rooming houses, apartments, private homes, all full. No one had been able to help. He hadn't even gathered any ideas for where to start tomorrow. Ray was beginning to believe that finding a saboteur would be easier than finding even a temporary place to stay. At least he could find his way around. Brunswick was laid out in a grid pattern of north-south and east-west streets and unlike Britain, which removed street signs and sign posts in May of 1940, Brunswick still retained theirs. Exhausted, Ray lay on the bed looking up at the ceiling. Fortunately, the hotel room would be his for one more night.

Chapter 16

Helen

*H*elen checked her watch and noted that it was time to tour the shipyard. She and William Browning had their routes they took every day to check on key workstations. The number of accidents that had occurred in the past three weeks concerned her. Yesterday's lathe mishap was the second major accident involving a serious injury to an employee in a week. In both of these incidents, all work in the area had come to an abrupt halt. Naturally, this caused havoc with the ship's building schedule. Constructing six ships simultaneously required strict adherence to a timetable. When programs got off target, her department had to step in to get things back on track.

Running a shipyard this size took a lot of orchestrated management. Very few seasoned shipbuilders had been hired. The men with the necessary skills were fighting overseas. Instead, the shipyard managers hired unskilled workers from all walks of life and from all parts of the nation. Most were put through a six week training program and then assigned jobs appropriate with their abilities. Highly motivated employees made up for their lack of skill with their desire to help in the war effort.

Helen slipped on her safety-yellow hard hat and turned to leave the cramped Industrial Efficiency office. To her co-worker, William Browning, she said, "I'm going out to do a little investigating about lathe accident that occurred yesterday. I'm surprised something like this happened. Those men are experienced operators."

"Why bother? I already looked into it and wrote it up." Browning pushed a single piece of typed paper on his desk toward her.

Helen quickly read the accident report which was so brief it contained little more than the operator's name and the date of his accident. She opened her mouth to say something, but Browning spoke first.

"You don't want to go over there. The machine shop is no place for a lady like you," he said condescendingly.

"Thank you for your concern Mr. Browning, but I don't mind finding out if more information can be added to your report." Helen said this tongue-in-cheek but the man didn't seem to notice.

"Welders, electricians, lathe operators, they're all experienced if they've been here more than a few weeks," said her co-worker. "Like my report says, the lathe operator received a nasty, heavily bleeding flesh wound on his right cheek. I let him get cleaned up before interviewing him." Browning smirked at Helen when he saw her stiffen at the words. "He didn't have much to say. Why interview him again? What's the big deal? He's back at work already."

"Mr. Browning, I am well aware that you don't necessarily approve of my methods, especially interviewing people immediately after an accident, but you know how important it is to learn all you can about the incident while it's still fresh in their mind."

Later, Helen reported to her boss, Burt Dixon. He sat in his shirt sleeves in front of a small oscillating four-bladed fan. Suffering from the late afternoon heat, he evidenced very little interest in her findings. After showing him Browning's report, she told him about her further investigation into the lathe accident.

"You didn't have to go to all that trouble, Helen," said Burt when she had finished. "William wrote up the accident shortly after it happened."

"I know, but I learn so much by talking to those involved in an incident. I can use the information to prevent future accidents. Isn't this what you want me to do—I mean, isn't my special assignment all about preventing accidents?"

"Yes, just don't get too carried away," responded Burt absently, his mind already on other tasks.

Helen paused with her hand on the doorknob to his office. She stood silently for a moment, deep in thought. "Burt, I can't help feeling that there is something odd about yesterday's lathe accident."

"Odd, what do you mean?"

"The operator, Charlie Timor, actually has a lot of experience operating lathes. When I interviewed him, Charlie told me that he had just finished setting a propeller shaft into the lathe when the whistle blew for break. To protect the slot or keyway cut in the shaft, a key had been inserted. Before wiping his hands and leaving the workstation, he removed the key from the keyway in preparation for the final polishing when he got back from break. Charlie set the key on his workbench like he has done dozens of times before. When he returned, he picked up where he left off."

"That sounds normal, what happened?" asked Burt, his tone uninterested.

"When the shaft began to rotate, the key flew out of the key slot and struck him on the face. It did a lot of damage to his cheek. It would have taken out his eye if it had been an inch higher."

"It's a good thing it wasn't—hey—didn't you just say he removed the key from the keyway?" Burt asked, more interested now.

"Yes, I did. That's what he told me he did."

"But if he took it out of the keyway how did it fly out at him? It couldn't have hit him, it wasn't there."

"According to Charlie, he put it on his workbench before going on break. The physical evidence, namely the bloody key and his damaged face, says otherwise," Helen said.

"So he just doesn't want to admit he forgot to take the key out."

"Charlie protested that he had. He didn't budge on that point and I'm inclined to believe him. He's experienced and not the careless type. I watched him operate the lathe. He has a rhythm to his work, a step-by-step procedure that he always follows."

"He slipped up this time. We've all made mistakes." Burt gave every appearance of wanting to dismiss the incident as worker carelessness.

"I don't think so. His memory seemed awfully clear on this point." Helen continued to stand up for Charlie.

"Then what happened?"

"I don't know. The only thing Charlie added to his explanation was that the key had to have been reinserted in the propeller shaft during his break."

"By whom? And more importantly, why?"

"Burt, I don't know the answer to those questions. I asked around and no one remembers seeing anyone in the area, except William Browning making his usual rounds. Of course, they were all on break and it wouldn't take long to insert the key. Anyone could have done it."

"But why? And I've got another question. Wouldn't Charlie have seen the key in the keyway?" asked Burt.

"I asked Charlie the same question. He said it would be easy to overlook if the keyway in the shaft was turned away from him so he couldn't see it. He distinctly remembered removing the key, so he didn't check; he just went back to work."

"So if Charlie didn't leave the key in the keyway, who put it back?"

"I don't know. I just don't know," admitted Helen. "I'd like to look into it further."

"Helen, listen, Charlie should have checked his work. It's another example of a guy not doing his job right. It doesn't call for more investigation. Don't waste your time."

Chapter 17

Ray

A spry middle-aged woman holding a feather duster and wearing what appeared to be a jeweled turban and matching apron peered through the screen door at Ray. Startled by her appearance, he took an involuntary step backwards.

"Well I declare!" the apparition exclaimed, clapping her hand over her open mouth. "It's Gregory Peck!"

Quick as lightening, she slammed the door in his face. Ray stood there nonplussed. If he hadn't been so tired from his exhausting house-to-house search for a room to rent, he would have turned around and left. Instead, he stood uncertainly on the broad veranda of a rambling Queen Anne-style mansion. Next door, sharing the shade of a huge live oak tree dripping with Spanish moss, its twin sat comfortably sagging with age. The air smelled of the marsh and the myriad of flowering plants that bloomed in profusion nestled against the porch.

"Sister, who's at the door?" he heard a fluting voice calling from deep inside the house.

"Gregory Peck! Can you believe it? Gregory Peck has come to visit us here in Brunswick! Quick! Help me out of my apron!"

Gregory Peck? The conviction in the woman's voice made Ray look back over his shoulder expecting to see the famous actor standing beside him on the front step. All day, he'd had a vague sensation of being followed, though not by Gregory Peck. Perhaps the excessive heat and cloying humidity made him imagine things. He'd heard of that sort of thing happening in the desert. Why not the humid South?

Abruptly, the door swung open again bringing him back around. Ray stared, disoriented. The same woman appeared again only, in the blink of an eye, she had changed her clothes. Instead of an apron and turban, she sported an apple green sundress. Ray blinked when she simpered, primped, and fussed with her hair.

Ray peered into the wide shadowed hallway beyond her shoulder. A second woman appeared or he should say the first woman reappeared, having disposed of the feather duster and swept off her turban and apron with remarkable speed. The two women so closely resembled each other, they had to be twins. In unison, they giggled and waggled their fingers at him in a girlish wave. Surely, they didn't think he was Gregory Peck.

"Sister, why did you slam the door in Mr. Peck's face? That wasn't polite, not polite at all," said the second woman in lieu of a greeting.

"I couldn't very well let him see me in my cleaning clothes, now could I, Sister?"

Though he was having a hard time keeping up with events, Ray could see the logic in that statement. He smiled at the two women and drew a breath to speak. In doing so, he missed his opportunity.

"Welcome to our home, Mr. Peck. May I say we—that is—my sisters and I—are honored by your visit."

Gregory Peck? Did they really think he was Gregory Peck?

"Mr. Peck, my sister seems to have forgotten her manners entirely. How may we help you? Perhaps you would like to come in out of the heat? Or perhaps you'd like a glass of sweet tea? You look positively parched! Georgia's heat and humidity can do that to a body. We'd be happy to share some of our tiny supply of sugar with a visitor from Hollywood."

"I've forgotten my manners? You're a fine one to talk. You slammed the door in his face!"

"Sister shush! We're ignoring Mr. Peck." The first woman wiggled her silvery eyebrows in his direction.

As they held the screen door open for him, Ray couldn't help but think the twins had been affected by the heat themselves.

"He's not Gregory Peck!" boomed a third voice from the interior of the house causing them all to jump.

"He certainly is, Sister. Just look at him," said the twin in the green dress.

"So handsome," simpered the first, fluttery, silver-haired woman.

"You both watch too many movies. This man is most certainly not Gregory Peck." The newest addition to the debate squinted at Ray, examining his features.

"How do you know?" asked the now turban-less sister.

"Gregory Peck does not wear a British Naval uniform," she announced with conviction.

"He might for one of his movies," argued the twin in the apple green dress, still holding her ground.

"Sisters! Do you think we're part of a movie?" That question prompted all three women to rush out onto the porch to look around for a movie camera and crew. Seeing none, their faces fell and they turned their attention back to Ray.

"Sister, what makes you think a movie company would come here to film?"

"Well, why not? Hinshaw Square is one of the loveliest squares in Brunswick. And since we're only a few blocks inland we still get a breeze off the marsh."

"That all may be true, but—"

"Quiet!" The women stopped chattering abruptly at their sister's command. The third sister, made imposing more because of her self-assured manner than her size, stared hard at Ray. "So, if you're not Gregory Peck, then who are you?"

She sounded so much like his commanding officer that Ray snapped to attention. "Captain Raymond Birkett, His Majesty's Royal Navy at your service, ma'am."

"See, I told you he's not Gregory Peck." Satisfied at last, she folded her arms across her ample bosom.

"Well, he could have been," sniffed one of twin sisters as she smoothed her dress and smiled up at him. "Mr. Peck, may I ask what brings you to our doorstep?"

"He's not—"

"Actually, ma'am, I'm trying to find a room to rent," Ray interjected, wanting to stave off another disjointed discussion about Gregory Peck.

"You and everybody else. We don't—"

"Are you really British?"

"Of course he is, just listen to him talk. He's got an accent! Isn't that exciting? Oh my heavens, Sisters, let him in! Have you completely forgotten your manners? We mustn't keep one of our allies waiting on the doorstep! What will the neighbors think?"

"But, he's only looking for a room and we haven't got one of those."

"Who says we don't?" countered the third sister.

Ray found himself looking into the bright, inquisitive eyes of three middle-aged ladies. Only their expressions were different. One smiled in welcome. One frowned at him. The third studied him shrewdly as if to see if he measured up to some secret requirement.

"But he's British."

"So is the King, but we haven't got room for him either."

"He doesn't look very imposing. In fact, he looks rather nice." The first twin peered at him closely. "Surely we can find a space for him somewhere."

"Yes, Sister. It's been so long since we've had a man about the house."

"But, we don't know anything about him."

"You're right, Sister. Young man, who are your people?"

"Sister, he's from England—you are from England, aren't you?"

Given their similar looks and voices, Ray couldn't keep track of the speakers. They left him thoroughly confused by their disjointed conversation. Hesitantly, he nodded yes.

The speaker continued, "See, he's from England, not from Charleston. Maybe they don't have people there."

"I declare sister, sometimes I think you open your mouth before you think. Of course he has people. Everybody has people."

"I know, dear. It's just that some people have better people, right?"

"There you go again—"

"Now Sister, no sense getting yourself worked up. Why don't we invite the young man in to see what he wants?"

"I'm sorry to have bothered you, truly I am," began Ray. He wished the cheerful bright yellow front door flanked by decorative planters had not drawn him to the big rambling house with its unusual occupants. It was proving to be a waste of time.

Before he could protest further, the third sister reached for him, gripped him by the arm and yanked him inside. Startled by her strength, Ray stumbled through the doorway after her. He found himself in a long hallway that bisected the house. Open doors at each end allowed a breeze to circulate dropping the temperature dramatically. In the dim light, he nearly tripped again over two blue-tick hound dogs.

"Mind your step," cautioned the woman in the apple green sun dress. "Blue and Beau always like to lie in doorways. The air flow must make them cooler."

"Hah! They just like laying anywhere they can be in the way."

"This one is Blue," said the first twin, pointing to the hound on the left. "And this one is Beau." She pointed at the dog on the right and then paused. She peered down at the dogs that hadn't bothered to lift their heads despite the commotion going on around them. "No, that's not right, this one is Blue and that one is Beau." She tapped her chin with her finger and contemplated the two hounds. "No, I think I got it right the first time."

Ray took a moment to study the hound dogs. As far as he could see, like the sisters, they were identical twins. No wonder she couldn't tell them apart. The third sister gave another powerful tug on his arm and guided him toward the parlor. Ray felt as if he had stepped through a rabbit hole and into wonderland. He wouldn't be shocked to learn that one of the sisters was named Alice.

"Careful now, Sister, the man does have a cane. Funny, I don't remember Gregory Peck needing a cane," said the second twin.

"Won't you join us, Mr. Peck? We're just about to sit down for some sweet tea," said the first twin sweetly. "I think your English habit of afternoon tea is wonderful. There is nothing like serving tea to provide pleasant and relaxing break in the late afternoon. Don't you think that's true, Mr. Peck?" The speaker continued without waiting for an answer. "Why, I declare, everything about afternoon tea makes a woman feel special, romantic, and well-cared for."

"Edna Jane!" the third sister bellowed to the maid. "Quit your dithering and bring us another glass and some more biscuits!"

"Sister! Really! Can't you just ring the bell pull like a lady? You're spoiling the mood."

"Ha! Despite everything your Momma tried, Miss Elva never did learn the finer points of being a lady," announced the maid, Edna Jane, when she entered the room.

Ray gratefully sank down on the couch, savoring the cooler temperature in the front parlor. A lovely eighteenth-century Japanese screen drew his attention. Its background of tarnished gold and great boughs of blossoms in the palest of pinks and faded reds set the color scheme for the room. White woodwork and moldings framed walls painted a delicate moss green. A worn oriental carpet covered the heart-of-pine floor. Upholstered furniture in cheery coral and moss green created an airy and comfortable affect. It was the kind of room that welcomed guests.

Around him, the sisters continued to flutter and fuss. Five minutes in their company and he was already thoroughly confused as to which was which. They all spoke at once, finishing each other's thoughts, losing him in their convoluted conversation. However, as they bustled around the room, he began to notice distinct personality differences between the three sisters. And they had to be sisters. Two were definitely twins, while the third, except for being slightly taller, had nearly identical features. All three women were good-humored, lively, and alert. Their eagerness and vivacity made them seem years younger than their true age. Though they looked alike, they did not, however, have similar personalities. Of the twins, the first he met was flighty and feisty at the same time. The second was quiet and reserved, almost painfully polite. The third woman asserted command over the other two with her take charge attitude.

"Never mind my failings. Let's start again, shall we? Now young man, we should introduce ourselves. I'm Elva Clay. I live next door. These are my twin sisters, Ora and Ida. This is their house."

Ray smiled. It all fit. Twin sisters, twin dogs, twin houses.

"There are two more of us," said Ora, the flighty twin, to Ray. She patted his knee. "Ulanalee Gibbons and our brother Afton Richard. He's married to Enid and they have four wonderful children. They live just across the square. Our sister, Ulanalee is married to Roger and lives in Atlanta. You'll be able to recognize her because she can play the violin beautifully."

"Ora, how could that bit of information possibly help him recognize Ulanalee? It's not as if Ulanalee carries her violin tucked under her arm all the time," remonstrated Elva.

"But she does play the violin beautifully," protested Ora.

"In case you haven't noticed, our parents had a thing for vowels: Afton, Elva, Ida, Ora, and Ulanalee," interrupted the sister named Ida. Then she made an abrupt segue that left Ray wondering how anyone followed a conversation with these women. "Do you play canasta?"

"Or bridge?" added Ora, looking at him expectantly.

"Yes, we certainly do need a fourth for bridge," admitted Ida.

"Ora! You can't ask a complete stranger if he plays bridge. There are niceties to be observed first," reprimanded Elva before Ray could answer.

"All I'm saying is that if a man is going to live with us, he might as well play bridge," said Ora. "Are you Church of England? You don't mind my asking, do you? We're Episcopalian ourselves."

Ora's tangential comment reinforced Ray's feeling of tumbling down a rabbit hole.

"Ora, you shouldn't be asking such questions. We've just met the man," said Ida.

"Like I said, I think we should know these things about a man if we're going to live with him."

"Ora! Hush your mouth! You should know better than to say such a thing." Ida's tittering giggle took the sting out of her admonishment.

Ray stifled a laugh. What an entertaining group of women. He studied the expressions on the faces of the three women. Delightful, they could only be described as delightful. Then he realized why he felt so much at home. "You ladies remind me of my aunts back home in Brighton."

"See, Elva, he has people!"

Chapter 18

Helen

*W*ould she ever be able to enter a room without searching for his face in the crowd? Would she ever forget the intense feeling of rightness she had felt when she danced in his arms? Helen stood poised at the door of the United Service Organization Club waiting for the quivering in her stomach to subside. Despite the briefness of her dance with Captain Birkett, she still missed his presence. She wondered if any of the love songs they played tonight would ever be for her. The voice of someone calling her name broke into her thoughts.

"There you are, Helen," Avis Lou greeted her friend. "It's great that you can be here at the USO Club tonight. Men outnumber women by at least four to one."

"Are you saying that tonight we'll be dancing so much we'll need to take our shoes off to walk home?" asked Helen with a smile. Experience told her her feet would ache in her poorly constructed wartime shoes made from cork and fabric.

"How much you want to bet that those soldier-boys from up North think that all us Southern women go barefoot?" giggled Avis Lou.

"If they see us walking home again tonight holding our shoes in our hands, they're bound to think so," laughed Helen.

"No complaining ladies. Corns for my country! That's what I always say," announced Hazel Ann, coming up to stand beside Helen.

"Hey, y'all give me any hints on how to deal with these GI's and their steel-toed boots?" asked Moria when she and Dot joined them at the buffet table.

"Honey, haven't you learned to choose your dancing partners carefully? Be brave, but not foolhardy. Pick the ones who take small steps. It gives you time to get out of his way!" counselled Avis Lou.

"It's always my luck to get the energetic guys," sighed Moria. She reached down and straightened the straps on her left shoe. "Why don't these smart-alecks learn to dance?"

"You won't believe what happened to me today!" said Dot breathlessly.

"What? Do tell!" said Moria.

"Well, I was walking down Newcastle Street on my way to the cinema when I could feel my slip sliding down my hips! The button holding it closed had popped!"

"Oh, how I hate not having any elastic for our undergarments!" exclaimed Hazel Ann.

"What did you do then?" asked Avis Lou, agog at her friend's predicament.

"What could I do? In two steps, it was puddled at my feet!"

"What did you do?" her friends asked in unison.

"I'd like to have died of embarrassment! I stepped out of it with one foot and with the other I kicked it up in the air. It came floating down like a parachute and I caught it as nonchalantly as I could." Dot's face turned bright pink despite her impish smile.

Her friends erupted into laughter at the image of Dot kicking like a drum majorette to launch her slip high into the air.

"I could just feel my cheeks burning with shame!" exclaimed Dot, clasping her hands to her face.

"I doubt anyone noticed," comforted Helen when her laughter subsided.

"On Newcastle Street? You must be joking! The whole world stands in line on Newcastle Street waiting to get in the cinema," said Moria.

"Moria!" protested Helen. "I'm trying to help Dot feel better. Can't you see how embarrassed she is?"

"Dot, honey, that's nothing," said Moria. "Don't y'all remember the time my dress made of that crepe fabric shrunk in the rain?"

"Do we ever! It shrank so fast that if we hadn't gotten you out of the rain quick you wouldn't have had a dress on at all!" said Hazel Ann over everyone's laughter.

Avis Lou studied the buffet table. "There's not much for the boys to choose from tonight, spam, macaroni and cheese, and Jell-O®."

"Rationing makes it difficult to come up with much," agreed Hazel Ann.

"Elastic, nylon, rubber, eggs, sugar, butter, just about everything important," added Dot. "I really miss elastic."

"And nylons," said Hazel Ann.

"Say, are my stockings straight?" Avis Lou strained to look over her shoulder at the back of her bare leg. She giggled at her own joke. "Do you think we'll ever get used to drawing seams on our legs? What I wouldn't give for a pair of real silk stockings!"

"Avis Lou, what would Bill say if he could see you now?"

"Heaven knows." Avis Lou smiled playfully. "My husband encourages me to do my part for the troops. Up to a point that is. Don't worry; I'm just dancing, not keeping company with anyone."

"Do you hear from Bill often?" asked Moria.

"Not as often as I'd like. His V-mail letters usually arrive in batches." Avis Lou referred to the Government Issue letters. "Aren't those letters amazing? First the men write their letters, and then they're censored and microfilmed. Once the film reaches stateside, they blow them up, print them on rice paper and mail them to us. I don't think I'll ever get used to the thin paper. Or the blacked-out sections either. I always wonder what Bill is trying to tell me."

"Everything is so secretive now," said Helen.

"Yes it is. Even so, I try to write to Bill every day."

"Every day? What do you find to say?" asked Helen in amazement. Then again, maybe it wasn't such a big surprise. She remembered all the little things she had wanted to write to Captain Ray Birkett over the past year.

"I never have trouble finding things to say. I tell him about all the mundane things that happen here in Brunswick and try to make it sound interesting." Avis Lou's face sobered. "It's not easy you know—always being upbeat and entertaining."

"No, I imagine it's not." Helen laid her hand sympathetically on her friend's arm. "I'm sure you'll give me pointers when Richard goes overseas."

"Ladies, it's time to put a smile on your face, here come the boys now," announced the matron. "Remember, first names only. Do not tell your dancing partner your last name. That's the rule. I'll remind you that it's for your own protection. And, I'm sorry to tell you that Milly Dorsett will not be joining us tonight."

Murmurs of concern went through the group of women. Helen asked, "What happened? Why won't Milly be here tonight?"

"Milly was involved in an accident at the shipyard. The nurse phoned me from the first aid station a few minutes ago."

Helen didn't wait around to hear anything more.

At the first aid station, Helen cringed when she saw Milly Dorsett's ankle swathed in bandages. It would be a long while before Milly would be dancing at the USO.

"Milly! Honey, what happened?" Helen asked, her voice full of concern.

"Oh Helen! It all happened so fast!" Milly's face twisted in pain. "The doctor says I've broken my ankle. They'll be taking me to City Hospital any minute now. It hurts so badly."

"Honey! That's just awful. Hang on, it won't be long." Helen hesitated before going further. She knew her friend really wouldn't necessarily want to talk right now, but she had to know. "Milly, I'm so sorry but I need to ask you a few questions for the accident report. Can you tell me what happened?"

"Oh, I don't mind. It will help me keep my mind off the pain. I was welding just like always. I gave a tug on the lines to roll my acetylene welding tank a little nearer. I've done that sort of thing a thousand times. The cylinders are on wheels, you know, to make them easier to move."

"Yes, go on," encouraged Helen.

"The wheel came off, just popped off! Next thing I know, the whole tank just toppled over right at me. The pressurized acetylene tank hit the ground with a clang! When it did, the valve snapped free and came shooting at me! It all happened so fast, I didn't have time to react. It hit my ankle and went spinning off. The doctor said my injury would be much worse if it hadn't been for my thick safety shoes and clothing."

"Oh Milly, that's terrible."

"Oh, the story's not over yet. What do you think happened to all that pressurized acetylene when the valve broke free?"

Helen suddenly realized that Milly clothes were singed and she could smell burnt fabric.

"Oh my God! A fire cloud!"

"You're right. The flame from my welding torch ignited a fire cloud. Fortunately, it didn't last long. All I can say is I'm glad I wear these heavy protective clothes and welding mask despite the heat. I would have been burned to a cinder."

Once she'd seen Milly safely ensconced in the ambulance, Helen went to Milly's work area. Swing shift workers had resumed production, but remnants of the first-shift accident remained. Helen stopped and stared, silently memorizing the area. The now empty acetylene tank on its one-wheeled dolly rested against the wall. Helen inspected the axle and unattached wheel. She couldn't find the pin and nut that should have held the wheel in place. That wasn't terribly odd since the small pin and nut could easily have gotten lost during the emergency. Helen spotted the valve partially wedged under the edge of a nearby pallet. She picked it up and studied it. Something puzzled her about the valve stem. Though she was far from an expert, she thought the threads looked stripped. Perhaps that could have happened during the explosion. She'd have to examine it later and ask a few questions.

"Hey!" shouted a tall, burly man as he approached. "What are you doing here?"

The man sounded angry and aggressive. Helen drew herself up to her full height. This sort of situation required her to be as confident as possible. She forced a professional smile on her face and moved bravely toward him.

"Hello, my name is Helen Stevens. I'm with the Industrial Efficiency department. I've been assigned to investigate this accident," Helen said pleasantly. Though officially a first shift employee, Helen decided to stretch her mandate from Burt Dixon to cover second shift activities.

"Yeah, I already knew that by the color of your hard hat. What's there to investigate? Milly got careless and toppled her tank. It's amazing she didn't get killed or worse, burn the place down. Browning's already been here and I told him all about it."

Two things annoyed Helen. First, Browning had already learned of the accident with surprising speed. Second, Helen thought the man standing in front of her was heartless, putting the building above Milly's life. However, she understood he was just doing his job. But then, so was she.

"All the same, Mr.—"

"Norris, Fred Norris" he said sharply, ignoring Helen's outstretched hand. "I'm the first shift supervisor in this department and I don't like you sniffing around bothering my men. William Browning already investigated. You don't need to be here. You ask me, women shouldn't be welders. They haven't got the strength or the brains to do it right. Milly's accident today proves it. Now I've got to work late cleaning up for tomorrow's production."

Helen bristled, clutching the valve in her left hand. The man was insufferable. She would never believe Milly caused the accident herself. Helen wanted to demand that Norris apologize but she sensed that an apology was not in his character. Helen vowed silently to herself that she'd investigate this accident to determine its real cause. Willing herself to be calm, she responded to his bad temper with as much force as she dared. "All the same, Mr. Norris, when an accident occurs, our department will investigate and determine what can be done to prevent future occurrences."

"All the same, Miss Stevens, I've got ships to build. Investigate on someone else's time. Now," he said with a note of threat in his voice, "Now, get out of here!" Fred Norris stood stonily in front of Helen until she turned to leave.

Though she had been planning to ask him about it, Helen slipped the valve and wheel into the commodious pocket of her coveralls and walked thoughtfully back to her office.

Chapter 19

Ray

*R*ay stood in the doorway of the USO Club and felt the hair rise on the back of his neck. Quickly he scanned the crowded dance floor. The room was full of white uniforms, the kind that submariners wear. They must have put into port for refueling and a night of liberty. There were very few women. Was Helen here? What other explanation could there be for the way his neck tingled? Or was it the song—their song— playing in the background that made hope beat like a drum in his chest?

Ray scrutinized each and every female in the room. His spirits sagged when his eyes failed to rest on anyone with luxuriant black hair and warm brown eyes.

"You look a little lost, sailor,"" said a moonlight and magnolia's female voice at his elbow. "I don't recognize your uniform. You're not with the submariners, I can tell that much. What branch of the military are you with?"

Ray drew a deep breath and focused on the woman at his side. Very pretty, she had a pixie face with wide-spaced blue eyes and high cheekbones. She wore bright red lipstick, the kind most women no longer could purchase. The woman regarded him with interest though her close inspection made Ray feel as if he was being appraised for some higher purpose.

"Captain Ray Birkett, His Majesty's Royal Navy."

"Winona Bunce, Brunswick Shipyard. In all my born days, I never thought I'd meet a limey at the USO."

Ray nodded in agreement.

"Why do they call you British sailors limeys?" Winona asked as if genuinely interested.

"I believe the term originates from the interaction of our two countries merchant marines. You see, British seamen were issued a daily ration of lime juice to prevent scurvy. Based on that, the US merchant marines gave us the nickname limey."

"You don't say. Limeys drink lime juice. Who would have thought?" Winona snapped her gum.

"It seems like everyone I meet in Brunswick is either in the armed forces or works for the shipyard," said Ray, continuing the conversation with the attractive woman.

"Not a lot of choices here in Brunswick. I work as a welder. Can you believe it? Me? A welder?" Winona made a sweeping gesture that took in her well-endowed figure from the toes of her fancy shoes to her pert little hat resting on her springy blond curls. "You certainly are a long way from England. So Captain, what brings you to Brunswick?"

"I'm at the shipyard on special assignment." Ray decided never to reveal more than that. Fortunately, he didn't have to do so. Winona Bunce caught sight of his cane and quickly lost interest in him as a suitable dance partner. He couldn't help but wince at the dismissive look that she made no effort to hide. Suddenly, she waved to someone across the room.

"I'm sorry to leave you," Winona said insincerely. "My friends are signaling me from across the room.

Ray watched her retreating back before making his way to the refreshments table. There he encountered a group of navy men talking shop. He waited for a break in the conversation before interrupting.

"Hello, I'm Captain Ray Birkett, His Majesty's Royal Navy. Pardon my interruption, but I was wondering if you might be able to help me." Ray noticed that the men seemed surprised to find him in a USO Club, so he explained. "Being a Brit, I had to beg my way in here. Maybe you guys could help me."

"Sure, what'cha need?"

"I'm trying to find an ensign by the name of Wayne Donaldson. He drove me from Brunswick to Jacksonville last year about this time. I have the impression he is, or was, stationed in this area. I was hoping to run into him again. Do any of you know him?"

"Sure," answered one of the sailors immediately. "I know Wayne. I hate to tell you this, but he's stationed down in Pensacola now."

Disappointment hit Ray with more force than he expected. Another lead to locating Helen Stevens lost. Bravely, he smiled at the men. "Well, thanks anyway. It was worth a try. If you ever run into Ensign Donaldson, tell him I said hello."

Chapter 20

Helen

"*H*elen, honey. You just missed our boarder," announced Helen's Aunt Ida when Helen stopped by on her way home from work the day after Milly's accident.

"Yes, honey. You did. He's such a nice man. You're going to like him," said Aunt Elva knowingly.

"I didn't know you had taken on a boarder," said Helen. No wonder her aunts had telephoned her mother to insist that Helen stop by for a visit. They were matchmaking again. If she'd known they had an eligible male in mind, she wouldn't have stopped by for some sweet tea. Helen always found it disconcerting that her Aunt Elva encouraged her to pursue a career on the one hand, while pushing young men at her with the other.

"He moved in three days ago. We've already gotten used to having a man around the house," said Aunt Ida.

"We did so want you to meet him. We just know you'll like him," added Aunt Ora.

Oh, please, Helen groaned inwardly, don't let her aunts begin acting like matchmakers. She could hear the radio playing in the kitchen. The incessant murmur of war news further dampened her mood. *"We now begin our radio newspaper program. In a second day of battle, our troops met with very stiff fighting. The enemy launched an armored counterattack, but was repelled with heavy losses..."*

"I'm sure he's very nice. I'm sorry I missed him," said Helen politely, even though she was anything but sorry about missing their new boarder. Inexplicably, Helen realized she didn't want a stranger sharing her aunts' house. She wanted one small part of Brunswick to remain unchanged. Why did the war, like the radio that broadcast news about it, have to intrude here too?

"He's British, you know," said Ora, her smile slightly out-of-focus. "Rather handsome too. Elva, what movie star did I say he reminds me of?"

"Ora, you're always comparing people with movie stars," said Elva.

"Do you remember, Helen, when your Aunt Ora thought she saw Clark Gable at the Bijoux movie theater?" asked Ida, smiling at the memory. "She caused quite a stir, insisting that all our neighbors follow her downtown so they could get his autograph."

"We had fun even if Clark Gable turned out to be old Mr. Haynes. I can't help it that our young man looks like a movie star!" protested Ora. She snapped her fingers. "Now was it Cary Grant? No, not suave enough. Jimmy Stewart? No, wrong accent. Gregory Peck! That's who! I knew he reminded me of a movie star."

Helen abruptly got up to leave. Once upon a time, she had danced with a man who, despite his limp, looked remarkably like Gregory Peck. There were several words—British and Gregory Peck among them—that reminded Helen of her few brief moments with Captain Ray Birkett. Today, instead of the usual sense of loss, Helen felt a rush of anger. Where was he? Why did he leave so suddenly? Why hadn't they had more time together? Why hadn't he contacted her? Why had he managed to send only a single postcard to her the very day after they met? Why not another?

The anger felt good as is coursed through her veins, certainly better than fear she usually felt. Fear that Ray was overseas. Fear that he had been captured. Fear that Ray was dead. Oh Lord, he couldn't be dead. Helen couldn't face a lifetime without Ray.

Feeling stifled by her aunts, Helen quickly took her leave, pleading housework at home. She briskly walked across Hinshaw Square to her house, trying to push thoughts of Ray from her mind with every footstep.

Entering her own home, Helen heard the radio playing from the kitchen. As she walked down the hallway, she knew she would find her mother at the rear of the house huddled by the radio or staring out the window into the backyard. When Helen entered the kitchen, as expected, her mother stood at the sink, her gaze had a faraway look to it that Helen would forever associate with the war years.

"I suppose Richard will never finish college now," her mother said upon seeing Helen.

"You never know, Momma. When the war is over, he could always go back."

Her mother's face took on a tight, pinched look. "When the war is over. When the war is over. Don't you know that things will never be the same when the war is over?" Her mother's voice rose an octave.

On the radio, patriotic organ music swelled, a sure signal that war news would soon be on. Hoping to avoid it, Helen switched off the radio. Like her mother, she didn't want to think about Richard or anyone else she cared about being overseas in harm's way. "Momma, don't upset yourself so. Come, sit down. I'll get you some tea to drink."

"Don't switch that off Helen! A few minutes ago they announced that Allied headquarters will be issuing a special broadcast!"

After turning the radio back on, Helen busied herself getting the tea. She added some of their precious sugar to help perk up her mother a little bit.

The radio began to hiss, crackle, and snap like it always did before an overseas transmission began. Helen braced herself for the special broadcast.

"We take you now to our correspondent stationed on a battleship in the Mediterranean Sea...Go ahead..." "Hello everyone. I am speaking to you aboard a ship in the Mediterranean Sea. You can hear the big naval guns bombarding enemy gun emplacements on shore."

Here the sounds of heavy artillery punctuated the air and drowned out the voice of the correspondent. The noise was indescribable. Helen's stomach knotted and she said a silent prayer for the men engaged in the battle. Through the reverberating noise, the correspondent's words came through in patches.

"Smoke and flames cover the area...Allied troops pushing the Germans out of North Africa are pinned down by enemy artillery fire. On the beach, enemy crossfire is mowing down our troops...To continue the assault, waves of landing troops must climb over the dead and wounded... The price of triumph is not cheap... Extensive preparations have been made for our casualties on land, sea, and air. Not all our men, your husbands, sons, sweethearts, friends, will be coming home when this battle is over."

At those words, Helen's mother sank slowly into a nearby chair. She fanned herself and looked disconsolate. This time, she didn't argue when her daughter snapped off the radio. In the ensuing silence, Helen didn't know quite what to say. She found it harder and harder to maintain a happy, upbeat demeanor in the face of her mother's worsening moods. Still, she had to try.

"Momma, I do wish you wouldn't listen to the war news every moment of the day. You know how it upsets you and makes you worry all the more about Richard."

"Of course I worry about Richard. He's in uniform!"

"Yes, but he's stationed right here in Saint Simons Island at the radar training school. For the time being, he's safe."

"You young people all think this is a lark. When you're young, you always believe there is a tomorrow, that you're safe! It's not until you're older that you learn the truth."

"Momma, you shouldn't fret so much. You'll make yourself sick." Helen handed her mother a glass of sweet tea. She returned to the sink and ran water over a wash cloth. Ringing it out, she folded it and placed the cool compress on her mother's forehead. A loud siren caused them both to jump.

"And the racket from the shipyard," complained Helen's mother. "It's bad enough we have to listen to the freight trains running around the clock, the noise of the heavy cranes moving about on their tracks, and the riveters shooting rivets. The public address system and warning sirens are just too much!"

"Hush now. Don't work yourself up into a fit." Helen understood the cause of her mother's distress. She'd been woken up by air raid sirens on multiple nights since returning home. She knew what it was like to lie awake in the dark with her heart pounding listening for the throaty thrum of plane engines or—heaven forbid—the whistling whining noise of bombs descending from the sky. Each time Helen fervently prayed in rhythm with the rising and falling of the sirens that this would be just another drill. Was it any wonder that the sleepless nights affected her mother's delicate constitution?

Chapter 21

Ray

"*O*h Captain Birkett. Captain Birkett," called Ida sweetly up the stairs.

"Will you be coming to our fundraising party? It starts in about an hour. We always take up a collection. This time, we decided that the proceeds will go to the British Widows and Orphans fund."

Ray hesitated before leaving his room. He had planned to take a walk to familiarize himself with the town. He'd never admit that what he really planned to do was look for Helen Stevens. He'd find her somehow, even if he had to knock on every door in Brunswick.

"We have lots of pretty girls coming," simpered Ora coyly. "Our niece will be the prettiest one of all."

"Of course she is," snapped Elva. "Everyone knows she's the prettiest young woman in Brunswick!"

"The smartest too," added Ida, nodding her head in approval.

"She looks just like Lana Turner," said Ora proudly.

"Ora, have you gone dotty? Lana Turner is blond. She looks more like Ava Gardner," corrected Elva.

"All right, Ava Gardner," agreed Ora. "Either way, she's as pretty as a movie star!"

"We're playing party games too," added Ida, getting back to the party. "And there will be music to keep everyone's spirits up." As if to emphasize this point, she moved to the radio and switched the dial from a war news program to a station playing big band music.

"How are we supposed to have a party with no eggs, no sugar, no flour, and no butter? We won't be able to make any cookies or cakes." Ora's face wore a hopeless expression.

"Ora, you know perfectly well that no one is expecting cookies and cakes. We'll make do with strawberry Jell-O®, cornbread, and a jar of the peaches we put up," said Elva.

"Peaches! That will be a big treat!" Ora clapped her hands happily.

"Will we be serving macaroni and cheese again?" asked Ida. "What I wouldn't give for a nice piece of beef."

"We mustn't complain. It's unpatriotic. If we're going to win this war, we all have to make sacrifices. Many people live much more frugally than we do," Elva stated. "Thank heavens we're well off. Some people have to balance their budget on two pins."

"Let's just hope the power company doesn't choose tonight to turn off our power in an effort to conserve energy," Ida said ominously.

"Don't be such a pessimist, Ida. If they do, I've got candles standing by." Elva often played the role of guiding and reassuring her younger twin sisters.

Over the past few days, Ray had grown accustomed to the shifts and drifts in conversational direction. He'd also grown remarkably fond of the sisters. Ray looked at their eager, expectant faces. Though he had no desire to be caught in their web of matchmaking, he knew he should make an effort and attend their party, at least for a while.

"Of course I'll stay, ladies." Ray's decision was rewarded with a clapping of hands from the three women.

"Wonderful," exclaimed Ora, still clapping her hands happily. "We can't wait for you to meet our niece, the one who looks like Ava Gardner. She stopped by the other day, but you were out. Pity." Her face fell as she remembered her earlier attempts at matchmaking.

"No use crying over spilt milk," said Elva.

"Now Captain Birkett, if you would be so kind as to help me set up the punch bowl. The crystal bowl is so heavy, I'm afraid Edna Jane or I may drop it. We keep it in our bomb shelter." Ida, seeing the surprised look on his face, smiled and said, "Well, our root cellar, really, but saying bomb shelter sounds so much more interesting, don't you think?"

Ray spent the next half hour awkwardly going up and down the stairs to the fruit cellar in search of extra chairs, coffee pots, and punch cups. The sisters didn't seem to notice that his cane prevented him from carrying very much on each trip. Ray was happy to be useful, happy to not draw attention to his infirmity. About the twentieth time he ventured downstairs, he began to wonder how many people would be attending. By his count, he'd set out enough cups and saucers to serve an army.

"Between the three of us, we have enough matching china to seat thirty-six people," commented Elva proudly as if reading his thoughts. "Our Momma was wise enough to make us all choose the same china pattern. It makes sense, even if white with a gold rim is rather plain. There are two sets in this house and one at mine."

That explained the abundance of dishware covering every available surface in the root cellar, thought Ray. He walked slowly toward the parlor, his leg paining him more than usual.

"Why Captain Birkett, you're limping!" cried Ora.

"Oh dear, we've asked you to do too much. All those stairs! You should have said something," exclaimed Ida, wringing her hands.

"I'll be all right," protested Ray. "I just need to rest a while."

"We have just the thing! Ora, go draw a bath. Ida, ask Edna Jane to get her healing salts," said Elva, taking charge as always. "Now, Captain, you take yourself upstairs for a nice long soak. Don't you come down until the party starts. Edna Jane's salts will help you feel so much better."

"Hello, Captain. Fancy meeting you here."

Ray recognized the feminine drawl as that of Winona Bunce. Using his cane to steady himself, he rose from the settee to greet her, disturbing Blue and Beau in the process. He was surprised the pretty woman bothered to speak to him. One quick glance around the room and he instantly knew why. She probably did so because she was among the first to arrive. Given her limited choices, talk to the other women or talk to him, the only male present, she'd chosen him. He knew she'd move on when some more men joined the evening's festivities.

It didn't take long for the house to fill with voices. Ray noted the eclectic mix of attendees, young, old, male, female. He recognized a few people, including Cecil Hudson from the Port Director's office and William Browning from the Industrial Efficiency department.

"Hello Captain Birkett," said Dot. "I've brought you some punch."

"Thank you, that's very kind of you Dorothy Dot Carson?"

"Aren't you just the sweetest thing to remember my name! Are you settling in okay?" Dot squeezed his arm invitingly.

"Actually, yes. I've taken a room here."

"Lucky you. The sisters are just about the kindest people I know. Save me a dance later, will you?" Dot asked, unaware of his cane.

"Sure," he said, knowing he never would take the sweet woman up on her request.

Ray watched Winona flit about like a hummingbird, flirting with every male present. Her happy attitude never failed to bring a smile to each man's face. After saying a quick hello to her, one man approached Ray and extended his hand.

"Hi, I'm George White. I've seen you around the shipyard in your uniform. You probably don't recognize me without my coveralls and hard hat. This is my buddy, Hank Stine."

"Hello, Ray Birkett," responded Ray, shaking one man's hand and then the other. George White was slight of build, but Hank Stine was one of those men with a wide grin and a bone-crushing grip to accompany his big-boned and sunburned face. "What do you do at the shipyard?"

"I work as a rigger. Hank, he's a gantry crane operator."

"What does being a rigger entail?" Ray asked, curious.

Before George could reply, outside several sharp blasts from a whistle accompanied a forceful knocking at the front door. "Home Guard. Open up in there!"

"Now, I wonder what he is on about," exclaimed Elva as she hurried to the door. The pounded continued. "Hold your potato, I'm coming."

"Mrs. Clay, you and your sisters have seriously violated blackout regulations," stated the warden as he pushed his way inside the blackout curtains at the door. Behind him the screen door slammed.

"Emmitt Mutterspaw, where are your manners? Who are you to come barging into my house—my sisters' house—without so much as a hello?" Stern of face and hands on hips, Elva blocked his path.

"Never you mind the hellos. You're in violation of blackout regulations!" The slightly overbearing and rather pompous warden stomped across the parlor and pointed dramatically to a spot where the front window curtain had parted slightly. "There!" Mutterspaw exclaimed, pointing an accusatory finger at the tiny opening.

Elva walked over and tweaked the curtains into place with a quick flick of her hand. "Emmitt Mutterspaw, do you mean to tell me that you got yourself all worked up over an eighth of an inch of light coming from our front window? For pity's sake man, not three blocks away the whole shipyard is lit up like Time's Square and you're worried about our itty bitty light."

"Not to mention the fact that we're several blocks inland and the window is covered by the veranda and that great big old live oak tree shades the front of the house," added Ora helpfully. "See Emmitt, even our houses know to hide under the nearest tree with the most Spanish moss whenever an air raid siren goes off. Mustn't leave any shadows."

Frustrated, Emmitt Mutterspaw scanned the window for further offenses. Finding none, he admonished, "Make sure you're more careful in the future."

Not willing to leave well enough alone, Mutterspaw couldn't resist firing a parting shot. "I'm surprised women in your position in the community continue to indulge in frivolities like parties."

"War is never the time to lose one's sense of humor," responded Elva succinctly. She stared him down. "It would serve you well to remember that."

Knowing he had been bested, Emmitt Mutterspaw marched angrily toward the front door.

"Mind you don't trip over Blue—or is it Beau—on your way out," said Ora, giving the irate warden a little finger wave. Emmitt Mutterspaw stomped out the door.

"Really Mrs. Clay, you shouldn't give Emmitt Mutterspaw a hard time. It's our civic duty to follow black-out restrictions and rationing laws," said Cecil Hudson.

"Oh, Mr. Hudson, you're so right. Sometimes though, Mr. Mutterspaw makes my nerves stand on end," said Elva in lieu of an apology.

"Well, he's gone now. Come on everybody, let's play a riddle game," said Winona, eager to restart the fun. She held up a copy of the party planning book that Elva always used when putting together her parties. The cover advertised that fifty-two parties and over six hundred games and stunts could be found inside. From the groans of the attendees, it was obvious that they were all too familiar with the types of riddle games the book provided.

"Oh, don't be such a group of party poopers. Riddles are fun!" exclaimed Winona brightly.

"That's only because you're so good at them," murmured a woman in the back of the room.

"She always makes a big point of showing off," whispered Hank to Ray. In a falsetto voice he mimicked Winona. "'All right, let's see if you can guess this one.'" People standing near them laughed in response to how funny the words sounded coming from such a large man.

"I only care about playing one kind of game with her," said George. "Winona's a real looker, she is. Maybe she'll let me play on her team."

Ray wasn't so sure he'd want to be on Winona's team. To him, she didn't seem the type of woman who would be easy to please. He decided to steer clear of her in the future.

Effectively ignoring the comments from the men, Elva clapped her hands and began pushing everyone around until they were neatly arranged on both sides of the room. Not for the first time, Ray marveled at her organizational skills. Perhaps he should recommend that Elva work at the shipyard's Industrial Efficiency department.

"Since she likes games, we'll let Winona choose. Ida, you keep score. Winona, go ahead and pull a riddle game out of this hat." Elva proffered a battered silk top hat. Winona reached in and pulled out a folded piece of paper.

"Oh!" Winona exclaimed. She opened Elva's party planning book to the chapter containing the riddle games. "This will be so much fun. This riddle game is called *'What letter is?'* I'll give y'all an example. What letter is an insect?"

"A 'B'," shouted Cecil, eagerly wanting to please Winona.

"That's right. How clever of you, Mr. Hudson." Winona smiled at Cecil who blushed happily. "Okay, try this one. What letter is a bird?"

"A 'Q'," shouted Alfred Smith.

"A 'Q' isn't a bird," said Winona, her voice laced with disdain. "What were you thinking, Mr. Smith?"

"A quail is a bird. Quail starts with a 'Q'," responded Alfred, trying to recover from her put-down.

"No, silly, the letter must be an actual word. Here's another example. What kind of word is a line? The answer would be 'Q' meaning 'queue'. Q-U-E-U-E." Winona spelled out the word.

Now that they understood what Winona meant, the others discussed the riddle among themselves before answering.

"Shush! Y'all have to come up with your own answers," announced Winona. She obviously enjoyed being in charge. "So what letter is a bird?"

"A 'J'," answered Ray easily now that he had time to think about it.

"That's right. Well done, Limey. Ready for the next one? What letter is a large body of water?" asked Winona.

"A 'C'," said Harold.

"That's right. What letter is a verb of debt?"

"Hey, these are hard," protested Mabel, a woman Ray recognized from the typist pool.

"What's the matter? Can't you get this one?" taunted Winona.

No one volunteered anything.

"An 'O'," said Cecil tentatively.

"That's right. You can owe someone money," said Winona with a smile. "What letter is a questioning letter?"

"A 'Y'," answered Cecil quickly.

"Right again. Now Cecil, give other people a chance." Winona waggled her finger at the man, causing him to blush. "What letter is a vegetable that rolls off of a knife?"

"You've got to be kidding," laughed Dot. She tugged on Ray's sleeve companionably. "You try, Captain Birkett."

"That's an easy one. A 'P'," said Ray.

"You're right. Chalk one up for the limey. Let's see if you can guess this one," said Winona when the laughter had died down. "What letter is a sheep?"

"A 'U'," answered George White.

"Yes, a 'U'," repeated Winona, obviously enjoying herself.

And so it went until all the letters in the alphabets were used up.

"Well done everyone. Cecil Hudson answered the most number correctly," said Ida. "So he gets the prize. A box of chocolates!"

Cecil Hudson grinned happily as he walked up to receive his prize. The others enviously eyed the tiny box of chocolates. They were a rare treat given the rationing of sugar, butter, and cocoa.

"Don't worry, Winona, I'll share them with you," he said shyly.

"Thank you honey. You're as sweet as those chocolates." Winona gave the man a luscious wink. Cecil Hudson blushed beet red to his hairline.

"Whatever in the world is keeping our niece? She should be here by now," fretted Ora as the party attendees broke into smaller groups.

"Now, Ora, she'll be here when she can. You know how hard she works at the shipyard."

The doorbell rang. Elva went to answer it. She returned a moment later and announced, "Captain Birkett, it's for you."

Ray went to the door and listened for a moment.

"I'm sorry ladies. I must go out. I'll try to be as quiet as possible when I return so as not to disturb you." Ray smiled at each of the sisters before taking his hat from the hall closet and leaving. Before the door shut behind him, he heard Ora say, "But if he leaves now, he won't meet—"

Chapter 22

Helen

*H*elen stayed late at the shipyard putting the finishing touches on a training program for new welders. She incorporated what she had learned from Milly Dorsett's accident. Well-designed training programs were crucial. In many cases, the people working in the shipyard had been field hands, farm workers, or unemployed before joining the swelling ranks of employees. Helen didn't mind putting in long hours. She wanted to make sure they could do their jobs well. Photographs showing every step in the welding process had been attached to a large board which would be used for teaching purposes. Trainees would learn to read blueprints, how to weld overhead or under head, how to handle steel, whatever it took to build a Liberty ship.

Enjoying the quiet, warm mid-June evening after the noise of the shipyard, Helen strolled across Hinshaw Square under the live oaks bearded with Spanish moss to her aunts' houses. Helen knew her parents wouldn't be expecting her until late since she'd promised to attend her aunts' widows and orphans fundraising party tonight.

In the waning light, Helen watched as a man leaning lightly on a cane got into a car parked at the curb in front of her aunts' house. Her heart skipped a beat when the lyrics from *I'll Be Seeing You* floated out the windows. The man looked so familiar that, for a moment, she thought it was Captain Birkett. Her whole being fizzed with joy. Just as quickly, Helen schooled her emotions. She didn't need to remember her course in probability theory to know that there was only minute chance that the man could be Ray. Would she ever stop hoping? Would her heart ever stop aching for a man she danced with once upon a time?

"Helen, honey! Welcome!" Aunt Ora greeted Helen in her usual exuberant style.

"You just missed our boarder again, honey," said Aunt Elva. "He's pretty sharp with riddles; I'll say that for him."

"Dot Carson sure seems to fancy him," added Ida.

Thinking it best to leave the new man to Dot, Helen gave each of her aunts quick hugs and then went to the refreshment table to join her friends.

"Hello Miss Helen."

Helen turned to see Alfred Smith standing nearby with a small bunch of flowers in his hand. He beamed hopefully at her. Inwardly she sighed. Alfred wasn't such a bad sort, really. Unfortunately for him—except for a certain Captain—she wasn't interested in anyone right now. Despite how she had grown and changed during the past year, Helen couldn't help comparing every man she met with Captain Birkett.

"Hello Alfred," Helen said politely. She looked at the man gazing at her with undisguised affection. Helen had been discouraging his attention since high school. Would she have to spend the whole evening with him?

"May I say Miss Helen that you set a room alight just by entering it?" Alfred Smith gave her a courtly little bow and handed her the flowers.

"Why thank you ever so much for your lovely compliment, Mr. Smith, but surely you exaggerate." Helen looked around desperately for an escape route. On the other side of the room, her Aunt Ida beckoned.

"I'm so sorry, Alfred. Please excuse me. I really need to go see what my aunt wants. Why don't you dance with Dot? She's quite a good dancer." Without a backward glance, Helen strode away.

"Helen, honey, I didn't mean to pull you away from that nice Mr. Smith. He dotes on you so."

"Aunt Ida, you best not encourage him. I don't want or need a suitor just now."

"All right, though he's such a nice young man. You should give him a chance. Anyway, listen to this, Helen, honey." Ida held the newspaper in front of both of them and proceeded to read in a loud and exaggerated voice. "'*The Stevens sisters sponsored another successful fundraising party. This time, the monies collected will be used to purchase materials and supplies for the newest Liberty ship under construction at the shipyard. The party was attended by Winona Bunce, Hazel Ann Crawford, Helen Stevens, ...William Browning, George White, Cecil Hudson, Alfred Smith, Hank Stine, Dot Carson, and many others. Guests acted out a short play for the amusement of all. Winona Bunce was voted the best performance of the evening and won a jar of Vidalia onion relish.*'"

"Isn't it wonderful our parties are so successful? Everyone will want to attend future ones. Won't that be nice? Think of the money we will collect for charity." Ida peered cautiously over the top of the newspaper, surveying the party-goers. Satisfied that no one was paying attention to them, she ducked back behind the newspaper. "Helen, honey," whispered Ida conspiratorially.

"What is it, Aunt Ida?" Helen whispered back. Recognizing her aunt's secretive smile, Helen crossed her arms over her chest and asked with mock severity, "Have you entered another contest?"

"I did better than that! I won another contest!" Without her meaning to, Aunt Ida's happy voice rose above a whisper. She quickly scanned the room to see if anyone overheard. Seeing no one nearby, she raised the paper in front of them and continued in a softer voice, "Wait until you see what I won! It's perfect for you!"

"For me? You've won something for me?" Helen's eyes opened wide in astonishment.

"Of course dear. Why not? You're the only one in the family who doesn't tease me for entering contests. Even after I won that new stove, your Aunt Elva thinks contests are nonsense."

"She's too practical to understand."

"A stove is practical!"

"Of course it is, Aunt Ida. Aunt Elva probably can't forget the time you won all that popping corn."

"Well, that was practical too. We enjoyed eating it and we put those leftover popped kernels to good use as packing material whenever we shipped anything."

"Whenever we shipped anything for two years," laughed Helen. Her expression softened when her aunt's face fell. Helen gave her aunt a reassuring hug. "So tell me, what did you win this time?"

"Come with me and I'll show you. It's up in my room." Aunt Ida led the way, still talking. "It came today. It's a good thing that I was home to meet the postman. You can imagine what your Aunt Elva would have done. She'd have turned it away."

"Oh, I don't think she's that against contests."

"She says it's not worth the spit it takes to lick the stamp needed to enter them."

"Surely after all the contests you've won, she doesn't say that!"

"Sure does, even after I've won upwards of twenty contests!" Aunt Ida entered her cheerful yellow room. On the bed lay a large box loosely wrapped in brown packing paper. "Helen, honey, I hope you don't mind that I've already opened it. I couldn't wait to see what was inside! When I saw it, I knew it was perfect for you so I wrapped it up again."

Helen sat on the bed next to the package. She removed the string and packing paper to reveal a box from a fancy dress shop in New York. Hurriedly, she lifted the lid. There nestled in an abundance of tissue paper was a strikingly beautiful royal blue tea-length gown.

"Oh, Aunt Ida, it's lovely! Absolutely lovely!" Helen exclaimed, her voice choked with emotion. She gently picked up the dress and held it to her body. It shimmered like a sapphire in the light. Caught up in the magic of a new dress, Helen twirled happily in front of the mirror.

"I checked the label and it's your size," said Aunt Ida, sublimely happy. "Now when you have an important occasion, like if they ask you to launch a Liberty ship, you'll have the perfect dress to wear. Look, it even comes with a fancy little hat and gloves. We'll pool our shoe coupons and buy you pretty shoes to match."

"I don't know what to say! What a perfectly wonderful prize! New dresses are almost nonexistent. You're much too generous. Don't you need a new dress? Shouldn't you return it for something in your size?"

"Something in my size?" Aunt Ida giggled. "What would an old woman like me want with a fancy party dress? No dear, you enjoy it. Maybe you can wear it when you have a date with our new boarder."

Chapter 23

Ray

$\mathcal{L}$ate in the evening, Ray stood in front of Admiral Jarabek's desk ready to summarize his findings. Even he had to admit it wasn't much. Ray half-wished he was back at the party vying for the attention of the beautiful Winona Bunce or the charming Dot Carson.

"How is your hunt for saboteurs progressing, Captain Birkett?" asked Admiral Jarabek.

"I'm afraid I have to admit that it's taking me longer than expected to settle in, sir. There is a lot to learn about ship building and the shipyard. Burt Dixon has been most helpful."

"You will need to speed up your efforts, Captain. I've learned another serious welding accident occurred the other day shutting down the entire department for several hours. Remember, time is of the essence!"

"Yes sir, I understand sir. While I've been familiarizing myself with the shipyard and the ship construction process, I've been compiling a list of the most vulnerable areas for sabotage. Like I said, Mr. Dixon has been most helpful."

"But you've found nothing of interest yet." Admiral Jarabek didn't look up from his cluttered desk.

"No sir, I haven't. As you requested, I've studied a number of recent accident reports in search of a pattern or opportunity for inflicting damage. An eye injury from a grinder, a burn when a worker failed to wear protective clothing, a metal key that flew off a lathe and struck a man in the face, and a broken ankle caused by an exploding acetylene tank. Though each incident halted work on the ships involved for a number of hours, none of the incidents appear to be anything but accidents."

"I see. You're certain about that?"

"Yes sir, I am.

The telephone on the admiral's desk shrilled insistently. Admiral Jarabek raised his hand as a signal to Ray to wait while he answered the phone.

"Hello." The admiral listened for a moment and then said, "Send General Dirner in, please."

"If you'd like me to leave, sir," said Ray as the admiral hung up the telephone.

"No, Captain, General Dirner has asked to speak with us both."

Ray wondered why a general would possibly want to speak with him. They waited silently until General Dirner entered the room. The tall man filled the cramped space with his commanding presence. Ray snapped a salute.

"Gentlemen." General Dirner returned Ray's salute and shook hands with the admiral. "You know I don't often make personal visits, Admiral Jarabek, but what I have to say is of the utmost importance." General Dirner eyed Ray pointedly.

"Thank you very much for stopping by General. This is Captain Ray Birkett, the British Naval captain I told you about. He's in charge of investigating suspicious activity around the shipyard," said Admiral Jarabek.

The general sized Ray up in a single penetrating glance.

"Captain Ray Birkett, His Majesty's Royal Navy," said Ray, snapping to attention and saluting again.

"Pleasure to meet you, Captain. Let's all sit down and I'll tell you what's been happening at the Navy Air Station's radar training facility."

"Whenever you're ready, General," motioned Admiral Jarabek.

General Dirner cleared his throat. "In June of 1942, German spies landed at Amagansett New York and Ponte Vedra Beach, Florida. Those men brought ashore significant amounts of explosives and planned to destroy multiple targets including U.S. aluminum and metal manufacturing plants, railroads, utilities, and the New York water supply. They intended to spread panic among the American people by setting off bombs in bus and train terminals and large department stores."

General Dirner stared at Ray as if expecting a response. Ray ventured, "Yes sir, I am aware of their intentions. It was on all the newsreels."

"Were you also aware that FBI agents working in Brunswick played an important role in monitoring telephone communications between the spies and their contacts here in South Georgia?"

"No sir, I was not," admitted Ray.

"Utility workers installing new telephone lines at the Hercules Powder Company reported that during the installation a man visited the worksite and asked a lot of technical questions about their electronics. Turns out, he stopped by whenever they were on-site working. Eventually, the utility workers reported him to the proper authorities. Based on his suspicious behavior, the FBI bugged the man's phone line where he was staying in a tourist court just south of Savannah."

"Tourist court, sir?" Confused by the term, Ray couldn't help interrupting.

"It's what we call a small motel where you park your car right in front of your room," explained the general without missing a beat. "Turns out the man was making a lot of calls to New York, coordinating the activities of the two landing parties of Germans. Well, he's out of it now—arrested and imprisoned like the other spies. You probably know that four of the Germans were electrocuted two months after their capture. Long story short—if it hadn't been for the work of the talented men who ferretted out the truth, imagine the damage the spies could have done."

"Yes sir, it was a lucky break that the saboteurs were caught."

"Lucky break, my eye!" thundered Admiral Jarabek. "It was hard work to capture the German spies within four days of their landing."

"Yes sir."

"There's more," continued General Dirner. "A few hours after the launch of the Liberty ship on May 19th, I received a message from the Navy Air Station radar training school over on Saint Simons Island. They picked up on a weak radar signal coming from this area. The men tried to use a loop antenna to pin-point its range and direction more closely, but the weak intermittent signal didn't give them much to work with, unfortunately. Are you familiar with loop antennas, Captain Birkett?" asked General Dirner.

"Yes sir, I am. You're referring to the wire loop antenna that rotates when operating. Transmitter locations can be pinpointed because the signal gets stronger or weaker depending on the orientation of the loop. When was the signal first detected? How long did it last? What frequency?" Ray asked the questions in rapid fire succession.

"It's all here in this report." The general handed Ray a folder marked confidential. "The signals began a few minutes after the ship launched and continued for about three hours. The signal was quite feeble, of short duration, and erratic."

"It's June 20th, sir. Has it or a signal like it been heard since the May launch?" asked Ray.

"No, nothing at all. We might be over-cautious, but we do have another ship about to launch. The radar station is listening twenty-four hours a day. I'll be sending over one of our operators to work with you. In the meantime, I'm here to ask whether or not you have uncovered anything suspicious concerning the ship that is about to launch."

"Suspicious? No sir. I was just telling Admiral Jarabek that there have been a number of small incidents in the past three months; burns, falls, and cuts. The only thing unusual is that there have been three unrelated loss-time accidents in the past ten days, which is more numerous than previous history would lead us to expect. I've studied the accident reports but have found nothing out of the ordinary," reported Ray.

"Nothing at all unusual about these recent accidents?" queried the general.

"No sir. One welder failed to wear protective clothing and received multiple minor burns. Another accident involved a lathe operator. The man was turning a propeller shaft on a lathe when the key used to mark a keyway flew out at him and cut his face badly."

"And you found nothing odd about the accident?"

"No sir. Apart from his claim that he had taken the key out before going on break, the incident is pretty cut and dry. He could have left the key in the keyway without meaning to do so. If the shaft was turned away from him, he wouldn't have been able to see it; thus the accident."

"And the third accident?"

"The third accident involved a female welder," Ray reported.

The general and the admiral both snorted softly. Ray knew to let their prejudices slide.

"The wheel came off her acetylene tank causing it to topple over on her. When the pressurized acetylene tank hit the ground, the valve stem snapped free and hit her ankle. The flame from her welding torch ignited a fire cloud. Fortunately, the flare-up didn't last long. The welder sustained a broken ankle," reported Ray succinctly.

"How unfortunate," the general said, dismissing the welder's injuries. "So what you are telling me is that we have nothing to go on in terms of sabotage."

"Yes sir, that's what I'm trying to say," admitted Ray.

"You're sure?" asked Admiral Jarabek.

"Yes sir."

"I hope that you understand the importance of your investigation, Captain," said General Dirner. "Let me ask you this, Captain Birkett. What if the FBI hasn't captured all the spies that might have landed on our shores? What if there are spies right here in Brunswick waiting to blow up the shipyard or the Hercules plant where they make components for explosives? What if there is a spy out there right now making calls to New York or some other place to report the ships being launched here in Brunswick or in Savannah? Think of the damage a single spy could do. The Brunswick shipyard has had a number of accidents in recent months that have delayed production. Is it the work of a spy? A saboteur? We need to know. I need for you to get familiar with the activities in the shipyard and determine if there is indeed a saboteur present. Do it and do it now! That will be all, Captain."

"Yes sir!" Ray snapped a salute at both the admiral and general before exiting the room.

Chapter 24

Helen

Saturday afternoon, Helen unlocked her bicycle and walked out the gate of the shipyard at shift change. Once upon a time, she thought she'd outgrown a bike. Now, she rode one everywhere. Just outside the gate, she found Alfred Smith waiting for her. Helen smiled at the young man she'd known since high school. Classified 4F because of his eyesight, Alfred now worked in the shipyard accounting department.

"Hello Miss Helen."

"Hello Mr. Smith. I didn't expect to see you here."

"Oh, please ma'am, there's no need to be so formal even though we're at work. We've known each other forever. Please call me Alfred."

Helen smiled tentatively at him when he fell in step beside her. She didn't want to encourage him by becoming too familiar, thus the use of his last name. She treated all the men she met this way. At least, she had until Captain Birkett. Inwardly, she laughed at her own double standard. If she wanted to keep all men at a distance, then why had she danced with Captain Birkett, a man she wasn't destined to see again? She wondered if Captain Birkett would always linger on the edge of her thoughts. Helen shook her head to dislodge the thought. She groped for something to say to Alfred. "Well, it's nice to see you again."

"It's nice to see you too," he answered shyly. "I've been hoping to meet you today."

Helen couldn't help but be flattered by his attention to her. It wouldn't hurt her to be nice to him; after all he looked so painfully shy. She smiled, happy to be away from the noise and commotion of the shipyard and in the company of such a pleasant young man. "I'm going to meet my friends the drugstore for a Coke®, would you like to join us?" she asked companionably.

"That would be really nice." Alfred's grin split his face from ear to ear.

"I've also got to turn in my empty toothpaste tube for a refill." Helen patted her purse where the empty tube resided.

"Yes, ma'am, the government is making sure we don't waste a single piece of metal, aren't they? You wouldn't think that a metal toothpaste tube matters all that much, 'cepting when you think about how all of us use them. Nationwide that adds up to a lot of metal toothpaste tubes."

Helen laughed, imagining an accountant just like Alfred calculating how many tubes of toothpaste Americans used. She was about to say so when her younger brother came toward them at a run.

"Randolph Joseph Michael Stevens, where are you going in such an all fire hurry?" Helen asked as she grabbed Randolph, better known as Mickey, by the arm and pulled him to a stop.

"They've got bubble gum down at the drugstore and I want to get some before all the other kids do," panted Mickey. "Then, I'm fixin' to go to the movies. Let me go! I don't want to be late and miss the newsreels!"

Helen marveled that young children like her brother appeared more excited than fearful when watching the newsreels at the cinema. Personally, the newsreels with their sights and sounds of war left her breathless with fear that weighed on her like a giant hand. Fear of invasion. Fear of bombing. Fear for her friends overseas. Fear of loss. Her emotions suddenly running away with her, Helen clung on to her brother as if afraid to lose him. Mickey struggled to free himself.

"Miss Helen, ma'am, you'd better let him go," Alfred said gently. He touched her arm, perhaps recognizing the reason behind her distress. "Bubble gum's scarce as hen's teeth these days."

"Yes—yes—you're right," she said, flustered. Helen took a deep breath to steady herself. "Mickey, maybe you should take my bike. Remember to lock it up. Now, give me some sugar before you go." Helen leaned toward him for a kiss.

"Ah, do I have to? There are people around," her brother complained. His face brightened and he added, "Hey Sis, can I have a dime for the movie and popcorn?" Laughing at his audacity, Helen handed him a dime and pushed Mickey on his way.

At the drugstore, everyone was discussing the war news and the upcoming launch of the next Liberty ship.

"I watched the newsreels at the cinema last night. There is so much going on. The Allied forces have driven Rommel and his army clean out of North Africa. And we might invade Sicily! Can you imagine? By this time next month, we could finally have a toehold in Southern Europe," announced Cecil Hudson.

"I've never even heard of these places our army is fighting!" said Hazel Ann.

"Do we always have to talk about the war?" whined Winona. "Isn't it enough that we have to go without stockings and lipstick? Why just yesterday, I went into the department store to buy a new blouse. Well, wouldn't you know they had the war news on the radio. It was so depressing; I couldn't bring myself to buy the blouse. It was such a pretty one too."

Helen winced at Winona's selfish comment. There was a war on. Regardless of the myriad of inconveniences they faced every day, it was unpatriotic to complain. Did Winona realize how shallow she sounded? Perhaps Aunt Ora was right, people see themselves differently than others do.

"I can't believe it's been a month since we launched the fourth Liberty ship," said William Browning.

"Yes, May 19th seems like ages ago," said Dot.

"Doesn't seem like that to me. It takes a long time to build something as complex as a ship," said Hazel Ann.

"The government thinks it's taken too much time. The keels for these first six ships were all laid last summer! It's taken over three hundred days to build each of them. Too slow. That's why they changed over the management of the shipyard. They'll probably be expanding our Industrial Efficiency department very soon," said William Browning importantly.

"I bet that's why they've got that good-looking British Naval Captain here poking around looking into things. Helen, have you met him yet?" asked Dot.

"No, I haven't." Helen really couldn't care less about meeting another man. Her mind preferred to dwell on the safety issues at the shipyard.

"He's ever so handsome and nice, though from what I hear, he asks a lot of questions," said Dot.

"I haven't met him either, but I've heard the same thing. I wonder what his job is," said Hazel Ann.

"*Thomas Todd*. Don't you think that's an odd name for a ship? What's the name of the one to be launched next?" asked Alfred.

"The *Robert Trumble*."

"I know the names are chosen to honor people, but they're not easy to remember," admitted Hazel Ann.

"With so many ships being built at shipyards across the nation, it's hard to come up with a unique name for each one. Every shipyard submits a list of names for government approval. Not that the name means much, they will operate at sea under a random number," said Cecil Hudson knowingly.

"Why is that?" asked William.

"We wouldn't want the enemy to know where they are from, what their mission is, or what cargo they are carrying. We also wouldn't want anyone to know in advance when they're being launched." Cecil Hudson puffed up with pride over the importance of his position in the Port Director's office. After the general manager and the assistant general manager, he was among the first to know a ship's launch date and time. His job entailed managing a detailed list of what had to be done, when, and by whom in order to prepare for a launch. He was responsible for making sure that the appropriate officials, dignitaries, sponsors, and workers would be ready an hour before the launch ceremony.

"Cecil sweetie, is that why you wouldn't tell me the exact launch date until yesterday afternoon?" Winona pouted.

"It's best that no one knows until it's for certain. For one thing, so many little things can go wrong and delay the launch. And then there is the security issue. Remember *Loose Lips Sink Ships*." Cecil smiled patronizingly at Winona.

"Do you think you'll ever pick me to be one of the ladies-in-waiting?" Winona wheedled. "Ladies-in-waiting get to wear pretty dresses, carry flowers, and get their picture in the paper and everything. Cecil, please pick me. You're my sweetheart. You'd do that for me, wouldn't you Cecil?"

"You've got your heart set on being one, don't you Winona?" he asked, all of his attention fastened on her well-endowed figure as she strained to move closer to him.

"What woman wouldn't want to be selected to serve in the court and have their picture in the paper?"

Chapter 25

Ray

*7*he evening following the launch, the Stevens sisters and Ray sat comfortably on the veranda. In the background, the radio provided a steady stream of war news intermingled with big band music.

"Tell us all about the launch of the Liberty ship today, Captain Birkett," insisted Elva. She handed Ray a sweating glass of iced tea.

"I'm sure you ladies would have enjoyed being there. Though I've made my career the navy, I've never been to the launching of a ship before this. I was taken aback at the amount of fanfare," Ray admitted. He took a long refreshing drink of tea.

"But Captain Birkett, why wouldn't the shipyard want to go all out and celebrate something as wonderful as the launch of a ship? After all, Liberty ships are so important to the war effort. Didn't I hear you say that the other day?" Ora asked sweetly. She refilled Ray's glass with iced tea.

"Oh, that reminds me. Captain Birkett, I have something to read to you," said Ida. She smoothed the newspaper she held in her lap.

"Now Ida, let's let him finish telling us about the launch before we tell him our news," said Elva.

"Of course, Sister, honey. I just don't want to forget," responded Ida.

"I declare, the newspaper is laying right there in your lap. How could you forget?" retorted Elva. "Sometimes I don't think you have a lick of sense."

"Speaking of something else I shouldn't forget," said Ida, ignoring Elva and her comment. "Ora, I met Mrs. Pickles in town today. She thought I was you and started talking before I could straighten her out on who was who. You know how she is. Well, before I forget, she wants your recipe for Vidalia onion relish."

"Ida! We were talking about the launch with our guest," snapped Elva.

"The launch," began Ray, drawing their attention away from their little squabble. "The launch included a master of ceremony, sponsors, co-sponsors, attendants, and the shipyard band. The champagne bottle, all wrapped up in red, white, and blue ribbons, hung from the bow until it was time for the sponsor to christen the ship."

"Captain Birkett, is it true that the sponsor who christens the ship is always a woman?" asked Ora.

"Yes, ma'am. That's in keeping with tradition. The sponsor, Mrs. J. Heck, received a huge bouquet of deep red roses. I'm sure you would have been impressed."

"Oh, isn't that precious?" sighed Ida. "Roses."

"I couldn't hear all the names of the participants, but I think the attendants were all female swing shift welders," Ray reported.

"Imagine, a woman working as a welder!" exclaimed Ora. "What's the world coming too?"

"The band played a number of patriotic tunes. Some were unfamiliar to me, but I'm sure you would have recognized them," Ray concluded.

"Thank you for telling us about the launch. Perhaps someday, we'll see one for ourselves. Before you get busy doing whatever it is that you do, we have something to show you," announced Ora proudly.

"Captain Birkett, I simply must read to you the newspaper article telling of our most recent party. Your name is mentioned!" Ida waved the paper around proudly.

"You ladies sponsored a wonderful evening. It was a charming party."

"A charming party! Oh, you British," blushed Ora. "Charming sounds ever so much prettier than 'swell'."

"Oh, it was nothing at all," said Elva. "Any Southerner will tell you that all it takes to make a good party is lively conversations and good cocktails."

"Ladies, I am deeply honored that you chose the British Widows and Orphans as your fund of the week." Ray bowed causing the women to simper happily.

"Captain Birkett, you are such a gentleman," said Ida.

Flustered by his bow, Elva said, "We're just like 'Bundles for Britain.' We provide clothes and blankets for people who have been bombed out of their homes."

The telephone rang noisily in the back of the house. Elva went to answer it. Moments later she appeared at the door.

"Captain Birkett, you're wanted on the telephone. The man sounds very official," Elva said.

Ray went to the telephone and the sisters tactfully remained to the veranda.

"Hello, this is Captain Birkett."

"Captain Birkett, this is Admiral Jarabek's assistant. I've been trying to reach you. Please hold for Admiral Jarabek." A series of clicks followed, and then the admiral's voice came on the line.

"Captain Birkett, General Dirner contacted me a few minutes ago. Shortly before today's launch, they picked up radio beacon signals. This time, they definitely were able to pinpoint the shipyard as the source. They were quite strong at first and then faded. One of the radar operators said that it reminded him of the sound of a ship going out to sea. General Dirner has sent a man over to meet you at the shipyard gate immediately. You are to meet with him so that he can fill you in on the details. Also, there has been another accident at the shipyard. Something about mixing acid and water incorrectly. I want you to investigate it and report back to me."

Chapter 26

Helen

Helen hurried to the source of the agonized screams echoing off the corrugated metal walls of the building. Ahead of her, Helen could see several people trying to restrain a struggling woman. For a moment, they parted allowing Helen to see Moria Painter who worked as one of the rust removers. The tormented young woman clawed at the skin that hung in strips from her face. Acid, thought Helen, only acid could cause such horrible disfiguration.

Horrified by the sight, Helen failed to realize William Browning had stepped into her path until it was too late. His black hard hat clattered to the ground. Flustered, she stooped and picked it up; noting absent-mindedly that it wasn't the correct color for their department.

"Mr. Browning, I'm so sorry! I was trying to get here as fast as I could," Helen apologized.

"You of all people should be more careful," barked Browning.

"Your hat—it's the wrong color," she said awkwardly as she handed it back to him. Her face red, Helen turned toward Moria.

"That's the least of our worries, don't you think?" he answered brusquely. Browning gestured at his hat. "I must have picked up the wrong one when I left the office."

Funny, thought Helen, I remember only safety yellow hard hats hanging on the pegs by the door. She chided herself. William was right, she should be thinking of Moria and her accident, not of trivialities.

"Here we go again, another accident investigation, another delayed launch. I wish people would be more careful," complained Browning with a remarkable lack of feeling.

Exasperated, Helen retorted, "Mr. Browning, it's not as if people get up in the morning and say 'I think I'll hurt myself at work today. That should be fun.'"

"Of course not, no one would say that. But everybody knows people who are involved in accidents are just naturally careless."

To Helen, he sounded more than a bit callous. Then she reminded herself that they had all been working very hard recently. Unlike the Southern men she grew up with, many of the men she worked with were curt in both their words and behavior. The ambulance crew had hardly taken Moria out of the building before William Browning spoke again.

"It looks to me like Moria mixed acid and water incorrectly. Too bad, now the next launch will have to be delayed while they clean up the work area and find someone else to do the work. I'll write up this accident. There is no reason for you to stay. It's past shift change anyway." William looked blandly at Helen. His expression showed nothing but professional interest in the scene in front of him.

Sensing that he would write it off in a perfunctory manner, Helen said, "If you don't mind, I'll hang around for a while."

Helen stayed because she wanted to find out the answers to a lot of questions including: what would have motivated Moria to deviate from her training? Even Helen knew the proper procedure for mixing the two liquids. Always pour the acid into the water to dilute its power, never the reverse. Pouring water into acid causes the acid to react and foam.

Under some circumstances, if the concentration is high enough, a small amount of water mixing in acid could explode. Moria, careful and attentive to details, should never have made that mistake. Helen swallowed her anger at his insensitivity and reminded herself that William Browning was an experienced safety professional.

Browning gave her a long, assessing look. "Suit yourself, if that's what you want." With that, he turned and walked toward Moria's supervisor.

Helen took her time surveying the accident scene. She worked silently, concentrating on the small details. In her mind, she replayed her professor's lectures. She reminded herself not to stop at the obvious cause. Helen believed William had jumped too quickly to his conclusion of operator error. Stopping at the obvious reason limits a person's ability to find and fix the real cause of the problem.

Gingerly, Helen knelt down and used a pencil to shift the containers marked acid and water. Both had toppled over on their side, the contents making puddles on the floor. If she was going to prevent future accidents, she needed to determine the root cause of this one. Her boss expected her to create a culture of people who worked smart. Helen told herself to be objective and analytical rather than fault finding. Perhaps that's what annoyed her about Browning's manner. He assumed it was Moria's fault that the acid exploded, a classic case of blame the victim.

Under her breath Helen repeated the steps to take when investigating an accident. "Isolate the accident site. Record all the evidence. Photograph the scene." She didn't have a camera, but Helen used pencil and paper to make several small sketches from different angles. She also stood still for a time in order to allow her memory to soak in the scene. "Identify and interview witnesses," she murmured. Moria had been taken away by ambulance. Helen would speak with her later at the hospital, if possible. Given the state of Moria's injuries, she might not be up to having visitors. Rose Price and Evelyn Mehaffie, Moria's co-workers, worked nearby. She would speak to them immediately.

When Helen felt she had learned as much as she could, she planned to analyze the information and fix the problem. At least she hoped she would. Helen straightened up from her investigation of the containers and sighed. Despite her training, she couldn't help but wonder if this was just another mistake made by someone who took a risk. She truly hoped not. A horribly scarred face would be a terrible price for Moria to pay.

She turned to interview Rose and Evelyn but stopped and took another look at the containers marked acid and water. It was then that she realized that something didn't look quite right about the labels.

Chapter 27

Ray

$\mathcal{D}$espite the late hour, Ray intended to visit the accident site to take a look around. Based on his findings, he would prepare a detailed report for Admiral Jarabek and General Dirner. If he waited until tomorrow morning, everything would be cleaned up leaving no trace. Ray invited the young lieutenant from the Navy Radar Training school to tag along. The noise in the shipyard prevented Ray from catching his new co-worker's name when they were introduced. He'd ask again later, when they were in a quieter area. They entered the corrugated metal building though the side door.

Half hidden in the shadows, a figure knelt by the accident site. Ray cleared his throat as they approached. The woman turned toward them. Suddenly, Ray found himself face-to-face with Helen Stevens. He stopped mid-stride, spellbound, completely taken aback by her unexpected reappearance in his life. He couldn't believe his eyes. He rubbed them and blinked. Without thinking how she would react or what he would say, he hurried over. The lieutenant followed on his heels.

"Hi Sis," said the lieutenant.

Sis? As in sister? The lieutenant was related to Helen Stevens? Utterly unprepared for the unfolding events, Ray remained speechless. He wasn't sure what he should say anyway. After all, he hadn't seen her in over a year. For all he knew, she'd forgotten all about him.

"Oh!" Helen squeaked when she recognized him. Joy lit her face from within. With a radiant smile, she took two steps toward Ray and reached out to touch him. Abruptly Helen checked herself, as if realizing it wouldn't do to behave so unprofessionally, especially in front of her brother. "Hello Richard. Hello Captain Birkett," she said coolly.

"You two know each other?" Richard Stevens took a good look at Ray's face. "Say, I recognize you now. You're the Captain who danced with Helen in the hallway! I thought you looked familiar but I couldn't place you."

Helen's face flamed visibly at the reminder.

"Hello Miss Stevens. It is wonderful to see you again after such a long time," Ray said respectfully, keeping his emotions in check. In reality, every fiber of his being strained to remain polite and professional. What he really wanted to do was sweep her into his arms and kiss her silly. What he really wanted to hear her say was that she lay awake at night remembering their single dance together. Instead, he stared longingly at the woman of his dreams.

"I didn't realize you were here or that you knew my brother." Helen gave her brother a quizzical look. She sounded so self-assured, so calm and collected while Ray's own heart raced uncontrollably. "You must be the Brit everyone is talking about. When did you two get together?"

"The powers that be have assigned us to work on a project together. We just met for the first time this evening," answered Richard.

"What's happened here?" Ray asked, striving to maintain an all-business attitude to match hers. He stepped forward and poked at one of the cans with his cane. It came in contact with the puddle of fluid beside them. Belatedly, Ray remembered that this was an accident scene and yanked his cane back.

"Hey! What are you doing? Don't you know you're supposed to maintain the integrity of the accident scene until all the evidence can be recorded! Can't you see I've isolated the accident site with these markers?" Helen asked forcefully.

Ray abruptly stepped back. Angry with himself over his gaffe, he responded more sharply than he intended. "Maintain the integrity of the accident scene? Isolated the accident site? Those are pretty fancy words you are using, aren't they?"

Richard touched Ray on the sleeve to caution him. He knew his sister would not take Ray's criticism well. "You best not open your mouth if you know what's good for you," cautioned Richard under his breath.

"I'll have you know I am in charge of investigating this accident," Helen said a bit pompously.

Her attitude continued to annoy Ray. He had hoped to see a face wreathed in smiles welcoming him into her arms; instead Helen Stevens remained aloof and distant. Without considering the impact of his words, he responded. "Investigating the accident? It seems pretty straightforward to me. Based on the briefing I received over the telephone, the woman mixed acid and water incorrectly. A foolish and dangerous thing to do. Accidents like this delay ship launches."

"People do not intentionally hurt themselves," Helen said through gritted teeth, fists knotted at her sides. "They do not intentionally act in an unsafe manner. I intend to investigate this accident thoroughly and determine what really happened here."

"You're wasting your time," argued Ray. "It was an accident, pure and simple. What do you know about accident investigation? You're not a safety professional."

In response, Helen pointed to his cane and his shoe that had touched the puddle. They fumed slightly from having come in contact with the acid. "Neither, it seems, are you, Captain Birkett."

Helen stormed away, leaving Ray to study his smoking shoe.

Chapter 28

Helen

*A*nger welled up in Helen. Anger that had been building for weeks.

Anger over the numerous accidents that had taken place. Anger over the senseless injuries that changed innocent people's lives irrevocably. Anger over the callousness of people around her—people more interested in launches than the fate of human lives. Helen intended to stand up for Moria and the others, even if no one else would.

Helen fumed. How could William Browning suggest that he conduct the investigation into Milly's or Moria's accident instead of her? Who was he to take over? After all, she was the first on the scene. And how could Captain Birkett insinuate that she was not a professional? What did he know of her training and abilities? She'd show her boss and Browning that she knew how to do her job. She'd show Captain Birkett too. She'd conduct her own accident investigation with great care. She'd find out what caused it.

Another kind of anger boiled inside her. Her first meeting with Captain Ray Birkett had gone very poorly. The moment she'd been thinking about—dreaming about—every night for months had none of the magic she had wanted or expected. Instead, their meeting had been perfunctory and business-like. She felt like crying. Captain Birkett's off-handed treatment of her hurt her deeply. He remembered her, she could tell that much. Unfortunately, it was obvious to her that he attached little or no significance to their dance. And she had. Night after night she had dreamed of him. His disinterest in her hit her like a bucket of ice cold water. Helen blinked back tears and remembered where she was. It served her right, she told herself firmly. She was no longer a starry-eyed love-struck teenager. She had no reason to expect Captain Birkett to attach romantic feelings to their single dance. Squaring her shoulders, Helen turned her attention to the job at hand. She marched over to where Evelyn and Rose were working, trying to make up for the lost production.

"Hello, I'm Helen Stevens. I'm investigating Moria Painter's accident. Do you mind if I ask you a few questions?"

"No, of course not," said Rose. "Anything to help poor Moria."

"I've seen you around," said Evelyn. "You're with the Industrial Efficiency department, aren't you?"

Helen nodded in agreement.

"Is Moria going to be okay? I mean, she didn't look so good, bless her heart." Rose shuddered at the memory.

"She's in a bad way. I'm going to try to see her tomorrow. I'll let you know if I learn anything."

"That'd be real nice of you, Miss Stevens," said Evelyn.

"Did you see what happened?" asked Helen. She knew it was better to ask open-ended questions to get people talking about the accident. "Evelyn, why don't you go first? Can you tell me what you saw?"

"We all work on the same types of jobs," began Evelyn.

"We joined up together and went through the same training classes," added Rose.

"Tell me about your jobs," prompted Helen. Even though Evelyn and Rose were describing the accident together, Helen knew better than to interrupt the flow of conversation. For the time being, she'd just listen and remain non-judgmental and objective. When they'd finished talking she would ask questions for clarification.

"We use diluted acid to clean metal, specifically to remove the rust. You know how this salt air causes everything to rust quickly around here. Before some of the welds can be made, we need to clean the metal. If we don't prep it right, the weld will fail."

"Can you show me how you mix up your own solution of diluted acid?" asked Helen.

"Sure," responded Rose. "First you take one of these containers of filtered water. They're already filled. Next you measure out the amount of acid you need. Then you slowly add the acid to the water."

"We learned in class to always pour acid into water, not the other way around. If you pour water into undiluted acid, the acid quickly reacts and becomes a boiling, explosive solution. They demonstrated it in class with just a little water. You wouldn't believe how it bubbled and fizzed," explained Evelyn. "I can't believe Moria would make a mistake like that. She's so much smarter than we are. She's always reminding us to follow correct procedures."

"She's so careful too. Today—today, when she got hurt, I saw her carefully measure the right amount of acid to add to the water. Just like we've been taught. You can see the measuring cup lying by the other containers." Rose pointed over at Moria's work area. She shuddered again and tears sprang up in her eyes.

"I saw her too. She poured out the right amount and then added it to the water, just like we've been taught. Suddenly there was this big whoosh and she started screaming!"

"It was horrible, so horrible! We tried to help, but by the time we reached her it was too late." Rose's tears ran unchecked down her face.

"I'm so sorry," murmured Helen. She was too. Moria was her friend too.

"It was terrible. She didn't do anything different than usual. There was just this great big whoosh and it was all over," sniffed Evelyn.

Helen left the two women to comfort each other and returned to her office in a thoughtful mood.

Chapter 29

Ray

$\mathcal{D}$isappointed by Helen's less than thrilled greeting following his long absence, Ray didn't seek her out for several days after the accident. When he was feeling generous, he delighted in the thought that he had found her. He relished the memory of the sight of her bathed in a shaft of light. The brief flush of pleasure that shone in her face convinced Ray that she missed him. Unfortunately, at his clumsy and ill-timed intrusion into the accident scene, it had faded as quickly as it had come, leaving her beautiful eyes remote. Could he hope to rekindle the light he saw in her eyes the evening they first met? More importantly, after her chilly greeting, did he want to?

With difficulty, Ray turned his attention to General Dirner's phantom radar signal. He considered where it might be coming from. Realistically, there were two worrisome possibilities: from an enemy agent on land or an enemy vessel at sea. The radio signal hadn't received a response, so it served only to communicate information. What sort of information? Information about positioning? Information about activity? The weak nature of the signal meant that the parties communicating with each other would have to be in relatively close proximity, a couple of miles at most. Ray made a note to contact Lieutenant Richard Stevens to determine how far the signal would reach at its current strength.

His telephone rang. General Dirner's voice came on the line.

"Captain Birkett?"

"Yes sir."

"I've received authorization to share the following information with you.

"Go ahead sir, I'm alone."

"Following the launch, an enemy submarine was sighted off the coast of Saint Simons Island. An observation plane scouting the area was able to provide its coordinates to a nearby destroyer. The destroyer gave chase and dropped depth charges. But, no luck. We think the sub is still out there waiting for an unsuspecting ship. Fortunately the Liberty ship did not encounter the U-boat during its sea trials. We don't think it was a coincidence that the sub was in the area the same day that the ship was launched."

On the afternoon of the Fourth of July, the aunts held another one of their fundraising parties, this time a barbeque. Ray read the newspaper clipping one of the sisters had thoughtfully taped to the mirror in his room.

"The Stevens sisters—" Ray read aloud. He stopped abruptly. Why, in all their elaborate conversations hadn't the subject of their last names ever come up? They had asked him to call them Miss Ora, Miss Ida, and Miss Elva. The only last name he knew was Elva's. Since hers was Clay, Ray had never connected the three women with Helen Stevens. His search for Helen could have been over so much quicker. He could have met her under such much better conditions. He continued to read the brief article.

"The Stevens sisters sponsored another successful fundraising party. This time, in honor of their houseguest, Captain Raymond Birkett of His Majesty's Royal Navy, the monies collected will be donated to the British Widows and Orphans fund. The party was attended by Helen Stevens, Winona Bunce, Hazel Ann Crawford, Dot Carson, Cecil Hudson, William Browning, George White, ...Hank Stine, and many others. Guests played

142

an assortment of challenging games. Cecil Hudson provided the greatest number of correct answers and won a box of chocolates."

So Helen had been at the party. She must have arrived after he left for his meeting with General Dirner. If only the timing of the telephone calls interruption had been better. He could have met her then and there.

Ray fervently hoped Helen would be present at the barbeque. He also hoped that he would have a chance to speak to her alone and renew their acquaintance in an atmosphere more pleasant than an accident site. Despite his cold reception, Ray knew she was the girl for him.

Ray stood at the top of the stairs listening to the laughter and music wafting up in the warm summer air. He savored the moment before descending. Unlike Helen, the Stevens sisters made him feel welcome and appreciated. Every evening, regardless of the hour, one or all of them met him at the door, eager and impatient to hear about his day. Once seated in the front parlor or on the veranda, they would all beam at him while listening to what he had to say. They were always honestly glad to see him and they let him know it. Through them he had learned the meaning of real Southern hospitality and affection.

"Oh Captain Birkett, there you are." Ora Stevens winked at him when he came down the stairs. "I heard you whistling in the shower this morning. You sounded awfully happy." She patted his hand, her eyes twinkling merrily.

Ray knew the reason for his good humor—a certain lovely young woman he would soon be setting out to woo. Helen Stevens would make any man whistle in the shower.

"Hello Captain Birkett." Ida greeted him formally, as if he hadn't just walked down the stairs of her own house and into the parlor. He found her behavior and her response to his status as house guest charming.

143

"This is my sister-in-law, Enid Stevens. She's married to our brother, Afton." Ora smiled at him timidly. "I don't know if you have been introduced. Enid, this is our house guest, Captain Birkett."

Ray extended his hand. Enid did not.

"I remember your name! You're the young man who had the audacity to dance with my daughter in the hallway of the high school last year!" Enid Stevens' voice was sharp and unyielding, her posture unwelcoming.

Her attitude caught Ray by surprise. He had thought the incident long forgotten, remembered only by him and by Helen. He had attached such a warm and rosy glow to that magical moment that he was unprepared for Mrs. Stevens' frigid attitude. Stung, he didn't quite know how to reply. Not that it mattered; Enid Stevens hadn't finished chastising him yet.

"We don't do that sort of thing here in the South. We can make allowances for some behavior, but really, Captain Birkett, a man your age should know better." Having said her piece, head held high, Enid Stevens walked stiffly away.

Ida and Ora smiled up at him weakly. He smiled back, trying to reassure them that he was not offended by what had just taken place. Ray's attitude toward the sisters had become quite protective.

"Captain Birkett, there is someone else we'd like you to meet. Here she comes now," said Ora.

"Helen, dear, we'd like you to meet Captain Raymond Birkett of his Majesty's Royal Navy." With a bright smile, Ida gestured to Ray standing at her side. "Captain Birkett, this is our niece, Helen Stevens."

"Doesn't she look like Ava Gardner?" asked Ora breathlessly.

Ray had to agree. At this moment, Helen Stevens closely resembled an angry Ava Gardner. She was so strikingly beautiful, his breath caught in his throat.

"We've already met," said Helen in a frosty tone.

Aunt Ora looked from one of them to the other, confusion on her face. "But Helen, Captain Birkett is our boarder we've been telling you about." Sotto voce, she added, "Helen, he's a *nice* man."

Ray hid his smile behind his cupped hand. Apparently, the aunts were used to Helen's prickly behavior.

"Captain Birkett is your house guest?" sputtered Helen in disbelief. "Oh! Aunt Ora! How could you?" She ran off toward the kitchen.

"Captain Birkett—I don't know what to think," began Ora helplessly.

Ray extended his hand to comfort her. "It's all right. I don't seem to be having much luck impressing the Stevens women tonight."

Winona's voice sliced into this awkward moment.

"Let's play a riddle game!" she exclaimed happily.

Predictably this statement was followed by a chorus of groans.

"Captain Birkett," said Ora, mustering a smile. "You go right ahead and join the game." Ora gave Ray an encouraging push toward the parlor.

"Oh my! This time we get to finish old sayings!" Winona declared happily. "You know, ones like 'as busy as a bee'. This should be easy. I'll start this time. Let's see if you can guess this one. As light as—"

"A feather!" said George White.

"Yes, that's right. As light as a feather," confirmed Winona. "Here's the next one. As white as a—"

"Sheet!" shouted Cecil.

"How about—as sharp as—"

"As a tack!" said Hazel Ann laughing.

145

Since the old sayings were familiar to nearly everyone but Ray, the game was swiftly concluded. He noticed that Winona didn't seem at all disappointed when everyone dispersed quickly before she could suggest another riddle game.

Out in the backyard, the tables had been set up for people to enjoy the barbeque. Ray drifted over and joined Richard and a group of men supervising the cooking of the meat over a wood fire. The smells made his mouth water. The sisters had once again managed to procure a variety of food. Ora told him earlier that there would be pulled pork, She crab soup, sweet cornbread, beans, sweet corn, watermelon and all the fixings for a good barbeque. Ray couldn't wait to sample the watermelon.

"Hello Captain Birkett. Glad you can join us," said Richard. "I'd like you to meet my father, Afton Stevens and my uncle, Eugene Clay. You already know Alfred Smith from the shipyard. Gentlemen, Captain Ray Birkett. Ray is Aunt Ora's and Aunt Ida's boarder."

"Welcome Captain Birkett. My sisters have told me about you," said Afton Stevens. He shook Ray's hand firmly.

"All good news, I hope, sir."

"Of course. We're discussing the merits of different barbeque preparations. Care to join us?" asked Afton.

"Thank you sir. Don't mind if I do."

"As I was saying, here in the deep South we prefer pork whereas in Texas, barbeque is made with beef," said Eugene Clay. "Carolina barbeque is made with vinegar but up in Memphis they make it sweet. Certain hardwoods, such as hickory or pecan will give barbeque a stronger, smokier flavor. I prefer using fruit wood for a milder, sweeter taste."

"I'm picky about barbeque sauce," said Richard. I like molasses sauces better than peppered vinegar or thick sweet tomato-based sauces."

"Which do you prefer, Captain?" asked Afton.

"I must confess I have very limited experience with barbeque of any sort. I must rely on your judgment, Mr. Stevens," responded Ray.

"Spoken like a true gentleman," said Eugene.

"It's sad about Moria Painter's injury. She's such a nice person. From what I understand, she mixed the acid and water incorrectly," interjected Alfred Smith. He failed to notice that his unexpected and inappropriate statement immediately put a damper on the conversation. The others stared at him wondering how to overcome this social gaffe.

"Yes, that's my understanding," admitted Afton Stevens reluctantly. "Alfred, how did you hear about the accident?"

"I don't really remember. From someone in the shipyard, I imagine."

"Why don't we try some of this barbeque?" asked Ray, changing the subject.

"It's time for another game!" said Elva merrily as the evening sun dipped low on the horizon.

Ray couldn't remember Elva ever sounding merry. Perhaps she'd laced her punch with something strong.

"And this one is particularly fun," Elva continued, her arms laden with blankets and clothesline. "Gentlemen, I need your help."

As Elva and her helpers got busy stringing up the blankets across the center of the back porch, from the kitchen came the sounds of commotion.

"Oh, no. Aunt Ora, you've spilled blue food coloring all over my hands."

"I'm so sorry, Helen. It will wash out—eventually," said Ora, sounding none too repentant.

"Ladies, come over here and stand behind the curtain. That includes you, too, Helen." Elva's voice sounded like a command.

Yes, Ray concluded, Elva would have done quite well ordering people about at the shipyard.

"Elva likes to think she's in charge," giggled Ida who had come up to stand next to Ray.

Obediently the women on the porch went behind the blanket which screened them from view. Elva joined the young women there and began jostling everyone into place.

"Now ladies, one at a time each of you will raise your hand above the curtain. Also one at a time, each gentleman will have three guesses to identify whose hand it is. If they successfully guess whose hand it is, then the young lady and the gentleman will have a glass of punch together."

"Ladies, when it is your turn, I'll tap you on the shoulder," said Ora. She waved a glass punch bowl ladle in the air to make her point.

"We'll let our guest from Britain go first."

Feminine giggles emerged from behind the curtain. Ray stepped forward and a single slender hand rose above the curtain.

"Dot Carson?" he asked at the sight of the first hand.

"No," said Ora, peering from behind the curtain. "Next hand please."

"Avis Lou?" Ray really had no idea whose hand it was.

"Wrong again," said Ora, smiling brightly. "Next hand please. Captain, this is your last chance before you have to step to the back of the line."

When the third hand reluctantly rose above the curtain, Ray understood why Ora smiled so brightly. The blue stained fingertips left no doubt in his mind whose hand it was. He marveled at the aunts' subtle trickery to bring them together.

"Helen Stevens," Ray announced firmly.

"Right you are. Helen come out here and take your young man out to the front porch swing to enjoy a glass of punch." Helen protested as Ora propelled both of them quickly through the house and out onto the veranda.

"Of all the dirty tricks! Aunt Ora spilled that food coloring on purpose! I suppose you put her up to it," seethed Helen.

"No, not me," protested Ray. "Your aunts come up their own ideas." He wanted to add that they were far better than his own.

"For some reason, I don't believe you." Her body turned toward the street, Helen sat as far away from him on the white-painted swing as she could. She made a point of not looking at him.

"Brrrrr...we don't need air conditioning out here," teased Ray, trying to lighten the mood. "It's forty degrees colder with you next to me." He hugged himself and gave an exaggerated shiver. He wanted to make her smile. He longed to see her smile at him.

"Why you—arrrgh—Captain Birkett, you get on my last nerve! I could just scream! The other night, I thought you were just trying to test me, but now I'm not so sure. Leave it to you to say something so—so—oh, I don't know what!"

"Please don't hold what I said earlier against me. I was just caught off guard to find you at the scene of the accident." This was not the direction Ray had hoped the conversation would take.

"Captain Birkett, you certainly sounded as if you meant every word you said, including those about my being unprofessional," said Helen, unwilling to let the subject drop.

"Okay, well maybe you could overlook that comment. I apologize." Ray could tell by the look on her face that it would be a while before she would accept his apology.

"Then I'll have to overlook how you literally stepped into an accident scene."

"Yes, I hope you will. May I ask what you were studying so intently when your brother and I interrupted?" asked Ray.

"The labels on the containers, they were wrong."

"What do you mean, wrong?"

"They were the wrong color."

"They weren't supposed to be white?" asked Ray.

"No, the white part isn't the problem. The borders around the labels were wrong. The border for water should be medium blue, the one for acid, orange. Both of these labels were brown," explained Helen.

"You remember the color of a border that couldn't have been more than an eighth of an inch wide," asked Ray, his disbelief apparent from the tone of his voice.

"Yes, I do."

"That's unbelievable," scoffed Ray.

"Oh, so now, besides mocking my professionalism and judgment, you doubt my memory!"

"I didn't question your judgment, I merely asked—"

"Merely asked!" Helen cut him off. "You implied I didn't know what I was talking about! I'll have you know I have significant training in industrial safety. You just chose to put down my comments because I'm a woman."

"It had nothing to do with your being a woman. I never even noticed that you are a woman," he protested. Ray regretted the words as soon as they were out of his mouth. Helen's expression became furious.

"Never even noticed I am a woman! Do you find me that unattractive? Captain Birkett, I don't believe I've ever met a ruder person than you!" Helen marched off leaving him alone on the veranda.

Flabbergasted, Ray sat for a few moments in the dark humid air. Far off, Ray could hear the thunder from an approaching storm. At the other end of the veranda, a match flared.

"Captain Birkett, there is nothing as temperamental as a Southern storm, except maybe a Southern woman," chuckled a deep voice.

Chapter 30

Helen

*"M*iss Helen?" asked Alfred Smith.

"Yes? What is it, Alfred?" Helen was surprised to see Alfred at the USO. Her heart skipped a beat. Something must be very wrong for the matron to allow him inside. She stared at the message he held in his hand.

"I've been asked to give you this message, Miss Helen."

Alfred handed Helen an envelope inscribed with her name. Helen recognized the writing as that of her boss, Burt Dixon. Her stomach twisted in fear. If it pertained to the shipyard there must have been another accident, a serious one.

"Thank you, Alfred," Helen said absently to him as she used her fingernail to pry open the sealed envelope. She scanned the short note quickly.

"What is it?" asked Avis Lou, trying to read over Helen's shoulder.

"It's a message from my boss. I told him I would be here tonight. Apparently there has been another incident at the shipyard."

"Oh no!"

"Oh no is right. He doesn't say what happened. Burt asks that I report to his office immediately. Sorry Avis Lou, no more dancing for me tonight."

"Miss Helen, my car is outside. May I drive you to the shipyard?"

Helen hadn't realized Alfred had remained standing nearby. She studied the eager, yet wistful, look on his face and smiled gently. She knew what he wanted her answer to be. "That would be very nice, Alfred. Perhaps we could stop at my home first so I can change clothes?" she said with a dazzling smile.

"Hello Helen! Fancy meeting you here!"

"Hello Daddy! I thought you'd be home by now." Their hard hats clanged together when Helen greeted her father with a hug.

"I'm staying late because of this accident."

"Yes, that explains a lot. Though we both work in the same place, I rarely run into you, Daddy."

"Too many people around to find that one special one." Afton Stevens smiled down at his pretty daughter.

"You're right about that." In the back of her mind, Helen couldn't help but think of one very special person she would give anything to run into under better circumstances. Would every word or situation serve as a reminder of Captain Ray Birkett? Would they ever spend time together without fighting?

"How's my little Doll? I hear good things about you from the men. You appear to have charmed the entire shipyard in just the few months you been here. I must say, Alfred Smith is particularly taken with you."

"Oh, Daddy, surely you exaggerate. And yes, Alfred Smith is a nice young man and I am trying not to encourage him."

"What brings you to my neck of the woods at this late in the evening?" Afton gestured at the broad foredeck of the Liberty ship. Though it was night, spotlights lit the entire area making it as bright as day.

"An accident, what else? My boss dragged me from the USO dance when he couldn't find my co-worker William Browning."

"Funny, I thought I saw Mr. Browning earlier this evening. It was at a distance though, so I can't be sure. With so many people around, it's hard to tell."

"William Browning always seems to be around when an accident occurs," muttered Helen under her breath.

"What do you mean, Helen?"

"Oh, nothing, Daddy. It's just that I feel like I always have to fight with Mr. Browning to get permission to investigate an accident on my own. It's as if he and Burt don't believe I—don't believe a woman—can investigate an accident."

"We're not used to women doing a man's job. Give it time. Say, Alfred Smith told me you had quite an accident to deal with the other day. A young woman got burned?"

"Moria Painter was mixing an acid solution to use to clean the rust off pieces of metal and it exploded in her face."

"That's awful. Is she okay?" her father asked, truly shocked.

"She's in a bad way. Her hands and part of her face are horribly burned."

"Another bad accident, another delay in launching a ship," Afton Stevens said almost to himself.

Helen studied at his face closely and made a decision. She glanced around to see if anyone was nearby who could overhear them. "Daddy, can you take some time to tell me what happened tonight? And then can I ask you some questions about the other accidents too?"

"Fire away little lady."

"You're a superintendent here. Do you and the other supervisors ever talk about the accidents that have been happening recently? I mean, do you or the others think anything unusual is going on?"

"Of course we talk about the accidents. We'd sure like to prevent them. It's hard to say whether or not anything odd is going on. In general, the shipyard is very safe. What's been happening recently may just be a run of bad luck. After all, there are more than ten thousand people working here and more coming in every day. Building a ship, let alone five or six at a time, is dangerous work."

"Yes, I know. It's just that I can't help but wonder about some of the accidents."

"Which ones in particular?" her father asked.

"The keyway incident, the welding tank explosion, and Moria's accident. There is something about each of these situations that bothers me. And now tonight, what can you tell me about the rigger's accident?"

"Honey, it's a sight that I don't want to see again. I truly wish your boss had assigned this one to Mr. Browning instead of you." He held up his hand to ward off her protest. "It's not because I don't believe you'll do a good job investigating the accident. On the contrary, I think you will. It's not fitting to expose you to such a horrific death. You are, after all, still my little girl." Her father sighed sadly. "It happened right in front of me. Two steps to the left and I would have been right under him when he fell." Afton Stevens shuddered at the memory. "Ben McNeely had climbed nearly to the top of the main mast when his harness broke. He plummeted nearly forty feet to his death."

Helen shielded her eyes from the glare of the spotlights and craned her neck to look up at the mast standing so tall above the deck of the ship. The height of the mast gave her vertigo. She swayed slightly and shivered in the warm summer air. This was the first time she had to investigate a death on the job. She pulled herself together.

"Do you still have the harness? May I see it?"

"Honey, are you sure you want to see it? It's not been cleaned up or anything. A man falls four stories, there's bound to be a mess."

"No, I don't want to see it, Daddy, but I have to. I've been assigned to investigate this accident and I intend to do a thorough job."

"Your Momma will be fit to be tied if she finds out I showed it to you. It's in my office. We'll go there when you have seen enough here."

Helen looked around, taking in the position of the blood stain at the base of the mast. She possessed a nearly photographic memory and she used it now, standing as still as a statue at the accident scene, absorbing it all.

"When you're ready, we'll walk back to my office," said Afton Stevens, not wanting to disturb his daughter while she was deep in thought.

"Just a minute, Daddy. I need to talk to that rigger. I'll only be a moment." Helen pointed to a man wearing a red hard hat.

"I'll wait right here for you."

"Excuse me, sir. I'm Helen Stevens from the Industrial Efficiency department. I'm here to investigate the accident that occurred earlier this evening."

The shadows thrown by the various lights strung overhead made it difficult for Helen to see clearly. All the same, she thought she saw a calculating look dart across the man's face. In some ways, Helen had grown used to drawing less than welcoming responses from the men at the shipyard.

"I'm George White," said the dark-haired, dark-eyed man.

"I recognize you now. You've been at some of my aunts' parties—the Stevens sisters."

"Yes, I have. I recognize you too. Your aunts really know how to throw a good party." George White relaxed a little. "I don't know if I can tell you much. I wasn't here at the time. Sad about Ben McNeely. Nice guy."

"I'm sure he was. You're a rigger, aren't you?" Helen asked as she gestured at the web harness that he wore and his red hard hat.

"Yes ma'am. May I ask why they've sent a pretty little thing like you to investigate such an unsightly accident?"

"My co-worker, William Browning, might have handled it, but he is off for the night. May I ask you a few questions?"

"Sure."

"Can you demonstrate how your harness works?"

George White patiently explained the details of how the web strips crossed in the back and how the buckles all fit together. By the time he had finished, Helen felt she understood how to attach the harness safely.

"Just one more question, if you don't mind. Do you know why Ben McNeely climbed the mast?" Helen asked when the demonstration was over.

"Since I'm going up there myself, I know exactly why he did. He thought he saw something hanging loose and he wanted to check on it." Reflexively, they both looked up at the top of the mast. Helen could see nothing but a small black box about three-fourths the way up. "Personally, I don't see it, but my supervisor and the superintendent want me to check." George White nodded his head toward Afton Stevens.

"Well, I won't keep you from your work any longer. Thank you for your time," said Helen before she walked back over to stand by her father. Together they watched George White scamper like a monkey up a palm tree until he reached the top of the mast. There he fiddled about before returning quickly to the deck. After saying that he found nothing amiss, he left them alone.

"It pays to be careful, Helen. Tonight's accident will delay the launch, but it won't be long before this ship slides down the way and into the water."

"So soon after Ben McNeely's death?" she asked.

"The Merchant Marines need the ship, honey."

Back at his office, Helen's father showed her Ben McNeely's bloody harness. After taking a deep breath to steady herself, Helen inspected the device. Holding it up so that it hung as if it were on a man, she studied the webbing and clips. Mentally, she compared it with the one worn by George White. Something about the harness disturbed her.

"Daddy, are all the harnesses of the same design?"

"Yes."

"Then why doesn't this one have a clip at the back where the straps are supposed to cross?"

"What do you mean?" her father asked.

Helen flipped the harness over.

"Look at these straps. On the back of George White's harness, there was a center clip holding the straps in a crisscross pattern. He told me that was to ensure that the harness stays on a man's shoulders. This harness doesn't have one."

"Let me see that." Her father studied the harness for a moment before laying it gently on his desk. From a cabinet, he extracted a new harness. Laying the two of them side-by-side, he compared them.

"You're right. This clip is missing. That's odd."

"Would Ben McNeely have removed it? Could it have come off during or after the fall?" she asked.

"I personally assisted in removing Ben's harness. There was no clip to hold the straps together."

Helen turned the harness around.

"Look, someone has removed the orange tag marking the harness as defective. Only the loop used to hold it on remains. Did you see it when you took off the harness?"

"No, I didn't."

"What do you think this means, Daddy?"

"I don't know, Doll. I really don't know."

Chapter 31

Ray

*R*ay approached the next party with trepidation. He wondered if Helen had spoken to her aunts and filled them in on what had transpired between them. The more he thought about it, the more certain he felt that they already knew. The aunts, as he had come to call them, had an uncanny ability to be at the right place at the right time. He stood on the veranda and watched Richard Stevens cross Hinshaw Square.

"Captain Birkett, I feel like I ought to apologize again for my sister's treatment of you the other night," Richard said when he met Ray on the veranda. "She should be more polite seeing as how you're a guest of our aunts. 'Course, it wasn't very gentlemanly of me to be eavesdropping either. I just couldn't figure out a way off the veranda when Aunt Ora hustled y'all out there." Richard extended his hand toward Ray in apology.

"It's all right, Lieutenant Stevens. Your sister and I just got off on the wrong foot." Ray shook the offered hand.

"Call me Richard, please. After all we're going to be working together. General Dirner and Admiral Jarabek want this radar mystery cleared up and fast."

"It's going to be very helpful to have you around, Richard. I've got a lot of unanswered questions about that radar signal you picked up."

"Ask away. We've got a few minutes before the party begins."

"I can't believe they're hosting another party so soon after their big Fourth of July barbeque. I've never known women so indefatigable."

Richard laughed. "My father calls them a force of nature. They really want to do their part to help with the war effort. For the past year, they've held a party every other week or so without fail. They make sure the parties never fall on the same day or time of the week so that everybody gets a chance to attend at least one every couple of months. At each party, they take up a collection for a worthy cause."

"Yes, I know. If only we could apply their energy and resourcefulness to finding concrete evidence that something was amiss at the shipyard," said Ray, only half-joking. "These launch delays are worrying. Have you heard the signal recently?"

"No. We'll start listening again in earnest when we've been given the new launch date. Naturally, we'll be paying close attention to any anomaly. The launch isn't too many days away now."

While they stood on the veranda discussing the activities at the shipyard, they acted as informal greeters, welcoming everyone to the party. George and Hank arrived together, deep in conversation.

"George, I'm sorry to hear about Ben McNeely's death," said Ray. "You worked with him, didn't you?"

"Yeah, it was a sad thing," said George. "That's what Hank and I were talking about on our way over here."

"I don't know how it could have happened. Ben was a careful sort of guy. It's not like him to make a mistake," added Hank Stine.

They all stood around awkwardly, unsure of what to say next. Eventually, George said, "Come on Hank, let's go inside. I want to see if Dot or Winona are here." He half-dragged the other man into the house.

"It looks like Cecil Hudson will have some competition tonight," commented Richard.

"Winona will enjoy having three men eager to win her favors," agreed Ray.

Ray could see William Browning approaching from the opposite end of Hinshaw Square. Instead of coming up the front steps, he walked past them and began to climb the stairs of Elva Clay's house next door. Knowing that the two houses were nearly indistinguishable, Ray and Richard laughed at his mistake.

"Hey William," called Richard. "What are you doing going up to the wrong house? The party's over here."

Confused, William swiveled his head from one identical house to the other. Recognizing his mistake, he looked chagrinned and gave them a small wave.

"Don't worry about it," said Richard. "It's easy to get them confused. Since Ora and Ida are twins, my aunts like the idea of twins. Twin houses, twin dogs. They like being mistaken for each other."

"Thank you for pointing me in the right direction."

Blue and Beau rose from where they were sleeping on the veranda. They growled at William as he mounted the stairs.

"That's odd," said Richard. "Beau and Blue are usually friendly to people they've met before. They didn't growl at George and Hank."

William hesitated on the front steps and waited until Richard had pulled the dogs aside. When they were safely out of the way, William turned toward Ray and asked, "Have we met?"

Startled, Ray responded, "At the shipyard. I was with Burt Dixon. I met you briefly at one of the Stevens sisters' parties, too. I'm Captain Ray Birkett."

162

"Oh, yes, Captain. I remember now. I meet so many new people at work, I forget who is who. I'm not good with faces. It's nice to make your acquaintance again." The two men shook hands.

"Come on in Mr. Browning." Elva swung the screen door open and greeted the newcomer. "Why are you hesitating? It's not as if you haven't been here before."

"Thank you, ma'am," said William as he walked through the doorway without a backward glance.

"I suppose Winona will want to play her riddle games again," sighed Richard as they turned to go inside. "It's starting to get tedious."

"Oh I don't know," said Ray. "The riddle games get everybody talking. Those short plays at the Fourth of July party were great fun, too. Your aunts have a marvelous way of mixing up people into different situations. It helps everybody get to know each other."

"They like seeing what happens when they do," agreed Richard. "I wonder what surprising party games they've devised for tonight."

The party was well underway but Helen had not arrived. Ray could no longer linger on the porch waiting for her. Though he kept it to himself, Ray sincerely hoped he'd be able to spend time alone with Helen. It bothered him that their previous meeting had been overheard by Helen's brother. What did Richard think of Ray's cavalier attitude toward her job? Ray wanted to make amends for his lack of tact.

"Oh, look, we're supposed to guess the names of fish." Winona waved the slip of paper with the riddle game in the air.

"Being a seaman, Captain Birkett, you should excel at this game," said Dot, who joined Ray at the buffet.

Obediently, everyone began arranging themselves around Winona. Ray noted that Helen carefully made sure they were on opposite sides of the room. Since she arrived late, he hadn't been able to find a moment alone with her. Helen always seemed to have no shortage of male admirers. Tonight, Hank Stine and Alfred Smith competed for her favors. Every time she smiled her lovely smile at one or the other of them, Ray felt jealously course through him. Surely, thought Ray, there must be some way to convince her of his sincere interest in her. It was getting late and he wanted desperately to arrange a meeting with Helen. Could he count on the aunts to throw them together again?

Winona cast small anxious glances around the room before beginning the game. She studied the riddles in the party planning book, her pretty forehead wrinkled in thought.

"All right, let's get started. Remember, the answers will all be the names of real fish. Let's begin with this one. What fish does a miser love?" Winona asked.

"A gold fish," shouted Cecil, eager to please her.

"What fish twinkles in the sky?" she asked after telling Cecil his answer was correct.

"A star fish," said Hazel Ann.

"That's right. What kind of fish is a soldier's fish?"

"A sword fish," answered Alfred.

"Right. What kind of fish is musical?"

The audience groaned in unison.

"Won't anyone at least try to guess?" asked Winona.

No one offered an answer.

"A bass," said Winona.

"How were we supposed to guess that one? The two aren't even pronounced the same," complained Hank.

"All right, we'll disregard that one. Let's see if you can guess this one," said Winona. "What fish is a royal fish?"

"A king fish," answered George.

"Yes," Winona agreed. "A king fish. Now everything is all right."

"That's a strange thing to say. What do you mean, Winona?" asked Dot.

"Oh nothing, nothing at all." Winona smiled a secretive sort of smile. "I like it when people get the answers right. Here's the next one. What fish is like a bird?"

"Gee, that's a tough one," said Alfred.

"Captain Birkett, you're a sailor. Is there such a thing as a flying fish?" asked Dot, playfully tugging at Ray's sleeve.

"Yes, as a matter of fact there is a fish called a flying fish," Ray answered with a smile.

"And that's the right answer," said Winona.

Ray couldn't help but notice how satisfied Winona looked. She must be pleased with herself for coming up with so many fish-related quiz questions.

"Okay everyone," announced Elva, clapping her hands. "It's time to explain why you all received an envelope when you arrived this evening."

Ray couldn't help but admire how the aunts kept their parties moving along. It took a lot of effort to coordinate the food, activities, and decorations for each one. He noticed Elva had her party planning book tucked under her arm. Ray pulled the envelope with his name on it out of his pocket and waited to hear what would come next.

"Does everyone have an envelope?" Elva glanced around. "Good. When we ring the bell—" She pointed to Ora who rang the little bell in her hand. "When we ring the bell, open your envelopes. Inside you'll find a postcard that has been cut in two. Your job is to go around the room and find the person with the other half of your postcard. When you do, find a quiet spot and share a glass of punch with your new partner. I recommend porch settin'. It's a lost art, sitting on the porch with your sweetie and staring at the moon."

"Is everybody ready?" asked Ora breathlessly. She rang the bell vigorously.

Ray opened his envelope and found half of a postcard very similar to the one he sent to Helen over a year ago. He turned it over and recognized his own handwriting. His eyebrows shot up in surprise. Then he heard someone else gasp in disbelief.

"Aunt Elva—my postcard—you cut my postcard in half! How could you?"

"Oh, I'm sorry, Helen honey. Was it important?"

"Important?" exclaimed Helen, obviously forgetting that she had an audience. "It's my postcard from Captain Birkett!" Then she blushed furiously.

"Of course it is, honey," said Ora soothingly. "Why do you think we chose it?"

"Hush Ora!" admonished Elva.

Ray studied the faces of Helen and her aunts. He could tell they knew how important the postcard was to Helen and now, he knew how important it was. Relief surged through him. The look on Helen's face left no doubt in his mind that she cared for him.

166

Chapter 32

Helen

"*G*ive me that back!" Helen tried to snatch the other half of the postcard out of Ray's hand once they were alone on the veranda. Holding the card aloft, he stood there grinning at her as if he couldn't believe his own good fortune. Despite her annoyance, Helen loved the way his grin made his face boyish and mischievous.

Laughing at her futile efforts, Ray said, "Miss Stevens, you never answered my question. What are you doing for the rest of your life?"

"I don't know, but one thing is for certain, if you don't give me my card back, I won't be spending it with you!" Despite her protests, Helen felt a warm glow of delight spread through her that had nothing to do with the heat of the summer evening.

"Does that mean that if I give it back you'll marry me?"

Marry Ray? Helen's heart somersaulted in her chest. Mid-reach, she stopped trying to grab at the postcard. Breathless with anticipation, she stared at him, her eyes searching his face. Even though Helen knew the moment they danced together that she wanted to marry him, Ray's audacious proposal both pleased and shocked her. She couldn't resist saying so. "Aren't you being a bit presumptuous, Captain Birkett?"

"Not at all. I've known all along we're meant for each other. Don't you see, Helen, we were meant to be. Will you marry me?"

"Marry you? Why should I marry you? You haven't even told me you love me!" Helen folded her arms across her chest and turned her back on him. This was getting much too serious, yet she yearned to hear him say the words.

"I apologize for my oversight." Ray dangled the postcard over her shoulder. Into her ear he whispered, "I love you Helen Stevens. I have since the first moment I met you."

"I—" began Helen. Abruptly, she sat down on the wooden porch swing. She hadn't expected to hear those words spoken with such intensity. Helen blinked back tears. She fought to breathe against the constriction in her throat. Although it was what she wanted, events were moving too fast for her. Should she dare to love in a time of war?

Unfazed by her reaction, Ray sat down beside her, took her hand, and looked hopeful. Under his breath he hummed the music from *I'll Be Seeing You*. A smile crept over her face. Since their dance, Helen had always thought of it as their song.

"Your aunt is right. Porch settin' is rather pleasant. It's peaceful sitting here, looking at the stars." Ray began to sing in his rich baritone, "*I'll find you in the morning sun and when the night is new. I'll be looking at the moon, but I'll be seeing you.*"

Hiding her smile, Helen continued to stare off in the distance. She liked his voice, very much. His singing sent pleasant tingles up and down her spine.

"Do you think we should get married before or after we finish our sweet tea?" Ray asked lightly after another few moments of silence. He gestured to the two glasses thoughtfully provided by her aunt.

Helen stared at him, nonplussed, and then she laughed. "Captain Birkett, you are nothing if not persistent." She plucked the postcard from his hand.

"I'd rather be irresistible." His eyes sparkled wickedly.

"Irresistible men do not propose over a torn postcard. It's just not done. Your foolishness is enough to give a body a headache."

Helen looked into his deep blue eyes and her heart admitted what her mouth would never say. She found him irresistible. In fact, if her aunts hadn't been doing such a fine job of throwing them together, she would be plotting meetings of her own.

"So my charming Helen, what about my question? Should we get married before or after we finish our sweet tea?"

He truly was irrepressible—and irresistible. A smile spread slowly across her face. "After. Unlike many women nowadays, I prefer a long engagement."

They smiled at each other, reveling in the moment. Then Helen frowned. Surely, if Ray was serious about marrying her, he wouldn't be so flippant. Fear and doubt began to invade her thoughts, threatening her happiness. From their joyous high, her spirits plummeted to a new low. To hide her dismay, Helen bent down to scratch Beau and Blue who had joined them on the porch.

"Ah, I see that you do not believe my proposal is a serious one," Ray said, reading her mind. He lifted her chin tenderly with his fingers.

"I have no doubt you are merely teasing me, Captain Birkett." Helen sat straighter and smoothed the folds of her flowered sundress. She had seen the result of risking to love in a time of war. Rather than allow her emotions to carry her away, she would approach his proposal with caution.

"Marry me, Helen," Ray said softly with conviction.

Helen looked up at Ray and it astonished her to realize how much she loved him. Just like that, she loved him completely. The thought terrified her so much that she drew back to put distance between them.

Frightened at the prospect of loving him when the world was so uncertain, Helen cried out, "I can't! I just can't!"

Swiping her hand across her face to dash away her tears, Helen fled the veranda.

Chapter 33

Ray

"*M*ust we play the memory game?" Helen asked dispiritedly when she returned to the party.

"That's the game we pulled out of the hat, dearest. You know the rules," answered Aunt Ida, a note of apology in her voice.

"Helen, you should excuse yourself. It's not polite for you to play a game everyone knows you will win. Heaven knows your memory is only a useful party trick," said her mother, Enid.

Helen flushed bright red under her mother's pointed criticism of her skills. Ray stood on the other side of the room watching her, wondering what was disturbing her. She seemed more distressed about being back at the party than she did about their little scene on the porch.

"Helen has a fabulous memory, Captain Birkett," gushed Dot Carson who stood next to him. Dot wrapped her arm around his, earning him a glare of disapproval from Ora. The pretty young woman smiled playfully at Ray. "It's almost photographic. Just wait until we play the game, you'll see. She's upset because she doesn't like to draw attention to it." More loudly, she said, "Helen, you've got to play! It's always so much fun when you remember everything on the tray."

"Helen will be one of the judges," said Aunt Elva firmly. She clapped her hands. "All right everyone. The rules are simple. We've prepared three trays, each with ten different objects on them." She pointed to the covered trays being carried by Ida, Enid, and Ora.

"One at a time, we'll remove the cover on each tray. You have ten seconds to study the objects. When we cover it back up, you write down what you remember seeing," added Ida.

"No cheating!" Ora wagged her finger from side-to-side at the assembled audience.

She's right," continued Elva. "Don't write anything down until we've covered the tray. When everyone is finished, we'll uncover another tray. When all three trays have been shown, Helen will tell us what is on each one. Then we'll count up all of your answers. The person who lists the highest number of correct objects will win."

One by one, the women briefly uncovered the trays. Ray wrote down as many as he could remember, but listed only five items for each tray. The others in the room scored similarly.

"Helen, are you ready to tell us what is on each tray?" asked her Aunt Ora. "You never even wrote anything down."

Looking very brave and mildly annoyed, Helen drew a deep breath and responded firmly, "Yes, I am."

"Go ahead and list the items on the first tray," said Aunt Elva.

"A woman's compact, a pencil with the eraser chewed off, a dog's identification tag with the name Blue on it, a tube of lipstick, an old toothbrush, a folded square of paper, a man's brown glove in need of mending, a small glass rabbit, a needle, and a bit of sponge."

Dramatically, Ora whipped off the cloth covering the first tray.

"She's right!" exclaimed Dot. "Helen, do the next tray."

"A cork from a bottle, a small photo of my father, a hairpin, a stamp, an empty sample tube of perfume, a hairbrush—Aunt Ora's I think—a bottle cap, a book of Robert Burns poetry—"

"I love the poetry of Robert Burns," sighed Ora.

"Shush Ora! Don't interrupt Helen!" admonished Ida.

"A toothpick and a small black stone," finished Helen.

Ida slowly peeled back the covering on the second tray to reveal that Helen had once again named all ten objects. The people in the room clapped, all except Helen's mother Enid. A fact which was not lost on Helen.

"And now for the third tray," announced Aunt Elva.

"A drum roll, please," piped George White. Cecil Hudson willingly obliged, beating a drum roll with his fingers on the edge of the coffee table. The young people in the room all laughed and poked each other.

"A juice glass and a fork," Helen began confidently. "A pink napkin embroidered with an 'S', a monogramed handkerchief—'E' for Elva, a curtain ring, a book of matches from the smoke shop—those must be Uncle Eugene's, a spool of thread, Aunt Ida's favorite green glass pin in the shape of a four-leaf clover, a biscuit cutter, and a hat pin."

Ray couldn't believe his ears. Helen, without missing a beat, had listed thirty items from three different trays. She hadn't mixed the items up on the wrong trays. She hadn't hesitated for a moment while listing them. The woman had a photographic memory. No wonder she remembered the borders on the labels and could describe accident scenes so clearly. No wonder she resented his accusations. He whistled softly under his breath.

"That was quite impressive," said Ray as he stood next to Helen by the punch bowl.

"It's nothing, really. Just something I've been able to do ever since I can remember. You heard my Momma. It's not good for anything but a party trick," Helen said. Her tone conveyed how much her mother's comment had stung.

"I don't agree with that statement," countered Ray, hoping to smooth over the bumps in their relationship. "It must come in handy at work."

"Yes, I suppose it does." Helen smiled weakly at him. "I'm so used to it, I don't even think about it. Captain Birkett, I'd like to apologize for my behavior on the veranda earlier this evening. I know you were just being nice."

"No, Miss Stevens—Helen—I meant what I said. I want to apologize for doubting you—your professionalism, your judgment, and your memory. In the future, I promise to take you and what you say and do seriously."

"All because I can recite things on a tray from memory?"

"No, it's more than that. Helen, can we start over again? Please? Can we go back to our first dance together and start all over again?"

From inside the house, they could hear the opening bars of *I'll Be Seeing You*. Ray gathered her in his arms and they danced together like they had that very first night. For Ray, it was magical to have her in his arms again.

After their dance, she stood there silently studying him, her arms crossed loosely in front of her, as if she were hugging herself. Ray considered her tense face and wondered what he could say to set things right. "Helen, I really do want to know what you're doing for the rest of your life."

Helen let out a deep breath and her face softened a little. She turned away from him before speaking. "I don't really have an answer to that, Captain Birkett, except to say that I'm not sure. I'm not the girl you left behind over a year ago. Since you never told me where to write to you, you don't know the impact your postcard had on my life. None of us knew that a simple postcard would change the course of my life. I would never have gone to Atlanta if you hadn't insisted that I leave Brunswick. Thanks to you, I've got a start on my education and I have a good job that I like doing."

"So you're telling me you're twice as independent as you were the first time I met you." Coming up behind her, Ray cradled her elbows in the palms of his hands and rocked her toward him.

"Twice as independent? What made you say that?" Helen turned around to face him, her surprise evident.

"Only an independent young woman would have dared to dance with me in the hallway of the high school," teased Ray.

"I paid a stiff price for that. Even without your postcard, my Momma planned to ship me far, far away from the Golden Isles."

"And look at you now. You're back and twice as independent. Her plan backfired, didn't it?"

His question finally drew a smile from Helen.

"Yes, it did. I've got a brain and I want to work. I like working. It gives me a lot of satisfaction, a feeling of fulfilment that I've never had before this. Captain Birkett, right now, I don't want to get married, raise a family—" she faltered before adding softly, "and become a household drudge."

"Regardless of what path you chose, Helen, I don't think you'll ever become a household drudge. Certainly no wife of mine ever would."

Chapter 34

Helen

"*H*elen? Oh! There you are," said Helen's mother as she approached the punch bowl.

Helen didn't doubt for a moment that her mother had timed her interruption down to the second. Sighing, she stepped away from Ray. "Yes, Momma, what do you need?"

"The guests are leaving and you need to help your aunts in the kitchen. And it's time for Captain Birkett to go home."

"Momma, Captain Birkett is home."

Momentarily caught off guard, Helen's mother rallied quickly. "Well, that won't stop you from going to the kitchen, will it?"

"No ma'am." Helen gave Ray one last lingering look before doing as she'd been told. *No wife of his...*

With her mother pushing her along down the hallway, Helen soon found herself in the kitchen with a dish towel in her hand.

"Momma, what are you upset about?" protested Helen.

"Your manners have been slipping, young lady. I'm sure it's the company you're keeping. All those men following you around like lost puppies. It's not done. It's just not done." Enid Stevens gave one of her characteristic sniffs.

"Oh, Momma, don't worry about Alfred Smith. He's a nice boy suffering from the throes of a crush." Helen laughed.

"Don't laugh, young lady. It's time you show some sense! Alfred Smith's comportment is never inappropriate. At least he behaves like a gentleman. Young men nowadays could learn a lesson or two from your father, your uncle, or even that nice man you work for, Burton Dixon. Real Southern gentlemen don't flirt so openly with a young woman. Of course, we have to remember that many of the men you're meeting aren't Southern at all, especially that Captain Birkett."

Helen's mother left the room as she often did in the middle of an argument.

"Don't mind her, honey," began Ora.

"Oh, Aunt Ora, you always say that," interrupted Helen.

"I know honey. It can't be easy having a Momma like Enid, but we all have our crosses to bear."

"Aunt Ora, why don't you or your sisters spend your life cautioning me against the world like my Momma does?"

"Honey, it's simply a matter of philosophy. We believe you can either move forward or stay mired in the mud."

At first, Helen began to laugh about Aunt Ora's statement but then she realized how succinctly it described the difference between herself and her mother. Helen didn't want to ever be mired in the mud. She'd taken great pains all her life to keep moving forward.

"Helen, I've known you all your life," continued her Aunt Ora. "You have always had the courage and the daring to go after what you want. The courage to experiment, the courage to seek, the courage to disregard stereotyped ideas, that's what I'm talking about. And mind you, I didn't say recklessness. Fortunately, you've always backed up your courage and daring with common sense."

Lecture over, Aunt Ora fluttered around the kitchen while Helen and Edna Jane companionably washed the numerous dishes scattered on the countertop and table. In the background, the radio provided its endless stream of war news.

"Today the Allies attacked focal points on inland road systems. Fighters escorting medium range bombers strafed and bombed enemy troop concentrations, gun positions, rail-yards, locomotives, oil tank cars, military buildings, armored vehicles, ammunition dumps, and airfields..."

Above the crackle and hiss of static from the radio, Helen could hear her aunt softly singing her favorite hymn *God of Grace and God of Glory.*

Cure Thy children's warring madness

Bend our pride to Thy control

Shame our wanton selfish gladness

Rich in things and poor in soul

Grant us wisdom, grant us courage

For the living of these days

For the living of these days

Hearing the words sung by someone she loved dearly brought peace to Helen's troubled heart.

"We all want to believe it's safe, don't we, Aunt Ora?" Helen asked when her aunt finished the verse.

"We live in a time of fear, honey. Just listen to the radio. You can hear his voice travelling all those miles under the Atlantic Ocean to reach us. Sometimes, I swear you can hear the bombs falling on London."

"What are we going to do?"

"Like I've been telling you, you can either move forward or stay mired in the mud. We'll get through this."

"She's telling you the truth, child," added Edna Jane sagely.

Helen pondered her aunt's words as she walked toward the front parlor to retrieve the remaining cups and glasses. On the other side of the door, she heard her mother and her Aunt Ida arguing. Having rarely heard her Aunt Ida raise her voice to anyone, especially Enid Stevens, Helen paused out in the hall and eavesdropped.

"Oh, I don't know," fussed Enid. "Life has turned inside out and upside down because of the war. It used to be that marrying was the thing to do—now, going to work is. How can a girl ever find a sweetheart?"

"Enid, dear, if you're so worried about Helen finding a sweetheart, you shouldn't stand between Ray and Helen," said Ida.

"It's a mistake for them to be together!" declared Enid.

"Well if it is, remember everybody's got a right to make their own mistakes," countered Ida.

"Oh, Ida, you're just a hopeless romantic. You and Ora always have been," grumbled Enid.

"Hopeful romantic, hopeful," responded Ida, unruffled by her sister-in-law's snappishness.

"Ida's right, you know," interjected Elva.

"Oh, not you too!" wailed Enid. "Elva! I thought at least you'd agree with me. You're the practical one. Surely you can see how impractical their relationship is. Think about what happened to Ida."

"I'm right here, Enid. And I don't need to ever be reminded of what happened," said Ida.

"For once I'm siding with love. Forget practical," announced Elva.

"And here I thought Helen got her practical nature from you! After all these years, I find out that you are a closet romantic," complained Enid.

"Enid, you have seen them together. Surely even you can see the love they have for each other shining out of their eyes," said Ida gently.

"Enid, haven't you noticed that they are oblivious to everyone and everything around them?" added Elva. "It's like they're in a fog of their own making."

"I've only noticed how little gets done when he's around," Enid said.

"Haven't you seen the electricity between them?" continued Elva, ignoring Enid's spiteful remarks. She understood that Enid's fussing was her way of coping with a situation that worried her.

"He's British!"

"Yes, isn't he precious?" asked Ida. "A real Southern gentleman, even if he is from England."

Finally, Helen could stand it no longer. She didn't want to be discussed like this, even by her own well-meaning relatives. She walked into the room.

"So what else makes a real Southern gentleman, Aunt Ida?" Helen asked lightly at the same time as her eyes flashed defiantly.

Undisturbed by her niece's sudden appearance, Ida answered without hesitation. "Well, Southern gentlemen are well-groomed. They're good dancers. They have flawless manners, like they know to hold a chair for a lady or to stand up when a lady enters a room. They're good at making conversation too. They know not to bring up topics distressing to a lady."

"I see. And Captain Birkett knows all these things?" Helen asked archly.

"Now don't you worry about Captain Birkett for the tiniest minute. He's been a perfect gentleman while he's lived under my roof," stated Ida firmly.

Wanting to avoid further words with her mother, Helen retreated to the kitchen. Edna Jane, up to her elbows in sudsy water, met her with an understanding smile.

"They giving you a hard time, are they?" Edna Jane asked. "It's just because they love you."

Helen rolled her eyes in exasperation.

"Well?" asked Aunt Ora, when she emerged from the pantry. Her inquisitive face was alight with curiosity.

"Well what?" responded Helen, perplexed.

"Well, has Captain Birkett kissed you yet?" asked Aunt Ora.

"Kissed me?" exclaimed Helen.

"Honey, now that you're walking out together, it's all right if you kiss him," said Edna Jane.

"Aunt Ora! Edna Jane! We are not walking out together! We are not dating! And whatever makes you think Captain Birkett wants to kiss me?" Helen's cheeks flushed a pretty pink.

"I may be old, but I'm not blind. Any fool can see that the man is crazy about you." Ora giggled happily.

"I can't believe we are having this discussion," said Helen. Ora's genuine innocent nature made it impossible to take offense to her prying questions.

"Helen, dear, you simply must realize that you are as romantic as you are practical," admonished Aunt Ora. "Now, answer the question—has he kissed you yet?"

"Of course not!" Helen's cheeks flamed with embarrassment over her aunt's prying.

"Well why ever not?" asked her aunt in surprise. "The electricity in the air between the two of you is enough to light a whole city block. Maybe you should wear your new dress. He'd kiss you for certain then."

"It's never been the right time or the right place!" wailed Helen.

"Honey, when it's love, it's always the right time and the right place," said Edna Jane, adding her two cents.

"I don't think I'd be a willing participant," announced Helen, primly ignoring her comment.

"Not a willing participant! Hah! Helen Shelby Stevens, you're always acting like you don't want to hear about him. What's more, you've been making all sorts of excuses to come over here to visit. You're always peering around corners hoping to spot Captain Birkett. Why, I've seen more of you since—"

"All right Aunt Ora, I get the picture!" protested Helen.

"As for the time and the place—girl—you're always meeting and meeting and meeting. You should be kissing and kissing and kissing."

"Really Aunt Ora!" Helen turned on her heel and left the room. Her aunt, the hopeless romantic had gotten it right. The big question truly was: why hadn't they kissed?

Chapter 35

Ray

$\mathcal{E}$nsconced on the comfortable couch in the front parlor, Ray balanced a tea cup on his knee and faced the three sisters.

"Oh dear, you're not making much progress courting Helen, are you Captain Birkett?" asked Ora kindly. "I can tell by the look on your face."

Unprompted, Ray related the whole story of his pursuit of Helen. He finished by saying, "Helen told me she's not interested. Rather firmly actually. She has made it clear that she doesn't want to talk about the future. I don't understand it at all. Women always want to talk about the future." Ray failed to notice that his comment brought smiles to the faces of the three sisters. Instead, he stared intently at his feet.

"Oh my, that does sound final, doesn't it?" asked Ida.

"It's not final at all. We've all heard how much she protests when we ask her about you, Captain Birkett," said Elva. "Haven't you seen the way Helen blushes whenever you speak?"

"No, not really." Ray shook his head sadly. "Mostly I notice that she's rude to me whenever we meet; either that or she talks about work."

"That is so like Helen, to take refuge in her work when she's nervous," commented Ida.

Ray never considered Helen's behavior from that point of view. He hadn't imagined a woman as unflappable as Helen as being nervous inside. The idea put a whole different light on her attitude toward him. The thought cheered him.

"Perhaps you should wait a spell and let her consider your proposal."

"Oh for goodness sake Ida, there is a war on. Captain Birkett doesn't have time to wait for Helen to come around," exclaimed Elva.

"Love is a funny thing," said Ora.

"Love?" asked Ray, perplexed.

"Yes, love. Helen exhibits the classic symptoms of a woman in love but who is unsure if she's loved in return," announced Elva authoritatively.

"Elva, you are so right. How does that saying go? *'I think the lady doth protest too much?'* Is that it?" asked Ora.

"Not quite dear. *'The lady doth protest too much, methinks.'* Shakespeare, Hamlet, Act III, Scene II," supplied Ida.

"Never use a Shakespearean quote when there is an English teacher present," Ora warned Ray.

"Captain Birkett, may I ask what you have done to make Helen feel loved? How have you expressed your feelings for her?" asked Elva.

"I'm afraid I haven't expressed myself at all well. Each time we meet, I either say something flippant or something to make her angry."

"Or you flirt with Dot Carson," stated Ora matter-of-factly.

"I only do that because Helen lavishes attention on that puppy dog, Alfred Smith," declared Ray in his own defense.

"Trading tit for tat won't win a woman's heart, Captain Birkett," stated Elva firmly. At her words, the sisters glared at him accusingly.

"You really must make an effort to do better," admonished Ida. "Remember, don't ever tell a woman what to do, especially Helen. She's got a mind of her own."

"Captain Birkett, do you mind if I ask the obvious? Why didn't you write after the first postcard?" asked Ora.

"I had the postcard hand-delivered by an ensign I met. I never knew Helen's address."

"Oh, I see," said Ora. She sniffed and pointedly looked at each of her sisters.

Ray was disconcerted when all three women gave him the eye. They acted as if his lack of knowledge of Helen's address, however difficult the circumstances, was no excuse.

"Ladies, let's get back to the topic at hand. Captain Birkett has a real problem," insisted Ida.

"I'm not sure what would be the right thing to do in this situation," began Ora.

"Captain Birkett, in our day, a man spoke to Father," interrupted Elva.

"All I was going to say—" persevered Ora, obviously used to being interrupted by one or the other of her sisters. "All I was going to say was that in my day, a man courted a woman before asking for her hand in marriage."

"And they asked, they didn't tell," added Ida.

"They didn't demand, they wooed," insisted Ora.

"Captain Birkett, it seems to me that you got off on the wrong foot," said Elva.

"Wrong foot, Elva? Wrong feet is more like it," giggled Ora.

Chapter 36

Helen

On the day of the launch, Helen felt a lightness of heart that she hadn't experienced in a long while. Her sister, Lilly, skipped along next to her, chattering incessantly.

"Helen, you're so lucky! You get to help christen a Liberty ship!"

"You're the lucky one, Lilly. I managed to wrangle an invitation for you, too. Promise me that you'll behave yourself," said Helen, smiling at Lilly who looked very pretty in her pale blue party frock.

"You know I will. I don't want to miss a thing! Will I be able to see you?"

"You will be standing with Daddy. I'm sure he'll have a great spot all picked out. I will be up on a tall platform erected at the bow of the ship. You should be able to see me without any trouble at all." Helen ruffled her sister's hair, glad that she would be there.

Just then a convoy transporting troops rounded the corner. Truck after truck shifted gears and growled forward drowning out all hopes of conversation. From the back of the trucks, young men in uniform waved, wolf-whistled, and called out "Hello beautiful". As they passed, they threw small objects at Helen and her sister. Lilly ran to retrieve them. She picked them up and put them in her dress pockets.

"Lilly, what are you doing" asked Helen. She bent down and picked up one of the three inch long brass objects. "These look like shell casings from bullets."

"Helen, look inside," instructed her sister.

From inside the empty shell casing, Helen removed a small slip of paper. "What's this all about?" Uncurling it, she read the firm masculine script aloud. "'Be a sweetheart and write to me.'" The man's name and address were written on the back.

"Didn't you know that soldiers put their names and addresses on paper inside shell casings just in case they see a pretty girl?" interrupted Lilly. "It's the easiest way to get a message to her when there is no time."

"No, I didn't know." Helen studied her little sister for a moment. "Lilly, have you collected these shell casings before?"

"Well why not?" asked Lilly defiantly. "All the other girls do!"

"Lilly! You're only fourteen!"

"Just because I'm young doesn't mean I should miss out on all the fun!" Lilly wanted so badly to grow up fast, but her eyes revealed how uncertain she was.

"Lilly! You're not old enough to correspond with men! Give me those shell casings before I tell Momma on you. You don't want to be locked up in your room until you turn eighteen, do you?"

With a mixture of exasperation and relief, Lilly handed over the dozen or so shell casings she had picked up. Helen put them inside her purse. "Thanks Lilly. Later on, I'll distribute them at the USO. There is no reason why someone—someone of a more appropriate age—shouldn't write to a lonely soldier."

"Tell me again what's going to happen at the launch," said Lilly, having given up on the idea of corresponding with soldiers for the time being.

"We're very lucky to be participating in a daytime launch."

"They launch Liberty ships at night?" asked Lilly in disbelief.

"They launch them whenever the tide is at the highest point for the day. Other rules apply. For instance, they don't launch on windy days in case the wind causes the ship to drift into the marsh."

"What if it's too windy today?" asked Lilly.

"They'll postpone the launch until the next high tide, twelve hours later."

"But that would make it the middle of the night!"

"Yes and you'd be in bed and miss the whole thing!" Helen playfully hugged her sister. "Personally, I think it is amazing how quickly they get everyone ready. Many times the sponsor and speakers don't know about the launch time until a few hours beforehand. You're also fortunate that several launches have already taken place."

"Why is that?" asked Lilly.

"Primarily for safety reasons, the first few Liberty ships were launched cautiously without very much fanfare. Today's launch will be a more festive affair. You'll get to hear the shipyard band play patriotic tunes in between speeches by important people from Brunswick."

"I don't know if I'll enjoy the speeches, but it will be fun to hear the band."

Helen laughed at her sister. "You won't have to worry. No one can talk very long because at exactly high tide, a loud whistle will give two short blasts signaling that the ship should be released from its shipway. There are lots of blocks, wedges, and cables that have to be removed. At the very last, the burners will burn away the final plates holding the ship in place. At the moment the ship begins to slide, the sponsor, Mrs. H. E. Whalen, will say the words 'I christen thee' and break the bottle of champagne on the prow of the ship. I'll be standing right next to her holding her bouquet."

"I hope it breaks! It would be embarrassing if it didn't."

"Yes, it would. Maybe Mrs. Whalen has practiced at home."

"Wow, I never thought of that. Won't the glass fly all over the place when the bottle shatters?" asked Lilly.

"Oh, no. The bottle is held inside a woven basket of red, white, and blue ribbons."

"After that will the boats moored nearby shoot off their cannons in salute? I saw that once in a movie." Lilly twirled around in her pretty frock, making it swirl.

"Yes, Lilly. I imagine the whistles around the shipyard will add their shrieks to the general noise and applauding."

"What happens then?"

"Hopefully, when the ship comes to the end of her shipway, she will splash gracefully into the water. That's the signal for the crowd to erupt with a giant cheer."

"I'll help with that!" said Lilly eagerly.

"I'm sure you will."

"Helen, will you get to wear a corsage?"

"Yes, the maids of honor are presented with corsages with red, white, and blue ribbons. We also receive souvenirs of the day. The best one is a silver pin in the shape of the Maritime Commission's Victory Eagle symbol. The name of the ship will be engraved on the front. The sponsor's pin is 10-karet gold. Imagine that! We also receive a souvenir program and a photograph taken at the exact moment the bottle of champagne strikes the bow of the ship. The sponsor gets to keep the broken champagne bottle in a pretty wooden box. I'm sure Aunt Ora will clip out the article about the launch out of the paper for her scrapbook."

"That's so wonderful. I wish I could be a maid of honor. Or maybe I could be a flower girl!"

Helen could think of other people who would love the opportunity to christen a ship. She smoothed the skirt of her beautiful tea-length sapphire blue dress courtesy of her Aunt Ida's skill at winning contests. Suddenly, she didn't really care if other people wanted the honor. Helen was very happy that she had been chosen.

Outside of the drugstore, Helen and Lilly met several of their friends.

"My oh my, you two are all dressed up in your finery today," said Hazel Ann with a smile.

"We're going to the Liberty ship launch!" announced Lilly.

"Is that a new dress, Helen?" asked Winona.

"Why, yes, it is."

"What did you have to do to get the funds for such a fancy new dress?" Winona asked suspiciously.

"I didn't do anything," said Helen defensively, angry with Winona's insinuating tone. Winona's curiosity often made Helen uncomfortable.

"Did you buy your dress on the black market?" asked Winona in a censorious voice.

"No, most certainly not," said Helen as lightly as she could. As much as she liked Winona, Helen didn't appreciate the way her friend tended to find fault in other people's good fortune. "My Aunt Ida won it in a contest."

"Aunt Ida's always winning contests," added Lilly helpfully. "Maybe next time she'll win something for me."

"It should be me serving as maid of honor! It's my turn!" Winona glared resentfully at Helen.

"You two better get on your way," urged Hazel Ann. Seeking to avoid a confrontation with Winona that would spoil the day, she made shooing motion with her hands. "You don't want to be late. Oh, look. Here comes Captain Birkett."

"Hello ladies. Your aunts told me that if I hurried, I just might be able to escort you lovely ladies to the launch," said Captain Ray Birkett.

Giggling, Helen linked her arm in his. Walking along beside Ray under the shade of the live oak trees, an unbelievably strong almost unbearable feeling of love flooded through Helen. Her chest ached from the strain of trying to contain her swelling heart. She understood that her heart didn't really belong to her anymore, it belonged to Ray. She was merely holding on to it for him.

Chapter 37

Ray

*R*ay stood beside Richard on the foredeck of a Liberty ship. The vessel, in preparation for launch, swarmed with men making last minute additions to the ship's superstructure. Richard held the loop antenna in front of him, rotating it in an arc as he tried to detect a signal.

"Nothing here," Richard said, discouragement creeping into his voice.

"It must be here somewhere," stated Ray firmly. "Signals have been detected on the past three launches. Chances are we'll hear something on this one too. The signal might come from the ship itself."

"Is that why you have us up here sweeping the deck? Truthfully, that sound could come from anywhere, even on-shore."

"You're right, Richard. The good news is that right now we just need to make sure that it's not coming from this particular ship. What should I be looking for?"

"Are you familiar with radio components? Basically the device will be similar. We're looking for a box big enough to contain a few tubes and knobs. Of course, it won't have a tuner. The device will be simple, only able to emit a signal." Richard stopped talking and fiddled with the dials on his antenna.

Left to his own thoughts, Ray pondered whether or not they should also keep their eyes open for a bomb as well. A saboteur could do a whole lot of damage with a single well-placed explosive device. Admiral Jarabek continued to discount the idea of that sort of attack, but the proximity of the Hercules powder manufacturing plant provided an excellent source of munitions.

"All right, Ray, let's get this show on the road. We'll start at the bow and work our way to the stern. Chances are, if there is a homing beacon somewhere aboard, it will be on deck. That would ensure the best transmission. We'll check the crew superstructure too." Richard continued to swing the loop antenna slowly from left to right.

"If we have time, we should check out as much as we can below decks," said Ray. He wasn't in a position to discuss sabotage with Richard, but he could widen their search. Ray knew others were also sweeping the ship, completing their final inspections.

"Ray, be sure to keep your eyes open for anything that looks out of place. This antenna will only pick up transmissions. For all we know, the device might be on a timer or remotely activated. It's too bad we couldn't arrange to be on the boat during its sea trials. If, like you think, the transmission came from the Liberty ship, we'd be in a good position to find, isolate, and destroy it."

As he toured the ship with Richard, Ray couldn't get over the feeling of being followed. Several times, he stopped and listened for footsteps behind him. Twice, he thought he saw shadows of figures on the walls in the distance. Once, Ray even pointed the form out to Richard.

"Come on, Ray. No one's paying attention to us. It's all in your imagination. There are so many people on this ship, no matter where we go you'll hear footsteps."

"Not in here," said Ray as he opened the door to a small room near the boilers. "This would be the place to hide. Look, even its door is hard to see."

"You're right. It's the perfect place to hide someone, but not the something we are looking for right now. It's too near the engine room and the boilers. All this metal will prevent a signal from escaping. Let's go back up topside and complete one more sweep. It's almost time for the launch. I don't want to miss seeing my sister get soaked with champagne when that bottle breaks."

Ray didn't entirely agree with Richard. This small room, so near the engine and boilers, would be a perfect location for a bomb.

Chapter 38

Helen

"*H*elen, we need to talk," said William Browning as he approached Helen the next day at the shipyard. "Let's walk back to the office. I'm going that way, are you?"

Unhappily, Helen trailed along in his wake. She dreaded any confrontation with William. She hated it when he fixed his intense stare on her. With his thin face and prominent aquiline nose, he reminded her of a bird of prey preparing to strike. Their opinions and attitudes toward accident investigation were miles apart. Any discussion between them was bound to end badly.

Browning waited until they were out of the hot July sun before rounding on her. "You dragged on your accident investigation until management had to move the proposed July seventh launch of the *John Catron* until the eleventh! That is simply unacceptable. You've got to get your work done and get it done quickly!"

"I'm just trying to be thorough," protested Helen.

"Thorough is one thing, slow is another!"

"But Mr. Browning, accident investigations must be conducted methodically and that takes time." Helen did not think that now was the time to tell William how sloppily his previous investigations had been done. His bad mood would prevent him from hearing her suggestions. Then again, given his attitude toward her, perhaps her boss, Burt, would be the best person to talk to about what she had learned from investigating the keyway, welding, and acid accidents. Before Helen could reach Burt in his office, Browning marched quickly to the door.

"Burt, I was just explaining to Helen that she needs to get her accident reports done more quickly. She doesn't see anything wrong with delaying a ship launch," said William, getting his side of the story in before Helen could even greet Burt.

"Hello Helen. Hello William," said Burt, trying to give William time to calm down.

"Hello Burt. Actually, what Mr. Browning says isn't true. I do care very much about the timely launches of ships. However, I care equally much about the safety of our employees."

"The launch has been delayed four days! All because of her making such a big fuss about thorough accident investigations!" shouted William.

"Now, William, we're all under pressure here. As you know, investigating an accident correctly and implementing safeguards based on what we learn is the only way to prevent future accidents," said Burt reasonably.

"The only way to prevent accidents is to hire smarter people. The folks we have working here," William looked pointedly at Helen, "some of them don't know nothing."

"Mr. Browning—"

William cut Helen off. "All I'm saying, Burt, is that she needs to get her work done more quickly!" Having said his piece, William stomped off in a huff.

Burt ran his hand through his hair. The fan hummed noisily in the still room.

"Helen, you know I believe your methods are valid, but you must realize that we have ships to build. Yes—" Burt held up a hand to stop her from protesting. "Yes, I want results, but we can't delay production. Several of the supervisors have been complaining about your presence in their departments. They say you disrupt the work while you talk to employees. Fred Norris has been particularly verbal in his complaints. Steer clear of him and any of his departments for a while."

Defeated, Helen left the office to walk around the shipyard to check on the safeguards she had installed.

"Alfred, don't you see? They don't believe in my work! William Browning couldn't manage his way out of a paper bag let alone write up an accident report! Why did Burt side with him?" Helen sat at the soda fountain with Alfred Smith. He'd been waiting at the gate for her after work again. Needing to vent her frustration, Helen agreed to have a soda with him. While he listened sympathetically, she described her confrontation with William Browning and her boss's response.

"Miss Helen, I know it's hard, but you shouldn't be so sensitive to criticism. That's how things are in the world of business. Mr. Dixon and Mr. Browning have some valid arguments. I know it's not easy to let something go, especially when it's something you really care about, but you need to look at things from their point of view too."

"It's just that—" Helen broke off when a man came through the door of the drugstore. "Speak of the devil." She gestured at William Browning with a tiny nod of her head in his direction.

"Hello Mr. Browning," said Alfred politely.

"Hello Alfred. Hello Helen." William gave them a friendly wave. "Lovely day, isn't it?"

Nonplussed, Helen could only stare at him.

197

"I had a nice time at your aunts' party the other night. They really go out of their way to make sure everyone is having a good time."

Helen sat silently, disconcerted by his agreeable behavior. William Browning smiled and waited for her to respond. Alfred Smith nudged her elbow gently. After thinking about what Alfred had said, Helen decided to apologize. Alfred's comments hit the mark and made her realize that perhaps there were two sides to the situation. "William, I'm sorry about our little disagreement today. You and Burt made some valid points. I'll try to do better in the future."

William stared at her for a moment as if he had no idea what she was talking about. Then he gave himself a little shake. "Sure. Of course. No hard feelings. Well, bye now. I want to get some bubble gum." William quickly moved to the candy counter.

"He won't find any bubble gum there," laughed Alfred. "The store's been out for weeks. I think your little brother bought it all."

Confused, Helen watched William's retreating back. She didn't understand his pleasant behavior toward her.

"Alfred, after what I told you, don't you think Mr. Browning behaved strangely?"

"Not at all. It's nice that he wants to make amends."

"But, he acted as if he didn't recall our argument at all. It reminds me of the day that he and I collided. It was as if he hadn't expected to find me at the accident site. He was even wearing the wrong color hard hat. I don't know what to think about him. Do you think it's because neither he nor my boss take my accident investigations seriously?"

"I think you're worrying about nothing, Miss Helen."

Chapter 39

Ray

*R*ay dodged trucks, forklifts, and people as he walked along the broad pathway in front of the dry-docked Liberty ships. The huge vessels loomed skyward and cast long shadows. In his mind, he reviewed what he had learned about each of the recent accidents. Focused as he was, it took a few minutes for the sound of tormented metal to sink into his subconscious and make a connection. Suddenly alert, Ray knew where he had previously heard that sound. It had come seconds before a chain had broken loose on the deck of his ship. When the link had finally failed, the chain had lashed out with a force that had smashed a seaman's leg.

Adrenaline surged through Ray as he scanned the shipyard for the source of the noise. High above him, from the hook of a fifty-ton gantry crane, dangled a huge square piece of metal that served as a hatch cover for a cargo hold. Though Ray couldn't see it, he knew instinctively that the chain holding the many ton object was about to fail. Frantically, he ran toward the operator and waved his arms. "Get back everyone! Get out of the way! Get away from the tracks! The load is going to fall!"

In response to his repeated shouting, people scattered in all directions. Ray sprinted with an awkward gait, almost dragging his game leg behind him. He wanted to warn the crane operator, who he recognized as Hank Stine. He had to tell the man to put his load on the ground before it fell.

"Move! Everybody get out of the way and stay out!" Ray continued to shout. "Hank! Set your load down!"

Ray raced for the cab, with its boom and cable tower. Hank Stine, protected by a mesh cage, sat casually in his seat. The man didn't see Ray approaching. He couldn't hear the sound of protesting metal over the thrumming of the crane's engine.

Then it was too late. With a final rending screech, the enormous piece of metal dropped to the ground. The shock wave created at the moment of impact drowned out every other sound. An eerie silence followed its fall.

Slowly, almost unwillingly, voice by voice, the shipyard came alive again. People rushed to the scene asking if anyone had been injured. Ray raked his memory trying to determine if he had seen anyone under the shadow of the huge piece of metal.

"Captain Birkett, what happened here?" asked Burt when he and William Browning ran to Ray's side. Focused on the commotion around the crane, Ray hadn't heard the men approach.

"What was that terrific noise?" asked William Browning.

"The chain failed under the strain of lifting that cargo hold door," answered Ray.

"How do you know the chain failed?" William's voice sounded suspicious.

"I heard the metal screech as it failed," answered Ray. "It's a sound I've heard before, on-board ship. I shouted for everyone to get out of the way. I don't think anyone was underneath when it landed but I can't say for certain."

Chapter 40

Helen

Ｆirst her Momma, then her boss, and now William Browning. All three angry at her in such a short period of time was more than Helen could handle. Since the temperature had cooled down, she decided to take a walk to clear her head. She turned the events of the past few weeks over and over in her mind. Something was going on, something serious. Could a saboteur be at work in the shipyard? The frantic ringing of a bicycle bell snapped her out of her reverie.

"Mickey, where are you off to in such a hurry?" asked Helen. "Hey! That's my bike!"

"I've been collecting scrap for the war effort." Her brother gestured to the wagon he pulled along behind the bike. It was full of tin cans, old pots and pans, and dated newspapers. "It's for the scrap drive. Mr. Dorsett down at the filling station is going to give me a nickel for each full wagon. I've got to hurry."

"Before you rush off, tell me what are you going to do with your new-found riches?"

"That's why I've got to hurry. A new shipment of bubble gum arrived at the drugstore. It's selling for a penny a piece! After I get some, I'm fixin' to go over to Gus Finch's house. We're going to study his enemy aircraft spotter cards. Actually, they belong to his dad. He's one of the patrol wardens."

"Don't let me hold you up." Helen laughed and waved him on his way.

Helen walked on until she came to the Lover's Oak. She slipped up onto one of its broad tree limbs. There, hidden by the thick Spanish moss, she allowed herself a few moments to day-dream about Ray.

"I wish I was the guy you're thinking about right now," said Alfred Smith.

"Alfred! You startled me!"

"I'm sorry to disturb you, Miss Helen. You looked so pretty sitting here, your face all lit from within. Like I said ma'am, I wish I was the guy you're thinking about just now." Alfred hung his head bashfully. For him, this was a rather long speech.

"Oh Alfred," began Helen. Then, realizing it would be unkind to reveal her innermost thoughts to this shy, kind man, she changed the subject.

"I was about to go to the Tip-Top Café. Would you like to go with me? We can see if any of the gang are there." Helen knew she shouldn't encourage Alfred, even with something as small as a visit to the café, but her distressed nerves enjoyed his undemanding presence.

"I'd enjoy that very much, Miss Helen."

Helen decided she would have to introduce Alfred to someone special. He took his defeat with wonderful equanimity.

"Hi Winona, Avis Lou, Hazel Ann, Hank, George, Cecil." Helen greeted each of her friends by name when she stepped inside the door of the café. The radio played *Bluebirds Over the White Cliffs of Dover*," a big improvement over the incessant war news normally being broadcast.

"Hi Helen. We've been discussing the big crane accident," said Hank.

"Wasn't it amazing that no one got hurt?" asked Hazel Ann.

"Crane accident? What happened?" asked Helen. Busy in town on errands for Burt, she hadn't been at the shipyard that day.

"One of the fifty-ton gantry cranes dropped its load today, a big square hatch cover!" exclaimed Dot. "Captain Birkett saved the day! Isn't he wonderful?"

Jealousy swirled around inside Helen. She knew Dot was sweet on Ray and didn't like it one bit. In fact, Helen suspicioned that Dot went out of her way to attend her aunts' parties in order to see him.

"Only Captain Birkett realized what was happening. He told Burt and William that he recognized the sound of metal under stress. Luckily, he shouted his warning in time for everyone to get out of the way," explained George.

"It's amazing he was able to prevent a disaster," said Avis Lou.

Helen's stomach churned. Another accident—another major accident— had happened and it could have resulted in deaths. Though she wanted to dwell on the fact that Ray had played the role of hero, her mind raced. Was it an accident? Would there be any way to ascertain whether or not it was sabotage? Could she procure the failed link of chain to take it over to the metallurgy department for analysis? Would the analysis tell her if it really had been an accidental failure of the link? Would William Browning be placed in charge of the accident investigation since Burt had pulled her off her special project?

Thinking about the accident investigation brought Helen's anger over her boss's apparent lack of interest to the surface. "Not that it would matter, but we might have prevented the accident if Burt Dixon would listen to me!" Helen declared tersely.

"What do you mean?" asked Cecil, startled by her abrupt announcement. The others looked at her curiously.

"I'm sorry. I didn't mean that the way it sounded," apologized Helen, instantly ashamed of her outburst. "All these accidents are unnerving me. They shouldn't be happening. They hurt innocent people and they delay launches. We've got to find a way to prevent them."

"There have been a number of accidents, haven't there?" asked Winona.

"Mostly, the accidents have been minor. For instance, the worker who failed to wear protective clothing and received minor burns. Or the two men who used a pallet mounted on the forks of a forklift instead of a ladder, the man on the pallet fell off and sprained his ankle."

"But some of them have been pretty bad," said Avis Lou.

"Remember the lathe operator who was struck by the key. He swears that he removed the key and set it on his work bench before taking a break," said Alfred.

"And what about Milly's accident?" spoke up Hazel Ann. "She broke her ankle when her acetylene tank fell over and the valve shot loose and hit her."

"What a nasty accident!" exclaimed Winona.

"One that should never have happened," agreed Avis Lou.

"No, the valve shouldn't have come loose," agreed George.

"And then there's Moria's horrible accident," said Alfred.

"There is a possibility that the labels on the water and acid containers were labeled incorrectly," answered Helen.

"Wouldn't she have been able to tell?" Dot asked, appalled.

"Not easily. Both liquids are clear." Helen didn't tell them that she had had the remnants of each container tested. Analysis proved that water was in the acid container and acid in the one marked water.

"And then there was the rigger. Ben McNeely's death was sad, wasn't it?" asked Cecil Hudson.

"Something needs to be done to prevent these accidents," Helen said, repeating what she had said earlier. Suddenly tired, she didn't want to think about it anymore. "Let's talk about something else, shall we?"

Chapter 41

Ray

$\mathcal{B}$ased on his discussion with Helen's aunts, Ray decided he should get to know Helen's father better. This would be no hardship because he liked the man's affable charm. Elva obligingly arranged for Ray to accompany Afton Stevens on his evening patrol of Jekyll Island. The two men brought Blue and Beau along, knowing the two blood hounds would sniff out any irregularities. Now the dogs ran to and fro between the breaking surf and the dunes, scattering the shore birds in their wake.

They had come by boat to the island and were now walking the beach. Without the benefit of any man-made lights, they relied on the half-moon to light their path. Ray paused to stare up at the immense, impenetrable blackness of the sky. Punctuated here and there by stars, the vault overhead reminded Ray of his time in a lifeboat on the North Atlantic. The smell and sounds of the ocean brought back other memories as well. Memories of men flaming like torches, the smell of burning skin, the fear that can paralyze a man. Ray wished Helen was beside him to drive the memories away. The sheer weight of his thoughts made his limp more pronounced.

"Captain Birkett, I have been remiss. You're limping. I should have considered your injury when I proposed that you accompany me. Do you need to rest?" asked Afton.

"No sir, I'm fine. Just a little stiffness that needs to be worked out."

"Richard told me how you ran to get those people out of the way of the crane. It couldn't have been easy on you. I've got a small flask of bourbon along for medicinal purposes if you need some. Please let me know, it's no shame to admit you've been wounded."

They walked in silence while the dogs sniffed the edges of the dunes.

"I was in the Great War," volunteered Afton. "Learned to play polo from you Brits. Of course now my polo ponies are being used for patrolling the beaches on Jekyll Island and Saint Simons Island."

"Is that how you pulled this duty?"

"Yes, I suppose so. On top of my work at the shipyard, once a week, I work an eight hour shift on beach watch. Our sole mission is to alert our command of any landing of German troops on U.S. shores. Naturally, we are to apprehend the enemy if possible. Some nights I ride while on guard duty. Other nights, like this one, I prefer to walk with the hounds. The beaches on these outer islands are patrolled twenty-four hours a day, seven days a week. Besides the patrols, the Coast Guard uses small craft like fishing and pleasure boats to conduct surveillance from the water. So far, no spies have landed, but we can't be too careful after that group that landed on Ponte Vedra Beach last summer."

"It's peaceful tonight along the beach," said Ray. Mentally, he removed 'long romantic walks on the beach' from his list of things to do with Helen. Being challenged frequently by members of the beach patrol would put a damper on the romance.

"The breeze keeps you cooler in the summer. It was hotter than blazes today. Makes me glad I'm on night patrol."

"I imagine it does." Ray looked ahead in the distance where he could see the blimps, illuminated by the huge lights, floating above the shipyard.

"Captain Birkett, what are your thoughts about the Battle of the Atlantic," asked Helen's father.

"You mean, aside from it being the longest continuous military campaign in history?" Ray asked. He never found it easy to talk about the battle raging on the stormy Atlantic Ocean. Inevitably people would question him about his experience. Happy as he was to have survived, Ray was disinclined to relive the sinking. "Truthfully, sir, I believe we are through the worst of it. We've been sinking more German U-boats this year than previously. We've also sunk several *Kriegsmarine* warships. What is important now is that the convoys continue to supply Britain and Russia. I can't over-emphasize how dependent my country is on imported material. Without the millions of tons brought in by Liberty ships each week, Britain wouldn't be able to fight. In fact, I doubt if Britain would be able to survive."

"So what you're saying is that the Battle for the Atlantic is basically a tonnage war," said Afton.

"That's right, sir. I've heard it said that on the field of battle that numbers, surprise, and confusion are key, but I've always believed that its success hinges on supplies. Material from merchant ships enables us to battle the Axis powers."

"Your answer leads me to believe you don't mind that my daughter has taken the unusual course of working at the shipyard," said Afton.

"No sir. The work that she and thousands of other women do nationwide is vital to the war effort. Why, just the other day, I saw her put into place some very clever jigs and fixtures that will save hundreds of man-hours over the long run. The faster the shipyards build sturdy ships, the better able we'll be able to fight on."

"Even if it means that a woman is doing a man's job? And before you answer that question, let me add that I've always been very proud of my daughter and her accomplishments. She's a woman who is ahead of her time. It's hard on her to be out-of-step with other women her age."

Ray knew Afton Stevens was referring obliquely to the heated discussion between Ray and Helen the night of the party. He tried to think of some way to put the man's mind at ease. Ray decided to be direct. "Sir, I think your daughter is a very intelligent woman. I've seen some of the training tools she's created and read her accident reports. They show her sound judgment and common sense. There is no doubt in my mind that she is a valuable asset to the shipyard."

"Despite your earlier misgivings?"

"Yes sir, I've changed my mind completely."

"That's good to know, Captain."

Chapter 42

Helen

*H*elen found her father sitting alone in the kitchen. For once, her mother wasn't hovering over the radio twisting her handkerchief round and round in her hands or staring sightlessly out the window with a distant look on her face.

"Allied forces have beaten back fierce German and Italian counterattacks. Allied long range bombers have been bombing bridges, railheads, and other military targets. American troops are making considerable progress despite stiffening resistance..."

Helen walked across the room and switched off the radio. Afton Stevens looked up from his paper.

"Hi Daddy. You don't mind that I turned off the radio, do you?"

"Hello Doll. You look pretty as a ripe peach today. If I don't watch out, some young man is going to steal you away from me."

"You don't have to worry about that, Daddy." Helen came over to where he sat, draped her arm around his shoulder and gave him a little squeeze.

"Don't I? Doll, what's up? You're not your usual bundle of energy today. Where is that twinkle I usually see in your big brown eyes?" Her father took her hand in his and gestured to the seat next to him. Helen sank into it gratefully.

"Oh, I don't know. I just got back from the picture show. The newsreels showed our army advancing through Sicily. The pictures were so disturbing! Oh, Daddy, so many people are dying. You've heard the news on the radio. Sometimes I don't think there is anything left on this earth that's been left unscathed, untouched by the war. Daddy—I'm afraid."

"Everyone's afraid, honey. We all are. It's war."

Helen stared bleakly out the window.

"When this is all over—after the war is over," she began. Then she slapped the table top in frustration. "Oh! I promised myself I wouldn't say that! Everyone always says that. When the war is over—what a phrase! Sometimes I think it will never be over. Sometimes I think things will never be the same."

"Helen, honey, they won't. The world has changed whether we like it or not. Remember what your Aunt Elva always says 'time has a way of moving on and dragging us along with it.'"

"I know, Daddy." Helen stared out the window. She shook her head as if to clear it. "Look at me! I'm star-gazing just like Momma does. Daddy, why does she do that? Sometimes I just want to shake her until she snaps out of it."

"Helen, your Momma's doing the best she can to cope with the difficult circumstances. She's worried about your brother. We can't fault her for that."

"Richard was eager to enlist. He told me that he believed that it is necessary to fight for the things you hold true."

"Richard told your Momma and me the same thing. She understands, but that doesn't make it any easier."

"At least he hasn't left Brunswick yet."

211

"No he hasn't, but the day will come when he will. And that's what your Momma is worried about. It will only be a matter of time and he'll be one of the over eight million men in the armed forces overseas."

"I know you're right. But, she upsets me so. You can feel her fear, can't you?"

"Yes. I can. That's why I try to help her the best I can. We all should. Remember, she's already gone through one war."

"I know, Daddy, it's just that—" Here Helen broke off, unsure of what to say.

"The war isn't really what we're talking about here, is it?" her father asked sagely. "It's not really what you're afraid of, is it?"

"No, I suppose it's not. Things are changing so fast. And then there is Ray," Helen said in a small voice.

"Ah, yes, Captain Ray Birkett. Helen, do you have feelings for this young man?"

"Oh, Daddy! I just don't know, really I don't." Helen burst into tears and sought the comfort of her father's arms. Into his shoulder she said, "Daddy, if I'm not careful I'll fall in love with him."

"Don't be too careful, honey. It's not such a bad thing to love someone."

"But what happens if he leaves Brunswick? How will I bear it?"

"You must know he will leave eventually. You can't hold him here. He's got too much sense of purpose to not do his part to win this war. Love in a time of war is never easy." Afton Stevens hugged his daughter tighter.

"I guess more than anything, I am afraid to love him," Helen said in a small voice.

"Loving in a dangerous and uncertain world isn't for the faint-hearted. It requires a leap of faith—a hope for the future. That man of yours has a lot of hope for the future despite all he has been through. Helen, honey, you must never be afraid to live—to love."

Chapter 43

Ray

*R*ay joined the congregation as those around him sang the moving hymn; *Eternal Father Strong to Save.*

Eternal Father strong to save

Whose arm hath bound the restless wave.

Who bidd'st the mighty ocean deep,

Its own appointed limits keep.

Oh, hear us when we cry to thee

For those in peril on the sea.

After the service, as he followed Helen out of the church, Ray noticed the tears on her face.

"Helen, what's wrong?"

"Nothing, I suppose," Helen said lightly as she daubed her eyes.

"Tell me. I can see you're upset. What's wrong?" Ray touched her arm gently.

"It's nothing, really. I get all teary whenever the minister intones the words of prayer, *'We most humbly beseech thee, in thy goodness, O Lord, to comfort and succor those in need.'* I just get upset when I look at the people kneeling in prayer. I know that one is a mother of two sons overseas, another is the father of a prisoner of war, yet another has lost a son or brother to the fighting in Sicily. What becomes of the hopes, dreams, and plans of those whose lives are lost?" Ray squeezed Helen's hand reassuringly. "And soon, Richard will be joining them. And then, perhaps you, too, will leave," she finished softly.

"Let's not think about the future, darling. After all, we have right now." Ray pulled her closer to him, tucking her arm in his. "Walk with me."

On their way to the Lover's Oak, Ray took a deep breath of the tangy air. In the distance, church bells rang. The hot summer weather had moderated slightly leaving the sunny day freshened by a light breeze.

"It's the kind of day that gives you hope for the future—our future—doesn't it, Helen?"

"There you go again talking about our future, Captain Birkett."

"Don't you believe we're going to have one, Helen?" Ray grasped Helen by her upper arms, lifted her, and swung her around. "And if we're going to get married, we should use our first names."

"Captain Birkett—Ray—you are a persistent man, aren't you?" She laughed and struggled in his arms.

"I won't give up until you say yes," Ray said refusing to put her down.

"Now isn't the time. There may never be a time for us," Helen said soberly.

"Helen, you can't mean that!"

"But I do, Ray. There is a war on and days like today make me wonder if I am doing my part."

"What do you mean doing your part? Isn't it enough that you work at the shipyard, volunteer at the USO, and utilize any remaining time in your busy life to participate in fundraising events?"

"I know you think I'm busy, but when I look at the people around me, like I did in church this morning, I want to do more. Take, for instance, the accidents happening at the shipyard. So far, I've done nothing to prevent them." She turned to face him, her eyes wide with concern. "Ray, do you think that they are just accidents? Is there even a tiny chance that they may be sabotage?"

Ray nearly stumbled at her suggestion. How had she jumped to this conclusion? He had assumed only he and Admiral Jarabek considered the possibility of sabotage. He framed his answer carefully.

"Sabotage is a very serious accusation. In reality, we shouldn't even be discussing it. Helen, word has gotten back to me that you have talked about the accidents that have been occurring at the shipyard outside of your department."

"Did Dot or William tell you that?" A look of anger crossed Helen's face. "So what if I have? It's not as if they are secret. Everyone knows about the incidents and accidents at the shipyard. It's not unusual for people to talk about them. No one seems to care at all. They all brushed off my comments."

"That's true, but have you ever considered that if—and it's a big if—if there is a saboteur and he heard you talking about investigating sabotage, he might think about stopping your efforts."

"I doubt any saboteur would bother with me. My own boss and coworkers ignore me, why wouldn't he?"

"Helen, I'm concerned about your safety."

"That's sweet of you, Ray, but you don't need to be." Helen thought for a moment. "Ray, do you honestly believe I'm wrong about sabotage?"

"Yes, I do. I've studied these accidents and I just don't see how they could be acts of sabotage."

"Well, maybe not all of them are," Helen countered. "Maybe they are so cleverly done, we just don't see it. Why don't we review the accidents now and see what we come up with?"

"I had something slightly more romantic planned for this afternoon," said Ray with a smile. Ray lifted her up onto one of the low boughs of the Lover's Oak.

"My mind won't rest until we talk it through," said Helen. She put out her hand and pulled Ray up next to her.

Ray let out an exaggerated sigh. "If you insist, my lady."

"Let's start with the key that flew out of the keyway."

"I read about that accident. The man should have been more careful. It's easy to forget a step in a process that you're used to doing, especially if your mind is on your upcoming work break."

"So you don't believe someone reinserted the key?" asked Helen.

"No, I don't. I know the man swears he took it out, but like I said, it's easy to forget."

"What about the valve accident?" asked Helen. "I picked up that valve after the accident. I want to ask someone in the machine shop about it. The threads look stripped or filed down and I wonder if someone tampered with it. What I am trying to say is, could a file be used to create the same damage that the valve has? Or would damage like that occur if the pressure in the tank had forced the valve loose?"

"I wouldn't know," answered Ray truthfully. "Okay, let's say the valve might have been tampered with at some time. The problem with that conclusion is that a saboteur couldn't have known what effect his tampering would have. If he wanted to cause a problem, he would have chosen a method that would guarantee success, so to speak."

"Ray, I agree that he couldn't have predicted the outcome. However, any sort of explosion from the tank would have caused problems in the work place. In many ways, things could have been worse. The flash could have ignited a fire."

"True. But you'll never convince me that the rigger's death was anything but an accident."

"Why is that?" asked Helen.

"You said in your report that the harness had been marked for disposal. It's sad to say, but the rigger failed to notice the orange tag." Ray shook his head unhappily.

"Then what happened to the rest of the orange tag? I never found it."

"Most probably it came off sometime after the man fell. A lot of people handled that harness, including your father."

"You have an answer for everything, don't you, Ray?"

"Not really. I don't have an answer for those switched acid and water labels. I can't believe anyone could be that careless."

"I can't believe that no one thought of using an inexpensive dye to color the acid so a person could distinguish between the two liquids."

"Thanks to you, they do now," said Ray with admiration in his voice. "Enough talk about accidents and incidents. Let's talk about us."

Chapter 44

Helen

"*H*elen, I want to have a party to announce to Momma and Dad that Hazel Ann and I plan to get engaged," said Richard. "I'm concerned about how they'll react."

"What are you worried about? And why a party? Isn't that rather silly since you've been sweet on Hazel Ann for ages? It's not as if they don't know her."

Helen's brother sighed hugely. "See, even you don't get it. How can I expect Momma and Dad to understand when even my sister doesn't get it?"

"What are you two young people doing with your heads so close together?" chirped Ora happily when she entered the room.

"Hello Aunt Ora," they chorused.

"Aunt Ora, Richard wants to tell Momma and Daddy that he's serious about Hazel Ann," giggled Helen. "He wants to have a special party to announce their engagement."

"Engagement! Oh Richard, how wonderful! I'm so happy for you, honey!" Ora gave Richard an enthusiastic hug. Abruptly, she released him and looked up into his face. "Oh dear, oh dear. You're getting married. Yes, this will have to be handled carefully, very carefully. It's wise of you to choose to make the announcement at a party. Yes, very wise."

"Am I the only one who doesn't understand?" asked Helen.

"Helen, I'm surprised a smart girl like you doesn't see the problem. You know what your Momma is like. Take Ora's word for it, this will have to be handled carefully," said Aunt Elva when she arrived with a tray of iced tea. She set the tray down on the table. "Lord, I'll be glad when we can have sweet tea again. In the meantime, drink up."

"Richard, this is a wonderful announcement! Congratulations! We've known all along that Hazel Ann is the perfect girl for you. Your Daddy is going to be so happy, but you'll need all the help you can get when you tell your Momma," said Ida.

"Ida's right." Aunt Elva tapped her chin, thinking. "It wouldn't hurt to have a stranger present to keep your Momma on her best behavior."

"Yes, Elva, that's a wonderful idea," said Ora.

"Why don't we have it here?" asked Ida.

Helen marveled at her aunts' ability to take control when it came to a party. Lounging on the couch, her brother appeared perfectly content to let them do so. Richard probably had it all planned from the very beginning.

"That's a good idea, Ida," said Elva. "Let's see. We'll invite the five of us, Eugene, Hazel Ann's parents, your parents and your brother and sister. With Hazel Ann, that makes thirteen."

"Thirteen! Oh, that will never do," exclaimed Ida.

"Why don't we invite that nice Captain Birkett?" asked Ora, clapping her hands with excitement. "He would make fourteen."

"Captain Birkett?" squeaked Helen in surprise. In a more normal voice, she continued, "Surely he wouldn't want to have dinner with us."

"And why not? He's got to eat somewhere," said Ora.

"After all, he lives here," added Ida.

"That settles it. There will be fourteen of us," said Elva with an air of finality.

"Oh dear," interjected Ora.

"What's wrong Ora?"

"Well, I was just thinking. This is a special party and we'll want everything just right."

"Yes?" Elva drew the word out.

"Well, what about the place settings?"

"What about the place settings?" asked Elva, mildly annoyed.

"This is such an important occasion and we'll want to make the table look special. I'd like to use those new dishes, the blue ones, not the white plates we always use. A new beginning together deserves new dishes. Hmmm, maybe we should give the blue plates as a wedding present."

"That would be lovely. I can picture those blue place settings against Momma's snowy white linen table cloth," sighed Ida. "The napkins are all starched and ready. And I know just the flowers from the garden to use in the centerpiece."

"Well, it can't possibly work," stated Elva firmly. "At last count we had twelve dinner plates, eleven bread and butter plates, twelve salad bowls, nine coffee cups and saucers, eleven water glasses and ten goblets that match." Elva ticked off each type on her fingers. "I think we have enough serving bowls and platters."

Helen wondered how her Aunt Elva kept track of such a complex list of serving pieces. She never thought about the fact that she did it herself all the time.

"I don't see why we didn't just buy a complete set of matching dishes when they offered them at the movie theater," said Ida.

"I seem to recall that at the time we didn't have the money for such frivolous purchases. Nobody did," answered Elva.

"It was so much more fun exchanging our ticket stubs for dishes whenever we went to the picture show. We never knew what they were going to offer," exclaimed Ora. "But we can't collect them anymore. Everyone in town goes to the movie theater now so they don't need to offer incentives." Ora's face fell at the thought.

"That's because it's air-cooled," added Ida. "Why, I've seen lines stretching out the door and clear down the street!"

"In my day, air-cooled meant sitting in front of the fan with a bucket of ice," said Elva.

"What are we going to do about the dishes?" wailed Ora.

"It would have been smarter to collect all the pieces you needed before wasting your tickets on those serving bowls and platters. Then we wouldn't be short pieces," said Elva.

"But the serving pieces are so handsome!" responded Ora.

"Now Elva, Ora, no fighting. It's all water under the bridge. We have to help these young people," soothed Ida, used to a lifetime of squabbling between the sisters.

"What should we do?" Agitated, Ora fussed with her dress. "We've just got to make everything perfect."

Everyone sat there thinking for a few moments. Then Helen snapped her fingers.

"Didn't Mrs. Newcastle and Mrs. Pickle collect the same dishes as you?" she asked.

"Oh! You're right! We can borrow from our friends! This is going to be so much fun!" exclaimed Ora, once again happy. "We'll start right away. Elva, you make a list of what we need. Helen, Ida, you take the list and go around to the neighbors. I'll start writing out the place cards."

"Oh dear, I just thought of something else," said Ida.

"What now?"

"Our Victory garden will provide the vegetables, but what about the rest of the meal? With the way rationing is, we might not be able to come up with anything besides Spam or chipped beef. Sugar, leather, coffee, gasoline, meat, shoes, seems like everything is rationed nowadays."

Ever one to take charge, Elva already had a plan. "We'll send little Lilly down to the butcher. She can always talk him out of something better than kidneys, brains, heart, or liver."

"I was only a mere child—" began Ora. "But I seem to recall that those things were call offal when I was growing up. That certainly is an appropriate name for them."

"Hello Winona. Hello Mrs. Bunce." Helen greeted the women with a smile.

"Come in Helen. It's so good to see you. It's been far too long." Mrs. Bunce opened the screened door wide and welcomed Helen inside.

"Work at the shipyard is keeping me busy, Mrs. Bunce," admitted Helen.

"I imagine it does, though why in heaven's name pretty young women like you and Winona want to work at a shipyard is beyond me," said Mrs. Bunce.

"Mother, it's not like there is anyone our age around to date. There is nothing for us to do but work," said Winona grumpily. Helen joined in when Winona started to sing the popular song; *They're Either Too Young or Too Old*.

"They're either too young or too old,

They're either too gray or too grassy green,

The pickings are poor and the crop is lean.

What's good is in the army,

What's left will never harm me".

Helen laughed when they finished the refrain. "Winona is right, Mrs. Bunce. There isn't a lot to do in Brunswick since the men our age have been drafted. If it makes you feel any better though, my Momma says the same thing to me."

"I can understand why," said Mrs. Bunce.

"How is your son, Mrs. Bunce? Have you heard from him?" asked Helen politely. Helen couldn't help but notice that even though the Bunce's had a son overseas, there was no Service flag with a blue star hanging in the window.

"We haven't heard from him in some time," admitted Mrs. Bunce cautiously. "But, you know how hard it is for the mail to reach us from an overseas posting."

"Mrs. Bunce, I need to ask you a favor," said Helen, wanting to avoid the sensitive subject.

"Yes, dear, what is it?"

"Did you collect the blue glass dishes that the movie theater gave out each week there for a while?"

"I have a few pieces, yes."

"My aunts and I are hosting a small dinner party for the family and we were wondering if we might borrow a piece or two. We'll write down what you lend us and make sure we return it."

"Well, I don't see why not," said Mrs. Bunce after considering a bit. "What do you need? Do you have a list?"

Helen pulled the list from her pocket. "We're in search of two dinner plates, three bread and butter plates, two salad bowls, five coffee cups and saucers, three water glasses and four goblets."

"My, my, that is a tall order. Fortunately, I can supply two cups and saucers, two dinner plates, and four goblets."

"That would be wonderful! I left a box by the front door, let me go get it," said Helen. Quickly she retrieved the box and handed it to Mrs. Bunce.

"I'll go into the cupboard and get them. I won't be long. Winona, get your friend a cool glass of tea. Helen, rest your feet a minute."

"Oh, Mrs. Bunce, Winona, thank you. That would be heavenly."

While the two women occupied themselves in the kitchen, Helen wandered around the parlor looking at the photographs and other items decorating the room. She smiled when she happened to spy a party planning book on the end table by the sofa. She picked it up and leafed through the pages. Helen imagined that many households in town had the popular book. It didn't take her long to realize that someone, probably Winona, had marked all the pages with riddles. Helen wasn't surprised, Winona liked to win. She set the book down and moved on to the photographs displayed on the mantel. Several were of Winona in fancy dress; a few others were of her brother.

"Hey!" snapped Winona when she returned with the tea. "What are you doing?"

Startled by Winona's harsh words, Helen quickly returned the photograph she was holding to the mantel, placing it next to the one of Winona's brother. "I was admiring the dress you are wearing in this photograph. It's so lovely; I wanted to take a closer look."

"Oh—well—thank you," said Winona, preening happily. "I'm sorry I snapped at you. I like that photo a lot and didn't want you to drop it."

Before Helen could say anything in response, Mrs. Bunce returned with the dishes carefully wrapped in brown paper and in the box.

"Oh, Mrs. Bunce, this is wonderful. Thank you so much. We really appreciate it. We'll be sure to take good care of them and return them promptly after the party which is three days from now."

On her way home, Helen stopped by her aunts' house to drop off the dishes she had collected.

"Mrs. Bunce loaned us two dinner plates, two cups and saucers, and four goblets. Isn't that wonderful?"

"I found two salad bowls at Mrs. Newcastle's, three bread and butter plates at Winifred Pickles, and three cups and saucers at the Whitney's. We still need three water glasses. My heavens, I did a lot of walking today. My feet are tired of passing each other," said Ida as she sat down at the kitchen table. "And Mrs. Whitney, bless her heart, has three blue stars on her Service flag. Two of her boys are in Europe, one is in the Pacific. Thank heavens none of our friends are displaying a gold star."

"Mrs. Bunce doesn't have a Service flag in her window. Isn't her son overseas?" asked Helen.

"I heard he was, but I don't know in what capacity," answered Elva.

"Maybe he's a conscientious objector," said Ida, her eyes wide. "She might not want to draw attention to him."

"Well, it isn't our place to ask," said Ora. "While you were out, I called Melva Ingrams for the water glasses we need. I think that takes care of everything. Everyone was so nice about it, too."

"Yes, we're fortunate that everyone is letting us borrow the pieces we need," said Helen. A shadow passed over her face.

"What is it, dear?" Ora asked, concerned.

"It's nothing really. When you said that everyone was so nice, you reminded me that Winona Bunce got mad at me when she found me looking at her photograph on the mantel. I don't want to upset anyone when we borrow these things."

"There's no excuse for poor manners. She's no better than she ought to be. Of course, she has no people, bless her heart," said Ora.

"It's a good thing she didn't see me pick up her party planning book. There is no telling how she would react," said Helen. "Did you know she has a book just like yours?"

"Winona probably doesn't want you to know she studies the games in the book before every party," soothed Ida.

"That's probably why she does so well," joked Helen.

"You're right about that," cackled Ora. "She enjoys winning, she does. You can see that in her face."

"Did you know that I saw the same book at Mrs. Pickles? The funny thing is that she says her boarder, George White, studies the book regularly," said Ida.

"Another person who wants to win," said Helen.

"No, another man who wants to impress Winona," suggested Ora.

Chapter 45

Ray

$\mathcal{R}$ay felt honored to be asked to dinner with Helen's parents. The aunts had outdone themselves with the elegance of the table. The blue dishes glimmered like sea glass on the startlingly white table cloth. While waiting for everyone to arrive, Afton Stevens held court in the front parlor. He always enjoyed selecting an article from the paper and discussing it.

"I've been reading today's paper," he began. "There is an article about war bonds that you might be interested in, Elva, since you're always hosting fundraising parties. Did you realize that war bonds help control inflation by providing an outlet for all the money being earned today?"

"I read that per capita income has risen from $1,200 dollars in 1939 to over $2,000 today!" interjected Elva's husband, Eugene.

"All that money and nothing to spend it on but war bonds," sighed Enid.

"War bonds are a good investment," declared Afton, warming to his topic. "Today's paper was full of interesting articles. Were you aware that over one-third of the men in the armed forces have German parents, grandparents, or cousins?"

"I can believe that. Many Germans immigrated here. I wonder how they feel fighting against their relatives. At least, we Stevens know our relatives hail from England," said Ida.

"Captain Birkett, did you know our family hails from Afton, England? Every first-born male in our family line carries the name Afton. You already know Helen's father as Afton. Her brother is actually Afton Richard the third, but we call him Richard to avoid confusion," explained Elva.

"What about the Japanese?" asked Eugene, picking up the thread of the original conversation. "There must be at least a million of them here in the United States. Do you know how many have been interred?"

"According to the article, there are only about 127,000 Japanese living in the United States. Nearly eighty thousand of those are Nisei, meaning they were born in the U.S. of Japanese parents."

"Only that many?" asked Ray politely.

"I don't care how many. They deserved to be interred after they carried out that sneak attack on Pearl Harbor," said Elva heatedly.

At this moment, Richard and Hazel Ann arrived all breathless and happy.

Uh-oh, thought Ray when he saw the look on Enid Steven's face. She's none too thrilled with her son's appearance in his best Sunday suit and polished shoes. Hazel Ann looked quite charming in a new ruffled floral dress. Ray studied Richard's face more closely, and then switched his gaze to Hazel Ann. The two of them positively glowed. They looked bursting with health, vitality, and happiness. And secrets too, thought Ray. From the bubbling, exultant look of them, they wouldn't be keeping their secrets for long.

The family moved into the dining room where the conversation continued without a hitch.

"I read that article about the Japanese. Did you know that Japanese living in California park on the beach and point the headlights of their cars out to sea in order to signal Japanese submarines?" asked Eugene.

While Ray didn't doubt there was some truth to that, he had to stifle an urge to point out that the Brunswick shipyard served as a fine beacon of light every night on the swing shift.

"They couldn't do anything like that here on Saint Simons Island. Why, we can't even get to our beach house now that soldiers guard the causeway bridge. The last time we drove over to check on the place, they made us pay to cross the bridge. Imagine, paying to go to see our own property," complained Enid Stevens.

"It's not worth going there anyway, Momma. All the windows are boarded up after the big explosion blew them out. That was a night! I wish I'd seen the U-boat!" piped Mickey.

"Mickey, must you bring up that horrible night?" asked his mother.

"Would anyone like some biscuits?" asked Ora, waving about the sweet-grass basket filled to the brim with warm biscuits.

"I've heard that the Japanese living in California set forest fires to signal the Japanese fleet," said Hazel Ann, her eyes wide with imagined terror.

"I wouldn't be surprised. They're awfully sneaky," said Eugene around a mouthful of sweet potatoes.

"No wonder the government moved them away from the Pacific coast in February of 1942," said Ida.

From this point on, the conversation became more heated. Finally, Helen's mother, Enid, had had enough.

"Now Afton, a gentleman knows which topics are polite in mixed company and at the dinner table," Enid chided. "Let's not talk about war. Surely, there is some other topic that will interest all of us."

"Yes, Momma, actually, there is." Richard, who hadn't been able to sit still, blurted out the couple's secret. "Momma, Dad, Hazel Ann and I got married!"

Without so much as a squeak of surprise, Enid fainted. Afton rushed to his wife's aid in time to catch her before her head struck her dinner plate.

Seeing the stunned look on Ray's face, Ora commented, "Don't worry about Enid. She's having one of her fits."

"Enid thrives on her fits—so we like to surprise her every once in a while. Keeps her in practice," added Elva.

"We thought Momma might react like that." Richard pointed to his mother now lying on the floor, a pillow tucked under her head, her husband patting her limp hand. "Hazel Ann and I decided that it would be best to get on with it and present Momma with a *fait accompli*. We didn't think Momma would survive the preparations for even a small, simple wedding."

"I, for one, am glad that you ran away and eloped!" said Mickey. "Now I don't have to be an usher. Momma would have borrowed a suit two sizes too big for me just so I could be dressed up."

"Now Mickey, mind your elders. A little spit and polish never hurt anyone," admonished Aunt Elva.

"Oh Aunt Elva," groaned Mickey. "Dressing up is for sissies."

"Mickey! Weddings are important! You don't understand a thing about true love," Lilly said self-importantly.

"At fourteen, neither should you, Missy," countered Aunt Elva.

"Fourteen and she's already beginning to understand about love." Aunt Ora clasped her hands over her breasts and sighed.

Chapter 46

Helen

"*H*azel Ann, I'm so happy for you!" enthused Helen when the others had left them alone. "But eloping? I thought you had your heart set on a pretty wedding with white gladioli on the alter, tall candles, and big white bows on the pews."

"Oh Helen, what I've really always wanted is Richard. I know our wedding didn't have all the trimmings, but it was wonderful. Really, it was. Richard proposed two days ago and I said yes. When we realized that he'd be leaving to go overseas soon, we decided to go up to South Carolina and get married. You know you don't have to wait there. Aunt Elva arranged for a car. Aunt Ida found us a place to stay overnight. Aunt Ora located a willing minister."

"But Hazel Ann, wherever did you get enough gas?" asked Helen. "Everybody we know is allowed only three gallons per week! Even then, you can't be sure the filling station will have any. Why just last week I saw that the filling station in town had run out of gas. They had a great big sign announcing they were closed until their next allotment of gasoline arrived."

"We borrowed gas ration coupons from just about everyone we knew and off we went. With the thirty-five mile per hour speed limit, it took forever! We didn't mind. It saved the tires and gave us more time together. I used all my clothing coupons so that I could get a proper dress. Do you like it? It's been so long since I've worn a new dress. I feel like a queen."

"You look wonderful. It's the perfect color for you. Clothing rationing is hitting everyone pretty hard. I'm glad you feel like a bride. I'm so happy for you."

"You're dress is lovely, too, Helen. I've always thought you looked good in sapphire blue."

"Aunt Ida won it in one of her contests!"

"She did?" asked Hazel Ann in surprise. "Why a new dress is ever so much better than all that popcorn she won!"

"It certainly is," laughed Helen. "It sounds like everything went perfectly for your wedding."

"It almost didn't. You'll never believe what happened!"

"What? Do tell," encouraged Helen.

"When we arrived, the minister said he couldn't marry us until after his bible study class. We told him we'd have dinner and come back. We were having so much fun at dinner, dancing and all; we didn't realize how late it had gotten. We rushed back to find him locking up the church! He and his wife were so understanding. Even though it was after ten, he performed the ceremony and here we are Mr. and Mrs. Richard Stevens!"

"Hazel Ann, can I ask you a question?"

"Sure, honey, what is it?"

"Did it take a lot of courage to get married so quickly? I mean, there's a war on and everything is so uncertain."

"Helen, in an uncertain world, love is the only thing that makes life worth living. I love Richard and I want to have as much time as I can with him. Now I have a question for you. You love Ray, so why don't you marry him?"

"I don't love Ray!"

"Oh yes, you do. Helen. It shows in every glance you send his way. Why aren't you willing to give in to that love?"

Chapter 47

Ray

*R*ay wandered over to where Helen's father now stood, his wife having recovered enough to make her way tearfully to a bedroom to lie down. On the way, Enid harangued her sisters-in-law about their role in the marriage of her precious son.

"Listen to my sisters go on. I can just imagine how much fun they had making the arrangements. Enid never stood a chance," acknowledged Helen's father. Afton Stevens poured them both a tumbler of bourbon. They clinked glasses and toasted the newly-weds.

"Thank you, sir. And yes, sir, they certainly are a force of nature. Living here, it didn't take me long to find that out." Ray hesitated, but decided to press on with his thought. "Your wife seems quite upset. Will she be all right?"

"Of course she will. She doesn't want to recognize what the rest of us have seen all along. Richard and Hazel Ann are in love, have been for quite some time now. As for my sisters' part in their running off to South Carolina to get hitched, well, Enid should have expected that too. After all, she's been friends with the Stevens sisters since first grade."

"First grade? As long as that, sir?"

"Yes, as long as that. Sometimes I think she married me in order to become their sister," Earl Stevens admitted ruefully. "As long as Richard and Hazel Ann are happy, that's all that matters to me. And now, young man, what are your intentions with my daughter?"

Ray, caught flat-footed, choked on his bourbon. "I—I—" he stuttered.

"Come on now man, I've seen the way you light up when my daughter walks in the room. My sisters didn't have to point out that you carefully choose a seat across the room from her so that you can stare at her without anyone really noticing."

Ray couldn't think of a single thing to say in response.

"Captain Birkett, the way I see it, there are two kinds of couples in this war. The bold ones marry quickly to grab all the time together that they can get. The cautious ones, they are the ones who choose to wait and trust in fate. Which one are you?"

"I intend to marry Helen, sir," said Ray, finding his voice.

"I know that. The question I'm asking you is when?"

"I—"

"Captain Birkett, have you proposed to my daughter yet?"

"Yes, sir, several times."

"And her response?"

"Well, sir, she's been less than receptive. She's coming around though."

"You want my advice? Be bold." Afton Stevens saluted Ray with his bourbon glass and went upstairs to check on his wife.

Ray stared out the window, watching Richard push his new wife on the swing in the backyard. Secretly, he envied Richard and his relationship with Hazel Ann. In a world where nothing stayed the same from moment to moment, the two of them seemed secure in their love for each other. Ray knew they were in love by the way Richard's gaze softened whenever his eyes met Hazel Ann's. The two of them looked at each other as if they shared a wonderful secret. Ray had so hoped to see Helen look at him that way. Instead she had withdrawn further and further from him. Maybe it was time to find out why.

Ray wandered out onto the veranda and found Helen sitting alone on the wooden swing. Seeing her there, his heart beat a little faster. The springs creaked slightly as she idly used her foot to keep it in motion. She sat, lost in thought, apparently unaware that he was there. The blackout curtains muffled the voices coming from the parlor. From the rear of the house, the faint sound of a telephone ringing could be heard. The dark night was filled with the scent of flowers and the marsh. Helen looked up as he approached, his shoes making a sandpaper noise on the worn boards. In the light cast by the moon, he could see her eyes shimmering with tears.

"Hello Helen," he whispered.

"Hello Ray," she said almost inaudibly.

Their eyes locked in an embrace that neither wanted to break. Ray joined her on the swing. As they rocked gently back and forth, he took her hand in his. She squeezed his fingers and their light pressure gave him the confidence he needed to once again declare his intentions.

"Helen, you look particularly stunning tonight. Sapphire blue is quite a becoming color on you. I'll have to remember that." Ray smiled when an unexpected thought came to him. "Your brother and Hazel Ann have set a good example for us. Why don't we take a little trip across the state line ourselves? Who knows, you might even consent to change your name to mine. At least I hope you will."

"Captain Birkett, your persistence never ceases to amaze me! That makes three unprecedented proposals! You can't possibly be serious." Helen's warm laughter and sparkling eyes invited him to say more.

"Of course I'm serious. The first time I met you, I knew I wanted to marry you. Haven't I told you that over and over again?"

"The first time I met you, I couldn't wait to see you again," Helen admitted as she turned toward him.

Her lips were close, much too close. Ray could hardly resist kissing her. Only the threat of her father being nearby kept him on his side of the swing. "Oh really," he murmured. "Then why was it that the second time I met you, you acted like you never wanted to see me again."

"To see if you would be bold enough to come around to see me a third time."

"The third time I saw you, I seem to recall asking you to marry me. You never gave me your answer." Ray took her in his arms and said fervently, "Answer me now, Helen. Say yes. We could leave tonight. Drive straight north and be married in the same church as Hazel Ann and Richard. Marry me, Helen. Please."

Instead of answering, she leaned into Ray and kissed him.

"There you are, Helen," said Elva as she broke into their little world. She sounded unnaturally hurried and upset. "Helen, I've been searching for you everywhere. Avis Lou needs you. Right now."

Chapter 48

Helen

*H*elen stared helplessly at her friend. She recognized the slip of paper clutched in the weeping woman's hand. Everyone with a son, husband, father, or relative in the Armed Forces dreaded receiving one. No one wanted Western Union to appear on their doorstep.

Avis Lou crumbled the telegram into a tight ball in her fist. "Why did they have to take my Bill?" she asked, her voice filled with agony.

Avis Lou had lost the one person she loved more than anyone else on earth. Along with him, she lost her hopes and dreams. Helen couldn't imagine a life consisting of open-ended days lived without direction or purpose—lived without the one you loved. Helen stood by mutely, having no answer that could ever bring comfort and happiness to Avis Lou's world again. Instead, it was Ora who tried to console the new widow.

"We'll never know the reason why some things happen, honey," soothed Ora.

"I can't go on living without him!"

"You won't be living without him, Avis Lou. You'll always have Bill in your heart. He'll never leave you. Remember, honey, grief can't bring back those we love or mask the pain of their loss. It's a hard lesson that many young women are learning right now. Oh, honey, you just go ahead and cry it all out." Ora wrapped her arms gently around Avis Lou and rocked her.

Over Avis Lou's sobbing, Helen could hear the war news broadcast. Would it ever end? Would the fear, grief, and hardship ever leave them? Seeing her friend's anguish, Helen wondered if it would be better to be alone—better to have no one to care or worry about. Helen thought about her unspoken love for Captain Ray Birkett. She had to admit that it made her feel alive. And, if she could not love him, then what reason would she have for living?

Helen knew what would have happened if she and Ray hadn't been interrupted earlier. She would have gone to South Carolina. Yes, she would have run right upstairs, grabbed her purse, and met him at the car. Instead, fate intervened again. Now she would never know if he was serious.

Regardless of the recent events, Helen still had work to do. She spent the better part of the next day trying to convince one of the men in the machine shop to talk to her about the valve and the wheel from the acetylene tank. Busy with preparations for the upcoming launch, no one had time to or was interested in speaking with a woman, no matter how friendly and flirtatiously she behaved. To make matters worse, Fred Norris appeared and rudely ordered her out of the area. Discouraged, she stopped at her aunts' home after leaving the shipyard for the day. She sat down at the kitchen table and traced the design on the tablecloth with the wheel.

"What have you got there?" asked Aunt Elva.

Helen held up the valve and the wheel. "They're a couple of parts I brought with me from work. I tried all day to get someone to tell me about them. Aunt Elva, why won't any men talk to me about work? And that supervisor Fred Norris, he all but chased me out of his department. That's the second time he's done that."

"Honey, everyone is so busy. You can't blame them for doing their jobs. Maybe having a woman in the workforce makes a man nervous. They're not used to having a smart woman asking so many questions."

"Thank you for the compliment, Aunt Elva, but I'm not all that smart. For the life of me, I can't figure out what this all means." Helen dropped the wheel and the valve on the table with a clatter.

"What you doing laying those dirty things on my clean kitchen table?" asked Edna Jane when the noise drew her from the pantry. "I declare Miss Helen; you're getting more like my husband every day. John is always bringing pieces of metal home from work to file on."

"Edna Jane, are you saying that John understands things like this?"

"He sure does. He's a right whiz at anything mechanical. He knows how to turn a lathe and work a grinder," Edna Jane said with pride.

"He does? Where is he? Can I talk to him?" asked Helen, already rising from her seat.

"'Course you can. He's out in the shed puttering around with the lawn mower."

Helen knocked on the door to the shed and smiled when John turned around to see her.

"What's you needing Miss Helen?" John asked amicably.

"John, Edna Jane told me that you might be able to answer some questions I have about this valve and this wheel."

"Sure. I don't know if I'll be much help. I'll try though."

"They came off of an acetylene cart."

"Let me see that valve first." Helen handed him the valve and John held it up to the light to examine it more closely. "I can tell that just by looking at them that somebody's gone and fooled with both of them. Do you see these file marks, here and here?" John held the valve close to Helen's face and used the tip of an awl to point out the file marks.

"Yes, I noticed them before but didn't understand what would have caused them. I've tried to get someone at the shipyard to tell me about them, but I haven't had any luck."

"These file marks have stripped most of the threads of this valve. Think of it this way, if this was the cap to your toothpaste tube, you wouldn't be able to securely close it. It would keep wanting to slip off the tube. Of course, this being a valve on a pressurized tank, it wouldn't take long for the pressure in the tank to send it flying. Bang—just like a rocket!"

Bang—just like a rocket—that describes exactly what happened, thought Helen. "John, could this kind of damage occur by itself? I mean, could the pressure in the tank strip the threads?"

"No, Miss Helen. Someone had to file on this valve. It's worthless now, same as this here wheel. Someone snipped off the cotter pin that holds the wheel on the cart. You can see the end of it right here."

Excitement coursed through Helen. She had proof that someone had tampered with the acetylene cart.

"Thank you, John. You've been a big help!"

"Glad to be of assistance, Miss Helen. But now, I've got a question of my own for you. Why is a pretty young girl like you worrying about valves and wheels and such? Why don't you let old Blue and Beau track down that handsome Captain of yours?" John pointed to the two dogs lazing around in the day's last rays of sunshine. "You should be spending your time with him."

Chapter 49

Ray

𝒯he photo of the Liberty ships docked in a row haunted Ray. Admiral Jarabek spoke of sabotage, but after weeks of fruitless searching Ray couldn't help but think that the shipyard faced other, graver dangers. He decided to determine whether or not the ships and the shipyard were at risk from enemy U-boat attack. To find his answers, he met with a group of flyers at the Navy Air Station on Saint Simons Island. The pilots were able to bring him up to speed on tactics for dealing with U-boats.

"If a German submarine was spotted off-shore, how would your planes deal with it?" Ray asked. "What I'm asking is how would you be able to protect the Liberty ships and shipyard until the Navy destroyers could arrive to deal with the U-boat?"

"Airplanes are the most effective weapon we have against German submarines," one young man stated confidently. "From our position in the sky, we have the ability to see great distances, making it easier to spot the enemy. We patrol the coastline in shifts, always on the alert for U-boats. If we were to spot a U-boat or other enemy vessel, we would immediately radio its position back to base. A destroyer would be dispatched to the area straightaway to protect merchant shipping and the coastline."

"It would be a lot easier to find the enemy in that great expanse of ocean if they'd send out a homing signal that we could pick up on our radios," joked one flyer.

"Yeah, that'd be nice," responded another flyer. "I almost got my hopes up once. It happened one day when I was adjusting my radio frequency. A consistent beeping came in loud and clear. I looked around, but the only thing I spotted was a Liberty ship out on her sea trials."

"When was that?" asked Ray nonchalantly.

"About a month ago, the ship that launched in mid-June."

Ray tried hard not to let his quickening interest show. Had anyone considered that the signaling device actually be aboard the Liberty ship? He would be sure to include this information in his report to Admiral Jarabek.

"What if the U.S. Navy vessels are not in the immediate vicinity? Could you attack? Are your planes equipped with torpedoes or bombs?" asked Ray.

"Yes, most of the planes based here on Saint Simons Island are equipped that way. Between May and August 1942, five U-boats were sunk of our coast. In each case, airplanes were involved."

"That gave the krauts something to think about. We haven't seen them around much since then."

"Can you tell me how you would engage the U-boat?" asked Ray. He wanted to understand the mechanics of their interaction with the enemy.

"Planes equipped with torpedoes have two key bombing methods. The first method involves an attack profile like this." The pilot drew a rough picture on a blackboard of a submarine travelling north to south. He added a plane approaching from the west. "Once a sub has been sighted on the surface, if it has seen the plane and begun to dive, the pilot of the plane has two options. The first option is to aim the aircraft and the torpedo at the point where the U-boat will be when the torpedo strikes. This is the most common method and it avoids lengthy contact with enemy anti-aircraft fire."

The speaker drew a line at an angle to the direction of the plane, connecting it with the submarine as it moved south. He drew a new diagram showing the U-boat travelling south and the plane approaching from the west. "The second approach works only if the pilot is able to pre-set the angle of the torpedo's rudder," he continued. "In this case, the pilot aims his plane at the U-boat at all times. After working out the angle and position of the U-boat at the time the torpedo will strike, the pilot sets the torpedo's rudder setting. This means that shortly after landing in the water, the torpedo will proceed on a collision course with the submarine and the pilot can veer off to safety."

"At the speeds you fly, the pilot must need to be quick at calculating the angle of attack," said Ray. "Most airborne torpedoes travel at a speed of thirty knots and have a range of about four thousand yards. The math can be a challenge since it all happens so quickly."

"You're right about that, Captain Birkett."

"I have another question," said Ray. "Do you think a German submarine would venture into Brunswick Sound? Could they get near the shipyard for instance?"

"Due to the shallow nature of the Sound, it's doubtful. They'd have to proceed slowly and follow the channel that's been dredged. If they did enter the sound, planes equipped with bombs would be a better choice to wage an attack."

"The planes I fly are equipped with bombs," stated another pilot. "Bombing a submarine from the air works best if the sub has surfaced or is slightly below the surface. The clear waters off the coast give us an advantage in this case, allowing us to see U-boats lurking just under water. It is important to launch the bombs well behind or in front of the U-boat, depending on your direction of travel. The forward momentum of the plane and the bombs will carry them into the contact zone."

"You, pilots, have a lot to remember," commented Ray.

"Yes, we do. Fortunately with practice, it becomes second nature. A pilot learns to feel the plane in his hands and knows what it is capable of doing."

"You must have nerves of steel," said Ray admiringly.

"Steel won't do you much good. Up in the air, down on the ground, at sea, you need nerves of rubber so that they stretch when you need them.

Ray sat in his make-shift office and studied the information he had spent weeks compiling. Admiral Jarabek and General Dirner informed him that the recently launched Liberty ship had been halfway through her sea trials when the Navy Air Station radar operators picked up a beeping signal from her. The ship had immediately been brought back to port. By the time it had docked, the signal had ceased.

Was he looking for saboteurs or spies? Were the incidents and accidents important or should he focus his attention on finding the source of the radio beacon?

Frustrated, Ray's attention shifted from paper to paper, intimately familiar with the words on their pages. Written primarily by William Browning and not particularly detailed, essentially, the reports told him nothing. Incidents and accidents. Some trivial, some life-threatening, some life-taking. All together, they delayed the launches of Liberty ships a matter of a few days at most. It was hardly worth the saboteurs' efforts, if indeed there were saboteurs. Ray had no evidence, no clue of anything happening. Yet, his gut instinct told him something was wrong. In disgust, he swept the whole bunch into one giant stack on his desk.

"Captain Birkett, is this a bad time?" Helen asked from the doorway. She managed to look quite fetching in her regulation brown coveralls. Today, she had braided her hair and arranged it like a crown on the top of her head. It suited her.

"Miss Stevens! Of course not—no—definitely not." Ray and Helen maintained the formality of last names while at work.

"Captain Birkett, I wondered if I could bounce an idea off of you. Actually, I wondered if you would take me seriously." Helen spoke earnestly, as if seeking reassurance from him.

"I promise I will do my best. What is troubling you, Miss Stevens?"

"It's these incidents and accidents," she began.

"Yes, as you can see, that's what I've been studying for quite a while now." Ray gestured to the stack on his desk. "By the way, your reports are very well written."

"Thank you, Captain Birkett." Helen blushed at the compliment. She didn't speak for a moment, obviously gathering her thoughts—or her courage.

"What I wanted to ask you is this," she finally said. "What if the motivation for a saboteur wasn't the accident itself but the result of the accident?"

Ray sucked in his breath. He had no idea Helen still considered the possibility of sabotage. After their previous discussion, he thought she had changed her mind. Ray quickly searched for the right thing to say. To give himself time and to protect them from eavesdroppers, he got up and closed his office door.

"Sabotage is a very serious charge, Miss Stevens. What gives you the idea that sabotage has been taking place in the shipyard?" Ray asked sternly.

Helen squared her shoulders defiantly before answering. "I have no real evidence that sabotage is occurring at the shipyard. As I explained before, I have only a few things that don't add up to merely an accident."

Inwardly, Ray breathed a sigh of relief. At least she hadn't said something about women's intuition or a gut feeling. Then he chastised himself. A few moments ago, he had been contemplating his own gut feelings.

"Go on," he encouraged.

"In several of the accidents I have found anomalies, things that don't add up. For instance, the valve that exploded from the acetylene tank had its threads filed down. And the cotter pin that holds the wheel on the tank cart was cut."

"Continue."

"The rigger who fell to his death was wearing a faulty harness, one that should have been disposed of and destroyed. Why did Ben use it? It had been clearly marked for disposal. He would have seen the tags. Did someone remove the tags? Did someone purposely give it to him?" Helen chewed on her lower lip. "And there is one other accident that bothers me—the key in the keyway. I believe the operator when he says he removed it. How did it get put back in? Who would do that?"

"Miss Stevens, I've read and reread all those accident reports. I don't see how the accidents resulted in anything that a saboteur could consider important. Yes, I know the launches have been slightly delayed and that people have been hurt and even killed. We can't overlook that, but where is the real gain from the saboteur's point of view? And, in the case of Ben, why switch from causing minor injuries to murder?"

"I understand what you're asking, Captain Birkett. Taken individually, I don't have an explanation, but I have an idea. I want to share it with you before taking it to Burt, my boss. I know you'll be sure to point out where it doesn't hold water."

Helen looked very discouraged, causing Ray to want to help her. He even found himself hoping a saboteur did exist.

"Miss Stevens, a minute ago you asked 'What if the motivation for a saboteur wasn't the accident itself but the result of the accident?' Can you clarify what you mean by that?" Ray asked gently.

"In one of my safety courses at the university—" Here she faltered as if she expected him to downplay the importance of her education.

"Go on," Ray encouraged. "What did you learn there?"

Helen studied his face carefully before continuing. "In one course, we discussed the unseen results of industrial accidents. These are results that people ignore or don't think about when the accident occurs. With this in mind, this morning, I took the time to graph four outcomes of poor safety: absenteeism, employee turnover, productivity, and cost overruns."

Helen slid a series of graphs across the desk top. She didn't say anything until Ray had studied them. What he saw there answered all his questions. His face lit up in surprise.

"So you see it too, don't you, Captain Birkett? Absenteeism, employee turnover, and cost overruns have increased dramatically since the first accidents began occurring. Productivity has decreased significantly too. Imagine what lower productivity will do to the creation of Liberty ships and the country's war effort. If our shipyard continues to have accidents and work slow-downs, we'll never meet our goals of producing a ship in under sixty days. If things get bad enough, the government may even choose to close the shipyard despite the huge investment required to create it in the first place. I think the saboteur is relying on the principle that no one wants to work in an unsafe environment. People will leave or at the very least work slower and more cautiously. Someone may be delaying launches in ways that aren't visible. What they are doing will have far broader reaching effects than most people realize. If there is a saboteur at work, we'll never be able to produce a ship in less than sixty days."

Chapter 50

Helen

$\mathcal{H}$elen felt ill-prepared to deal with a meeting with Burt, William, and Ray concerning the accidents. Even though she and Ray had spent time discussing her findings, she wasn't sure how receptive William and Burt would be to her ideas. As Ray said, sabotage is a harsh accusation. Helen gathered her materials and walked into the cramped conference room. In the open window, a small black fan oscillated back and forth but did little to dispel the afternoon heat. A trickle of sweat ran down her back uncomfortably. Ray and Burt had already taken their seats. William lounged in the doorway, smoking. As soon as she joined them, Burt began speaking. Much to her dismay, her boss approached the subject abruptly, without his usual concern for the individuals involved.

"Helen, I'm telling you that the time you've spent investigating these accidents isn't time well-spent. We've got a lot of other things to do in this department. In a few days, another ship launch will take place and we can't have any more delays," said Burt.

"But, Burt, accident investigation is important to prevent future accidents. You said so yourself," countered Helen.

"Of course it's important, but not to the level you're taking it. William tells me you've been spending all your spare time reviewing the accident files, re-interviewing witnesses, and checking safety precautions. That's noble, but like I've said before, you have other responsibilities. Several supervisors are complaining that you're interrupting employees at their work. Fred Norris was in here again today saying just that."

"I understand what you're saying, but take a look at what I've learned." Helen pushed her files across the table toward her boss. William casually picked up one of the folders and began to peruse it.

Burt rubbed the perspiration from the nape of his neck with his handkerchief, his expression both tolerant and annoyed. He took his time lighting a fresh cigarette. "I've read your reports. Mostly minor and unfortunate accidents."

"Burt. Please study the new information. Look at what I've learned about the acetylene torch cart and the rigger's harness." Helen's eyes pleaded with her boss. She desperately wanted her investigation to be taken seriously.

"Burt, Miss Stevens does have some new information that has merit," said Ray. He was curious to hear what Burt thought of her productivity theories.

Giving in, Burt said, "Okay, let's see what you've got. But make it quick. I've got another meeting to attend." Even as he opened one of the files, Burt looked skeptical.

William moved into the room and set his lit cigarette in the ashtray. He picked up another file. His face showed his annoyance at being asked to listen to Helen talk about past accidents.

Helen plunged ahead. "Let's start with the first accident. It occurred in early June and involved a worker who failed to wear protective clothing. He received minor burns. A few days later, two men used a pallet mounted on the forks of a forklift instead of a ladder. The man on the pallet fell off and sprained his ankle."

"Yes, Helen, is all this really relevant? I'm well aware of those minor accidents," said Burt wearily.

"That's actually the point, Burt. These accidents and a half a dozen others that occurred prior to mid-June are minor. After mid-June, that all changes." Helen waited for what she had said to sink in. She brought out the wheel and valve and laid them on the table.

"Go on," said Burt, more interested now.

Helen could tell by William's body language, that he, too, was significantly more interested in her findings.

"The next accident involved the lathe operator who was struck by the key that flew out of the keyway. He's still quite adamant that he had removed the key and set it on his work bench before taking a break. Then there is Milly's accident. The wheel came off her acetylene tank causing it to topple over on her. When it struck the ground, the valve shot loose and hit her ankle. I showed the valve and the wheel to someone who knows about these things and he said that the valve stem had been filed to strip the threads. Here and here." Helen pointed to the threads with her pencil. "He said the pressure in the tank could have caused the valve to come loose even without the help of the tank striking the floor."

"You mean someone tampered with the valve?"

"And with the wheel, too. There's more Burt. I think the labels on the water and acid containers in Moria's work station were switched."

"How could you possibly know the labels had been switched?" asked William.

"Two reasons. First, I noticed that the labels on both containers were trimmed in brown, but the water label should have been blue and the acid one orange. Both liquids are clear so it would be impossible to tell them apart just by looking. Moria would have relied on the label."

"And second?"

"I had the remnants of each container tested. The lab technician found acid in the container marked water and water in the one marked acid."

"You did these things without telling either of us?" asked William hotly.

"And you think the switch was made on purpose?" asked Burt, his face concerned.

"I don't know what to think." Helen shook her head sadly. "Then there is the accident that caused the most significant delay of a launch of the Liberty ship. The rigger who fell to his death—I think he was given a faulty harness. I don't know who would do such a thing! And don't forget the gantry crane that dropped its load. Who knows how that would have ended if Captain Birkett hadn't shouted a warning."

"Helen, you're making some pretty serious accusations against someone. Do you have enough proof to make them stick?" asked Burt.

"No, not really. I only have the valve, wheel, and containers," Helen admitted.

"Get to the point, Helen," said Burt, clearly uninterested.

"Burt, what if it's not about the accidents, but about the effects of the accidents?" Helen asked, finally getting to the point of the meeting.

"What do you mean?" responded Burt. He lit a fresh cigarette and looked at her through the smoke.

"Remember how we discussed the hidden costs of accidents? All I'm asking is that you take a look at the graphs for absenteeism, productivity, and employee turnover I've made. They show what I've discovered. Please study them. Maybe it will make more sense to you. Even I can see that these events could have simply been accidents. But, I can't help thinking of the posters we have hanging all around the shipyard. *If you see something, say something.* I guess I feel like I'm seeing something so I'm saying something. I wanted to bring this to your attention so that you can be aware of my findings."

"Burt, Miss Steven's findings on productivity are very interesting," said Ray.

"Burt, I know Helen's on this kick to prove that her fancy university courses taught her something useful, but this is ridiculous," interrupted William. "So what if absenteeism and turnover are up. Lots of these guys don't want to work hard so they don't show up after a few days. If we were able to hire better people, the whole problem with accidents and absenteeism would go away. I guarantee it."

"Helen, I tend to agree with William," admitted Burt. "This is all very interesting, but you haven't shown that any of these accidents could be more than accidents. Stop wasting time. In the future, I want you to follow William's lead. Investigate accidents like he does. That's sufficient. Nothing should delay the upcoming launch."

"Like he does? Sufficient? But Burt—" Helen sputtered in protest. She hadn't even had a chance to tell them what she had learned about the failed chain link from the crane accident.

"Helen, I've said my piece, now get back to work."

Chapter 51

Ray

*A*fter Burt and William left the room, Ray opened a folder Burt left abandoned in the middle of the table. While Helen straightened up the room, he read over the contents. Helen's strong, purposeful script reflected her organized personality. The reports were clear and concise, her conclusions based on fact, not supposition.

At the end of the report, several photographs clearly showed a proper rigger's harness. Ray compared those with photos of Ben McNeely's blood-stained harness. Then he laid out the photos showing a correct valve stem. Ray compared the valve in the photo with the one Helen had brought with her. He frowned in concentration. Helen was right. When seen side-by-side, the photographs made the sabotage obvious.

"Who took these photographs? They're good."

"I did."

Helen's reply surprised Ray. Before he paused to temper his response, he said, "You did?" Even he could hear the incredulous accent to his voice.

Helen turned to face him, hands on hips. "What? Don't you think I'm capable of taking a few photographs and putting together a training program? Or do you think I should be allowed to perform only secretarial duties like cleaning up this conference room?" Helen glared at him.

Ray, who found much to admire in Helen, opened and shut his mouth helplessly while he searched for the right words to say. "Helen, I'm sorry. I didn't mean that the way it sounded. It's just that I hadn't expected to be shown so clearly what is wrong. It took me by surprise, that's all. You've done great work. Really."

"Thank you Captain Birkett. Actually, it means a lot to me to hear you say that." Helen smiled at him.

Her smile went straight to his heart. Helen seemed to have a soul filled with a bottomless source of optimism. Did she meet all disasters without complaining?

"If it helps at all, Helen, I believe you. I think you're right about the unseen results of accidents. The shipyard's productivity is decreasing every day, delaying the launches of all future ships. Something has to be done to stop the accidents. Unfortunately, without concrete evidence, it's hard to prove sabotage."

"Thank you again, but I know you're just trying to cheer me up after the chewing out Burt gave me. He didn't even look at my graphs or my conclusions. What a waste of time." She paused in her cleanup activities, looked at the floor, and chewed on her lower lip.

Ray stood, gathered up the contents of the file and moved to the doorway of the small conference room. Admiral Jarabek would want to see this information.

Incorrectly taking his action as dismissal of her theories, Helen's smile became more cynical. "Now, I had better get busy straightening up this room. It's part of my job description you know."

"Can I help you?" asked Ray, reluctant to leave her presence.

"That's very kind of you, Captain Birkett. Thank you, but no. I have a system." She laughed ruefully. "Actually, some people say I have a system for everything. They're probably right. Look at me now. First, I cleared away the any remaining folders and papers and set them neatly on the small table at the rear of the room." She gestured to the tidy stack she'd made. "Then I gather up the pencils, pens, paperclips, and empty coffee mugs and place them on this tray to transport them later. Next, I throw the trash into the waste can next to the door. On my last pass through the room, I pick up any ashtrays full of leftover cigarette butts. And on my way out the door, I dump the debris in this can full of sand." She dumped the smoldering cigarette butts into the ash can and set the ashtrays on a nearby ledge. Helen brushed her hands together, her job complete.

Ray did a double-take at the ash can by the door. Dropping the files, he roughly grabbed Helen by the arm and yanked her bodily through the doorway.

"Look out!" he shouted.

A huge whoosh of air accompanied by a blinding white fire ball exploded where Helen had stood seconds before. Ray felt his skin tingling from the heat from the fire. He rushed Helen down the hall and outside while shouting a warning to the others.

"Fire! Fire! Get out of the building!"

It took hours for firefighters to get the fire under control. The plywood walls and offices full of papers provided excellent fuel for the hungry flames. Standing next to the smoldering remains of the building that once housed the Industrial Efficiency department, Ray and Helen surveyed the grim scene.

"Are you all right?" Ray asked.

"I'm fine thanks to you, Captain Birkett." She hugged herself tightly.

"I think it's time we dropped the formalities, Helen. After all, I did just save your life."

"Captain Birkett—Ray—what caused the fire ball?" Helen's voice shook slightly and she shivered despite the heat from the smoldering fire.

"Magnesium flares. Someone put them in the ash can."

"Magnesium flares?"

"Marine flares. They're made using magnesium because the highly reactive metal makes them easy to ignite and difficult to extinguish. Magnesium does not require an oxygen-rich environment to burn. It even burns well in water, making it perfect for marine flares. They burn with a characteristically brilliant white light which explains the flash you saw. Once started, only sand or dirt works effectively to extinguish the flare."

"Who?" Helen spoke around the lump of fear in her throat. "Who would put magnesium flares in an ash can?"

"I don't know, Helen."

"How did you know they were there?" she asked suspiciously.

"I was standing there watching you. Remember? I find myself watching you a lot recently." Ray touched her cheek with the palm of his hand.

"Watching me? Whatever for? I've never seen you watching me."

"Just because you haven't caught me doesn't mean I haven't been looking," Ray countered. He smiled at her and gripped her hand tightly. "Helen, I care about you. I think you know that by now. I'm worried about your safety."

"Ray, I don't understand why you are worried about me." Helen gave his hand a little squeeze and released it.

"I'm not asking you to understand why. I'm asking you to trust me." Ray grasped Helen firmly by the shoulders. "You're in danger. Someone wants to prevent you from looking further into these accidents. I'm serious, Helen. You have to trust me on this."

"Ray, I don't know where you got that idea. Why do you think someone wants to hurt me? There must be some logical explanation about the marine flares."

"There isn't time for me to explain my suspicions. Please, Helen, just trust me."

"But—" Helen protested, still not believing what had just happened.

"Helen, go home. Stay near your parents, your father especially. If they're not around, stay with your aunts. Whatever you do, don't go anywhere alone. Promise me you won't go anywhere alone." Ray gave her shoulders a little shake.

"But Ray—"

Ray sensed Helen would not give in easily. He doubted he would ever succeed in convincing Helen she was in danger unless he shared his suspicions with her. Knowing her, she'd probably see it as a challenge. "Helen, think about it. Those magnesium flares didn't appear by magic in that ash can. No one in their right mind would carry marine flares around and then casually toss them away. Helen, they weren't casually tossed away; they were snapped in half and buried up-right deep enough in the sand to hold them in place. All it took was hot ashes and a burning cigarette butt or two and whoosh—instant fire. Someone who knows your routine for cleaning the meeting room put them there."

"But why? Who would want to do such a thing? All my hard work! My files were on the table. I know I can recreate some of it from memory, but the photos, the parts, and the supporting documentation, it's all gone!" Helen gestured helplessly at the smoking ruins in front of them. "Look at all the data that was destroyed when the office burned. We'll never be able to recreate that information. Why would anyone do this? Why would anyone want to start a fire?"

"It was more than a fire, Helen. When a marine flare ignites, the flames shoot upward. If I hadn't pulled you out of the way, you would have been horribly burned, perhaps even killed. Just look at how long it took the fire fighters to put out the fire. I think someone meant to destroy the office—and you along with it."

"Oh, Ray. I don't understand why anyone would want to hurt me." Helen stepped into Ray's embrace and leaned against him. He wrapped his arms protectively around her.

"Helen, dearest, are you aware of what you do to me? Me, a confirmed bachelor and all I can think about is you. I haven't thought of anyone else but you for over a year now. Helen, I'd cross oceans and continents to win your heart," Ray said with a lightness meant to mask the depths of his feelings for her.

"I don't want you to cross any oceans, Ray. I want you to stay right here," she said into his neck.

"Helen, I—" Ray didn't finish his sentence, giving into his desire to kiss her instead.

Chapter 52

Helen

*A*fter Ray left Helen safely at home, she prowled the rooms of the house restlessly. Over and over in her mind, she pondered the recent events. Specifically, she thought about her feelings toward Captain Ray Birkett. Intuitively she knew she could trust him. She took his concerns for her safety seriously.

Helen felt all mixed up, full of feelings she couldn't identify. When she heard her mother come in through the front door, Helen knew she couldn't stomach listening to her mother discuss the fire at the shipyard. Unable to sit at home with her thoughts any longer, Helen ran out the back door and across Hinshaw Square to her aunts' house. She burst in through the kitchen door and flung herself down at the table where her Aunt Ida was stringing beans. The radio droned on in the background.

"The Germans have unleashed their considerable strength…"

Irritated, Helen reached over and switched off the war news.

"Well honey, this is a surprise. You look as if you're fit to burst."

"Oh, Aunt Ida, I'm beside myself! I shouldn't be like this!"

"Like what, honey?" Ida looked up from her beans to study Helen's flushed face.

"Oh, I don't know if I can explain it." Helen fidgeted in her seat. "Captain Birkett makes me so mad!"

"Why would you be mad at the man who saved your life?"

"I don't know. He just makes me mad. You live with the man. You should know!"

"Know what?"

"Oh—it's everything!" Helen exclaimed, frustrated by her Aunt Ida's obtuseness. "He just can't seem to stay out of my work. I see him everywhere!"

"I wouldn't think that's such a bad thing. The man sure is easy on the eye, especially going south."

"Aunt Ida!" said Helen, shocked.

"Well, why shouldn't I notice Captain Birkett? After all, he's a handsome man. A nice one too."

"He is not!"

"He's not what? Not handsome? Or not nice? Helen, honey, could it be that you're just a little bit in love with this man?" Aunt Ida cocked her head waiting for an answer.

Helen's face colored when her aunt stared at her, unblinking. She bowed her head and picked at the edge of the placemat on the table. "Maybe just a little," she said almost to herself.

"More than a little unless I miss my guess. Why don't you start by telling me what got you into such a state to begin with?"

"Oh Aunt Ida! It's all so silly! Today I caught myself gazing out my office window watching for Ray—Captain Birkett—I mean. I was filled with unimaginable longing, just like one of those heroines in a novel," wailed Helen. "Just thinking about him makes my heart beat faster. I find myself growing giddy whenever he is in the same room. And he's kissed me!"

"Well it's about time!" stated Aunt Ida matter-of-factly. "Sounds like true love to me,"

'No! It just can't be! I shouldn't be like this—I should be sensible and practical! I'm not an impassioned eighteen year old girl anymore. I've got a job—a career—I'm nearly twenty now. I'm too old to be indulging in fantasies."

Ida smiled at Helen's comment about her age. A year mattered so much to the very young.

"Helen, honey, you don't have to choose between being passionate and practical. Honey, you really don't." Aunt Ida pursed her lips and thought for a moment before continuing. "You know I don't often give advice."

Helen wanted to respond that her Aunt Ida rarely said anything at all. Aunt Ida was the most quiet, unassuming person Helen had ever known.

"I never thought I'd ever meet anyone like him," Helen admitted softly.

"Helen, I've watched you with Ray. The two of you have something special, something very, very special." Ida held up her hand to forestall Helen's protest. "I know what your Momma, bless her heart, thinks. But Helen—please don't waste your love like I did!" she finished with emphasis.

"Waste my love like you did? What are you talking about, Aunt Ida?"

Aunt Ida's eyes grew moist and introspective. She sat lost in her own reverie for a while and a small sad smile played on her lips. With that smile, the years fell away from her face and Helen could see the lovely young woman she once was. Aunt Ida's lips trembled and a tear rolled slowly down her cheek.

"I could have married Charles," she whispered.

Helen strained to hear her.

"Yes, I should have married Charles," Aunt Ida repeated more loudly.

Helen's eyes opened wide with surprise. Aunt Ida, spinsterish, shy Aunt Ida had a beau?

"I keep thinking that if I'd married Charles, things would have turned out differently. I thought if I had married him he would have survived the war. Somehow our love would have been strong enough to keep him safe," admitted Aunt Ida. Looking at her niece for the first time, Aunt Ida gave a little laugh. "What? Are you surprised that your aunt could have had a grand passion in her life?"

"But," began Helen.

"Well, whether you believe it or not, I did. And it was every bit as wonderful as what you and Ray have today! Oh how I loved Charles!"

Helen stared at her aunt, flabbergasted. Could it be that the inner strength and comfort she'd always sensed in her Aunt Ida had come from such a painful source?

"I still miss him, you know. Some nights, when it's real quiet, I can hear his voice singing our favorite song," Aunt Ida added softly.

"You do understand. You really do. You understand what I mean when I say I miss Ray when he leaves the room, if only for a moment. Oh, Aunt Ida, I love him. It's such a surprise."

"What is love, my dear, if not a surprise?"

"Did you feel like this, all sparkling all over?"

"Yes," laughed Aunt Ida. "I couldn't wait to tell everyone. Helen, dearest, you don't have to choose between your passion and your profession. It will all work out. Put on your pretty blue dress, brush your hair, and go tell Ray you love him. Don't waste another precious moment. Be happy while you can."

Returning home, Helen took her time dressing up and fixing her hair. She applied a bit of rouge to her cheeks and some of her precious lipstick to her lips. Her hands shook so much; she thought she'd never get it straight. Why was she so nervous? Why did she feel such a need to impress Ray—now—after all this time? It was early evening when she walked back across the square. She intended to surprise him on the porch where he usually sat after supper. Instead, he surprised her. As she passed the Lover's Oak, a voice called down to her.

"Well, look at you. Just look at you standing there as lovely as a picture." And he did. Swinging out of the tree to land in front of her, Captain Ray Birkett stared at her like he had that very first night in the auditorium, as if all his happiness resided in her.

Helen caught her breath. She knew when she looked deep into his eyes that he would take care of her. Not because she was a woman, but because he loved her. Ray truly loved her. It was a strange, not unpleasant feeling, to know that you would be cared for yet still retain yourself. Caught up in the thrill this knowledge imparted, a smile spread slowly across her face.

Ray took a step toward her. She reached out her hand to clasp his.

"You're smiling," Ray said softly as he drew her to him. "And you have such a lovely smile."

"I'm smiling because I know you love me."

"And, do you love me?"

"Yes, Ray, I think I do love you."

"When do you think you'll decide?" he murmured against her lips.

He kissed her then. To Helen, it was the kind of kiss that people wrote about in novels—the kind of kiss she would never forget.

Much later, she answered, "I don't think I love you anymore."

Ray stood up straighter, taken aback.

"Now I know I do. I really do love you, Ray." When she said the words out loud, Helen felt as if a huge hollow space deep inside her had been filled.

Ray picked her up and swung her around until she couldn't stop giggling. When he set her down gently, he kissed her again.

"I loved you from the first moment I saw you," Ray admitted as they started to walk back toward her home. "I've just been waiting for you to come around to what I already knew. We are meant to be."

"But, why Ray? Why would a man like you be interested in me? I wasn't anybody then, just a teenager," she protested. "I didn't deserve you so I set about becoming someone." As she said the words, Helen realized how true they were.

Chapter 53

Ray

*R*ay and Helen nestled close together on the sofa in the front room of her aunts' house. They'd tried for days to find some quiet time to be alone together. Unfortunately, it was not to be. Aunt Ora entered noisily from the hallway, tactfully giving them time to pull apart and straighten their clothing.

"Here you are, dears. I managed to scrape together enough sugar and honey to sweeten just a little bit of lemonade for you. I also brought in my scrapbook in case you needed something to do." Aunt Ora smiled sweetly.

"It's nice of you to bring us all some lemonade, Ora. A cool drink is perfect on this warm evening," said Aunt Elva coming in behind her sister. "I think I'll sit a spell here in the parlor where it is cooler."

"But, Elva," protested Ora before sitting down herself.

Ray groaned inwardly. Now that Helen had admitted she cared for him, he was finding it nearly impossible to see her without one member of her family or another arriving on the scene. They were all skilled at dispelling any romantic mood. Given her mother's attitude toward him, meeting at her parents' house was out of the question. Even with Ida's help, it was becoming increasingly difficult to spend any time alone with Helen here. He had no doubt they would eventually be able to meet only at the Lover's Oak. Beside him, he felt Helen suppress a laugh.

"Here, Ray, why don't we take a look at Aunt Ora's nice scrapbook?" Helen barely stifled a giggle.

Without much interest, Ray flipped through the pages until he found a photograph of the day Helen served as maid of honor at the ship launching.

Helen pointed at the photo. "Perfect timing, don't you think?"

The photographer had caught the exact moment when the champagne bottle exploded against the hull showering everyone nearby with foam. Though Helen was smiling, she had her eyes squeezed tightly shut to keep out the frothy spray.

"I had so much fun that day, even if I did get drenched in champagne!" exclaimed Helen. "Look at me, I'm a mess! Or maybe you shouldn't look. You may not like what you see!"

"You've no cause to worry," Ray whispered softly in her ear.

"Do you remember how angry Winona was to be passed over for maid of honor?" asked Helen, trying to cover her intense pleasure over Ray's implied compliment. "Winona goes on and on about it whenever she gets the chance."

"Personally, I thought Winona was going to ask you to step aside, Helen," added Elva.

"She was rather upset, wasn't she?" asked Helen.

"Upset? She was madder than a wet hen," exclaimed Ora.

"Fit to be tied," agreed Elva.

"That poor girl never seems to get her way as often as she'd like, bless her heart," said Ida as she entered the room.

Helen shifted beside Ray as if recognizing that they wouldn't be left alone tonight. Inwardly, he sighed. Time alone with Helen was precious. He smiled when Helen picked up a piece of paper and began to idly make notations on it.

"I wonder who Winona is mad at. Maybe I'll make a list," said Helen.

Ray understood that when Helen was agitated she needed to keep her mind and her hands busy. She flipped the pages back and forth as she compared parties with ship launchings. On her sheet of paper, Helen jotted down party dates in one column and launch dates in the next.

"Aunt Ora, you've done such a lovely job pasting articles about each ship launch. It's fun to see them all organized like this. Aunt Elva, I hadn't realized your parties occurred so close to ship launches," Helen said when she had finished.

"Yes, dear. Elva's always been one for liking things organized, in this case, ship-shape." Aunt Ora laughed at her own joke.

"Your timing is uncanny. Did you purposely plan your parties to coincide with ship launchings?" Helen asked her aunts.

"No dear. We just plan our parties two weeks apart, except of course for the Fourth of July. Their timing is coincidental. Remember, no one but the managing port director knows when a ship is going to be launched," said Ida.

"That's not quite right, Ida," corrected Elva, always a stickler for details. "Nearly everyone knows in general when a launch is going to take place. It's not hard to tell when a ship is nearing completion. We just don't know the exact date."

"And as you know, an accident can delay a launch. It was so unfortunate to have to delay launch near the Fourth of July. We had such a lovely surprise planned. Mickey had constructed a float and we were going to play act a Liberty ship christening. Of course, we wouldn't dream of doing so after what happened. It wouldn't have been fittin'," said Ora sadly.

"It's getting late dear," said Aunt Elva. "Don't you think Captain Birkett should walk you home now? He can escort me home too."

Ray swore it was like living with three chaperones. Did other suitors have this trouble? Sighing, Ray picked up Helen's piece of paper and folded it carefully before putting it in his pocket.

"What are you doing, Ray? That scrap of paper is just that, a scrap," said Helen.

"I'd rather think of it as a souvenir," he said with a smile.

Chapter 54

Helen

"*H*ello Hannah." Helen greeted her former classmate outside the drugstore. "It's nice to see you again. It's been such a long while."

"Hello Helen. It's wonderful to see you too. Please call me Anna now," responded the young woman. "I've changed my name from Hannah Thaler to Anna Taylor."

"Anna Taylor? Whatever for?" asked Helen, truly perplexed.

"I don't want to draw attention to my German heritage. My father's bakery is suffering from lack of business. No one wants to buy from a German, even one who has been in the States a long time. It is not so easy for those of us with German parents. My grandparents still live in Munich. At least we think they do. We have had no mail since Hitler's declaration of war on December 10, 1941. Such a long time with no news."

"But surely just because you are of German descent doesn't mean that people treat you differently." Even as she spoke the words, Helen knew that people did treat Germans differently. She'd seen it in the shops and on the street. Helen knew it didn't make a difference to anyone that fully one-third of the Americans serving overseas were of German heritage.

"Oh, Helen, remember how people used to wait in line at my father's bakery? Now, the store stands empty. As for the name change, my family thought it would be best, especially after my younger brother was bullied by the children at school. Even his teacher singled him out in class and insisted that he explain Hitler's plans. As if a boy of ten could possibly understand the workings of such an evil man."

"Oh, Hannah—I mean, Anna, I am so sorry for you and your family."

Just then, Ray approached. Happiness surged through Helen, erasing, as only love can, the sadness attached to Hannah Thaler's plight.

"Hello Ray." Despite being in public, Helen greeted Ray with a welcoming kiss. "Ray, I'd like you to meet my friend from high school, H—Anna Taylor. Anna Taylor, Captain Ray Birkett."

"Hello Miss Taylor. It's nice to meet you." Ray extended his hand toward the pretty woman with the sad eyes.

"Hello Captain Birkett."

"I know several Taylors back in England. Do you have any relations in Great Britain?"

Hannah flushed, visibly uncomfortable. She flashed an overly-bright, brittle smile. "It's lovely to see you again, Helen. Captain Birkett, it is nice to meet you. I really must go." Hannah spun on her heel and fled down the street.

"That didn't go well," said Ray, bewildered by Hannah's behavior. "What did I say that upset her so?"

"Walk me home and I'll tell you on the way."

Helen took Ray's arm in hers. As they walked down Newcastle Street toward their homes, Helen told Ray about people's response to Hannah Thaler's parentage and her name change.

"Right now, I have only one good thing to say about the Germans. I'd never have landed on the shores of the Golden Isles without them." Ray smiled at Helen and squeezed her hand. "But seriously, it's not an unreasonable thing to do—to change your name. I imagine many German families are Americanizing their name. They wouldn't be the first. King George V of England belonged to the House of Saxe-Coburg-Gotha. That all changed during the First World War. In 1917, anti-German sentiment caused George V to decree that the surname of his family would be Windsor, after the castle of the same name."

"How interesting. I didn't know that. I wonder whether anyone else in town changed their name," mused Helen. "Hannah, Anna, Thaler, Taylor."

"It reminds me of those riddle and word games we play at your aunts' parties."

"Oh, please, every time Winona wants to play a word game I want to strangle myself," Helen admitted with a laugh. Happily ensconced in their love for one another, she felt full of optimism.

"You know, for many names, it really wouldn't be too hard to make adjustments. Heinrich could become Henry or Hank, Wilhelm becomes William, Friedrich changes to Fred," Ray laughed, getting on a roll. "Gregor becomes Greg, Berthold becomes Burt, Joachim becomes Jack, Johann becomes John, and Stefan becomes Stephen." He paused for a breath.

"Don't stop there!" Giggling, Helen encouraged him. "What about women's names?"

"Women's names, let me think about that." Ray made a great show of wrinkling his forehead in thought causing Helen to giggle again. "Well, there's Brigitta who could become Brigit, Gertraud becomes Gertrude, and Irmgard becomes Erma. Now it's your turn." Ray bowed to Helen. "I'll start for you. Wendelin becomes—"

"Wendy," continued Helen. "What other names can you think of?"

"Let's see if you can guess this one. Wilhelmina becomes what?"

"That's a tough one. I don't know many names that begin with the letter 'W'. Wanda, Wallis, Winona. The only one I can think of for Wilhelmina is Wilma."

"Not bad. How about last names?"

"Do they have to be an anglicized version of the name? What about a translation? For example: Black for Schwartz. Or someone could pick Smith or Jones. Why stop there? For all we know, Bunz could even become Bunce," added Helen laughing. "Winola Bunz becomes Winona Bunce."

The instant she said that, they both stopped laughing and looked at each other a bit breathlessly. Suddenly, it wasn't a word game anymore.

"What made you say Winona? And Bunce?" Ray asked sharply. "Why mention someone you know?"

"I don't know, really. Just a flash of a memory of something my aunt said about her having no people. And then you mentioned the parties at my aunts' house. Winona loves to play riddle and word games. You even sounded like her when you said 'let's see if you can guess this one'. It just all came together in my mind. Why? What do you think—" asked Helen, faltering as her mind raced through unexpected possibilities. "Ray, what's wrong? Your face looks odd."

Chapter 55

Ray

"*We*'ve been trying to figure out whether or not sabotage has been taking place in the shipyard, right?" Ray asked, excited at the prospect of making progress in his quest for a saboteur.

"Yes, but Ray, I thought we had already decided it has been taking place. Even you can't deny that someone had tampered with both the valve and the wheel on the welder and the labels. You also were the one to point out that someone started the fire on purpose."

"Yes, I did, darling. And you are the one who pointed out that something bigger might be happening than just random accidents. Let me tell you what I've been thinking before you make any comments. See if it makes sense in that logical, ordered mind of yours."

Helen looked up at him expectantly.

"What if someone of German descent works at the shipyard and is trying to slow ship production?"

"Did this idea pop into your head because I said 'Bunz could become Bunce'? That won't work, at least not for Winona. She doesn't have the strength or the knowledge to tamper with equipment or set fires. You'll never convince me she is involved."

"Not necessarily Winona, I was thinking more about men who would have access to marine flares and the conference room. Berthold becomes Burt, Friedrich becomes Fred, Joachim becomes Jack, and Johann becomes John."

"Burt? Burt?" Helen focused on the name of her boss. Her eyes narrowed. "That's even more bizarre than accusing Winona! Burt's my boss and a truly fine man. He's my friend! He would never destroy our records. He's heartbroken over the destruction of our offices."

Seeking to divert her anger, Ray protested, "Hey, you're the one who said that Burt discouraged you from investigating accidents. I heard him myself in the meeting."

"Instead of accusing Burt, you should open your mind to other possibilities. How about Hank Stine, the gantry operator? He could really be Heinrich Stein. Or what about that supervisor, Fred Norris? I don't know what his surname would be in German, but he's an unfriendly man who bullies others. He certainly doesn't want me investigating accidents!" Helen stopped speaking and stared at a poster affixed to a wall of a building. She tugged on the sleeve of Ray's uniform and pointed. Below the banner that read: 'Careless talk brings tragedy in wartime,' were five vignettes. First, a soldier tells his sweetheart about troop movements, and then his sweetheart tells her father who repeats the information at his club where it is overheard by an informant who tells a spy.

Ray whistled softly when the importance of the message sunk in.

"Ray, do you think something like that is going on here—right now—at the Brunswick shipyard?" Helen asked in a small voice.

"It's a real possibility. If we could just figure out how."

"Means, motive, and opportunity."

"What are you saying, Helen?"

"I'm referring to the need to determine the means, motives, and opportunities for sabotage. Perhaps we should start with motive. If there is a spy or a saboteur, their motivation would be related to delaying the Liberty ships launches."

"That goes without saying," agreed Ray. "His means would involve how they get the information. There would need to be some sort of meeting or communication method that wouldn't draw attention to himself. And his opportunities would be the accidents themselves."

"Do you really think the saboteur has to be a man? Or that he would be working alone? Could it be two people or a group? Could a woman be involved? I thought by now you'd understand that women can do nearly every job a man can do." Annoyed, Helen folded her arms over her chest and glared at Ray. She didn't have to remind him that she never liked it when a man discounted a woman's ability.

"You're right and I did not mean to make a disparaging comment about women in the workforce. I'm trying to solve a mystery here. I'm the one who has been thinking much too narrowly," Ray said, deciding not to mention her earlier dismissal of Winona Bunce.

They walked on, both deep in thought, until they reached the shade of the large live oak tree called Lover's Oak. Ray was the first to speak.

"Seriously, Helen. What if someone of German descent works at the shipyard and is committing acts of sabotage in order to slow ship production?"

"Ray, don't you think we're grasping at straws here? Don't you remember my father talking about how over one-third of the men in the armed forces have German parents, grandparents, or cousins? There are probably thousands of people working at the shipyard who are of German descent. Why pick on ones we can guess German names for?"

Ray pulled a sheet of paper from his pocket. Helen recognized it as the paper she had scribbled on the night before.

"I can't believe you kept that silly list of mine," exclaimed Helen.

"I'll be the judge of whether or not it's silly." Ray studied the piece of paper intently.

His face had a tense, closed look that made Helen fall silent, not wanting to disturb his train of thought. After several minutes in silence, unable to control her curiosity any longer, she asked, "What are you thinking, Ray? What do the dates in the third column mean?"

"They're nothing, just some random dates I jotted down. Helen, nothing makes sense yet. I need a little more information before I can draw any conclusions." Ray could hardly tell Helen that the dates signified when the radio transmitter picked up unidentified signals. He couldn't share such an important secret with her. Despite hearing the signals following the most recent launch, he and Richard had not been able to locate the source of those signals even after sweeping the entire shipyard with a loop antenna. So far, they only knew that the signals lasted about three hours and weakened as the ship moved out to sea for its sea trials.

"What exactly are we looking for? Maybe I can help," suggested Helen, not at all put off by his silence.

"I'm not really sure. An idea is niggling around in my brain but it hasn't really taken form yet. I don't want to say anything until I've sorted it out. Let me think this through. When I tell you, I want your viewpoint to be fresh."

"Tell me, Ray. I can help you," insisted Helen. "We can solve this together."

"There is no 'we' darling," said Ray firmly. "You are not to get involved in this! Now, before we go making accusations, I want to run this by my commander, Admiral Jarabek. In the meantime, let me make sure I have dotted my 'i's' and crossed my 't's. Do *not* under any circumstances tell anyone what we talked about today." Having reached her home, Ray kissed Helen firmly on the mouth and left.

Chapter 56

Helen

*A*fter Ray left, Helen considered the poster's message. The chain of events brought about by the sharing of news from one sweetheart to another could happen so easily. It would be no trouble at all for sensitive information to reach the wrong person. The third vignette in the poster bothered her the most. In it, the father shares troop movement details with members of his club. Surely he spoke only in front of people he trusted. The club setting reminded her of her aunts' parties. Who wouldn't trust other attendees at such a delightful gathering?

Helen turned that thought over and over again in her head. Slowly an idea, a somewhat disturbing idea, began to form in her mind. To work it out, she needed to know who attended the last five of her aunts' parties. Since she hadn't been at all the parties, Helen only knew who attended some of them. Then she realized she didn't need to rely on anyone's memory. After each party the local paper printed a short article about the parties in their '*Heard Around Town*' column. Aunt Ora always cut the articles out and pasted them in her scrap book, along with other interesting news. Despite the distraction of Ray nuzzling her neck and kissing her ear, Helen remembered seeing the articles the other night.

Before thoughts of Ray could side-track her from this mystery, Helen crossed the square to her aunts' house and went in search of Aunt Ora's scrapbooks. Finding them, Helen sequestered herself in the dining room with a pitcher of cool water and a plate of crackers for refreshments. She could hear her aunts tittering happily outside the closed door. They probably thought she was planning something romantic. Not likely, thought Helen as she leafed through page after page of interesting bits and pieces of Aunt Ora's life.

She read the first short article aloud.

"'The Stevens sisters sponsored another successful fundraising party. This time, the monies collected will be used to purchase materials and supplies for the newest Liberty ship under construction at the shipyard. The party was attended by Helen Stevens, Winona Bunce, Hazel Ann Crawford, Dot Carson, Cecil Hudson,...William Browning, George White, ...Cecil Hudson, Alfred Smith, and Hank Stine. Guests played an assortment of challenging games. Dot Carson provided the greatest number of correct answers and won a box of chocolates.'"

On a hunch, Helen listed launch dates in one column, who attended each party in a second column, and in a third the party dates. She circled the parties that preceded launches. In a fourth column, she added the dates of the accidents. When she completed the list, Helen sat silently studying it. She compared the attendees with the launch dates. "I think who came to the parties is important. There is a pattern here," she whispered to herself. "But the pattern doesn't appear to be related to the accidents. What is going on here?"

The same six people consistently attend the parties scheduled right before a launch: Winona Bunce, Cecil Hudson, William Browning, Hank Stine, Alfred Smith, and George White. Helen turned the names over in her mind. Cecil followed Winona everywhere. Cecil knew the dates and times of the launches. Because she wanted to be a maid of honor, Winona always pestered him about the launches. Bunce could be Bunz. But, if Winona knew the launch dates in advance, who would she share the information with and why? Helen studied the other names on the list. William Browning could be Wilhelm Bruening. She didn't know about Stine and Hudson, but George White was Italian. Could he really be Giorgio Bianco? Did it mean anything that the same six attend each time or was she making something out of nothing? Surely, she was grasping at straws.

Helen furrowed her brow. Then she laughed. What was she thinking? Giorgio Bianco? Alfredo Smith? Quiet Alfred Smith a saboteur? Helen wasn't sure George was even Italian and she seriously doubted that he would engage in subversive acts. She knew Alfred came to the parties to see her. And what about the others? What about Ray? Or her family members? Surely she wasn't surrounded by saboteurs.

Instead of continuing that line of thought, Helen pulled out a clean sheet of paper. From memory, she wrote the party dates in the first column and the launch dates are in the second column. Then, Helen created a third column. Though she had seen it for only a few seconds, the information Ray had added in a third column came easily to mind. She didn't know what the dates meant, but she added them anyway. Following this, she put a star by the dates that Winona and the others attended the parties.

Remembering a group of articles in the scrapbook, Helen sucked in her breath. Quickly, she drew a fourth column. Flipping through her aunt's scrapbook, she sought out articles related to U-boats being spotted off the Georgia Coast. She wrote the dates in the fourth column. With a shaking hand, Helen circled the three rows in which all four columns matched. "Oh no," she half-whispered. "The dates of the parties attended by Winona, Cecil, Alfred, William, Harold, and George coincide with the dates Ray had added and align with the launches and submarine sightings."

Silently she stared at the paper, aghast at what the circled information revealed. It couldn't be a coincidence. Not three times in a row. That had to be more than coincidence.

Helen sat silently, holding her breath, her thoughts a jumble of remembered words and events. "Let's see if you can guess this one," she murmured under her breath. Aunt Elva's party book flashed across her mind. Without pausing to think, Helen ran off and soon returned with the book. She sat down and paged through it until she found the riddle games. She read each one, remembering that she had seen a copy of this book at Winona's house. It had writing on the pages related to riddle games. At the time, she remembered thinking that's why Winona always performed so well in the games.

"Let's see if you can guess this one." Winona always said that phrase in front of only one riddle and George White always answered it. Helen tried hard to remember which ones. She read through the riddles. Finally, she pointed to one. "This one. I know she said it in front of this one," she said aloud. "As light as a? The answer is feather, but what does that mean?"

The strangest idea popped into her head. As her uncle would say, it might be fantasy or there may be some truth in it. Helen shivered at the thought. She tried desperately to think it through. She chewed on her thumb thoughtfully. Could it be some sort of code? She thought some more. Yes, it could work. But what was the code? What were they communicating? And who was doing the communicating? To whom and for what purpose?

Helen sat there, unable to believe that one or more of the people who attended her aunts' parties could be involved in sabotage. Surely, her imagination was running wild, spurred on by the poster depicting people sharing important information without realizing the consequences. Helen reminded herself again that she mustn't jump to conclusions. She may not have discovered anything at all. For instance, Winona may have the party planning book simply because she wanted to excel at the games. It suited her personality, wanting to win all the time. And then, she mustn't forget that besides the five other people attended the same parties: Winona, Cecil, Alfred, William, Hank, and George; dozens of other did too, including her Aunt Ora, Aunt Elva, Aunt Ida, Ray and herself.

She felt a tingling in her hands and shook them to clear it. Could something really be going on at her aunts' parties? And if there was, would her aunts get into trouble?

The idea of her beloved aunts getting into trouble disturbed Helen. She would have to be very, very sure of her reasoning before mentioning her suspicions to anyone, even Ray. It could be just a coincidence, Helen thought half-heartedly. It must be! Only her curiosity drove her to investigate further, beginning with determining who else had a copy of the party planning book. She didn't know, but she could find out. Then she remembered her aunts telling her that the man who lives with Mrs. Pickles, George White, had one. Winona Bunce and George White. It was a starting point.

"Hello Mrs. Bunce. How are you today?" Helen smiled brightly at the woman through the screen door. She hoped her nervousness didn't show. She'd never done anything like this in her life. She'd never even *planned* to do anything like this. She had to know. Helen just had to see Winona's party planning book.

"I'm fine, Helen. What brings you here?" the woman asked cautiously.

"I'm looking for Winona, is she around?"

"No dear. She's out with her fancy man, the scheduler. She should be home any minute if you'd like to sit in the parlor and wait for her."

Helen couldn't believe her luck. The last time she visited, the party planning book had been laying out in full view on the coffee table in the parlor.

Once inside, Helen said, "Mrs. Bunce, would you mind fetching me a glass of water? I'm so parched I could just drop." Helen fanned herself with her hanky for emphasis.

"Oh! I'm so sorry! Where are my manners? This heat is fierce and the humidity almost unbearable! You sit right here and I'll be right back."

When Mrs. Bunce had left the room, Helen quickly rifled through the stacks of magazines and books in search of the party planning book. Finally, she located it on an end table underneath several newspapers. Helen tilted her head, listening for sounds of Mrs. Bunce in the kitchen. Judging that she had a little time, Helen flipped open the book. It was just as she remembered. Several riddle games were marked in pencil. She didn't look any further; Mrs. Bunce would be back soon. Silently, Helen slipped the book into the large purse she carried for that purpose. She sat down and arranged herself on the couch. Mrs. Bunce found her patting the perspiration on her face with her handkerchief.

"Are you all right, dear?" inquired Mrs. Bunce with some concern.

"Nothing that a cold glass of water won't cure. Thank you so very much. You're such a dear to take such good care of me," Helen said with more warmth than she felt. She drank the water. The insignificant natural act helped Helen recover from her nervousness. She looked around the room, searching for something to comment on. Finally, she spied a photograph of Mrs. Bunce's son.

"Is that a photo of your son?" asked Helen politely.

"Why, yes, it is. Would you like to see it?"

"That would be nice." Helen studied the photograph, noting that it appeared to have been taken fairly recently. Her heart quickened when she recognized a flag barely visible in the background. With difficulty, Helen continued to exchange small talk until she told Mrs. Bunce that perhaps she should call another time.

At home, up in the room she shared with her sister, Helen pulled Winona's party planning book out of her purse. Before opening it, she took out the chart she had created. Then she added the dates of the accidents and the names of the people connected to them. Concentrating hard, she also wrote down all she could remember about Winona's words and actions during the three riddle games. No, now that she thought about it, there were four riddle games. Winona had attended four parties, arriving very late at the party that followed the cancelled Fourth of July launch. The party coincided with the rescheduled launch on the eleventh of July. Helen paused, realizing what this could potentially mean.

After she satisfied herself that there was nothing else she could remember Helen flipped through the pages of the party guide. She found a bookmark on which someone had written the alphabet with each corresponding number next to it. One for an 'A'. Two for a 'B'. Three for a 'C' and so on. She studied both sides of the marker but couldn't attach any significance to it. Unsure of its purpose, she set it next to her on the bed.

Helen turned to the appropriate chapter containing the riddle games. In the margins, different riddles were marked with circles or stars. At first, nothing made sense. Of course, since Helen hadn't attended one of the parties, she didn't know which of the marked riddles Winona used then. She'd have to ask Ray. Still, that left her with three riddles. Frustrated, Helen took a different tack. She wrote down the riddles that she remembered Winona saying the words "Let's see if you can guess this one." Helen chose these riddles because she remembered that Winona's body language gave extra emphasis to these riddles. She wrote down with the answers. In her mind, Winona's strident voice rang out clearly. "What letter is a sheep? A 'U'. As light as a? A feather. What fish is a royal fish? A king fish."

The bookmark, with its numbered alphabet, flashed in Helen's mind. What was its purpose? Helen studied the launch and accident dates on her chart. "As light at a feather," repeated Helen. Suddenly it all became clear. The first letters of the answer represented dates. A 'U' stood for the twentieth. An 'F' represented the sixth. But that launch didn't happen. Helen remembered how agitated Winona had been at the party on the ninth. Winona had insisted on a riddle game. She didn't calm down until she said "Now everything is all right" after one of the answers. "What fish is a royal fish? A king fish." Winona had had to change that date when the accident had prevented the launch. The 'K' stood for the adjusted launch date of the eleventh. Helen remembered the woman's look of satisfaction, like a cat in the cream. Helen whooped with joy! Winona was telling someone about the launch dates! She must have gotten the information from Cecil Hudson since only he and a small handful of others knew about it more than a few hours beforehand. Now Helen only had to figure out whom and why. For that, she would need Ray's help.

Chapter 57

Ray

*R*eturning to his office, Ray placed a telephone call to Admiral Jarabek.

The man wasn't in, so Ray left a message asking the admiral to meet him later in his office. He knew the admiral and General Dirner would want him to move as quickly as possible since another launch was scheduled soon. But move where? Now that he'd had time to think about it, what did he really have? Nothing substantial, just a list of parties and a word-game involving Germanic pronunciations of Americanized names. Suddenly, Ray was glad the admiral was unavailable. It gave him time to come up with something more concrete.

Ray grimaced. All he needed was for that first piece of the puzzle to fall into place. Unfortunately, he didn't even know if he was dealing with one puzzle or two. On the one hand, there were the accidents, potential acts of sabotage. On the other hand, there were the elusive radio signals he and Richard had yet to track to their source. Ray had no idea whether or not the two were connected.

What did he really know? Walking back toward town, Ray reviewed the events of the past six weeks in his mind and came up the four questionable accidents, one death, three ships emitting untraceable signals, and one delayed launch. Nothing. He knew nothing. Disgusted with his inability to figure out what was going on, Ray kicked at a pine cone on the sidewalk in front of him. It exploded into small shards at the force of his blow. Ray stopped abruptly.

Wait a minute. He did know something important after all. He had a starting point. Someone had inserted marine flares in the conference room ash can. The resulting fire had demolished the Industrial Efficiency office and all of Helen's accident investigation work. Timed to coincide with Helen's presentation of her findings, the fire was definitely not accidental. All Ray had to figure out was who would want to destroy the records, including those in Helen's possession.

Excitement coursed through Ray. His fatigue vanished. Finally, a breakthrough. He walked faster, thinking hard. If he assumed that the fire was meant to eliminate all traces of Helen's work, then the flares could not have been in place very long. Helen had just completed her analysis. Who knew about Helen's quest to determine the causes of the accidents? Who knew about the meeting with Burt and William? Who had Ray seen in and around the Industrial Efficiency offices in the short period of time before the meeting?

It dawned on Ray that the answer to this last question was a short list: Burt Dixon, William Browning, and three others. He remembered seeing Cecil Hudson emerging from Burt's office shortly before the meeting. Fred Norris had been waiting to go in to see Burt. Ray had also seen Alfred Smith loitering in the hallway, presumably hoping to catch a glimpse of Helen. None of them were in the building when the flares ignited. It's not much to go on, but it's a start, thought Ray. I'll go see each of them.

Concocting a feeble excuse about planning another party, Ray visited Cecil Hudson's house. Hudson was the logical starting point because the man was privy to all potential launch dates. He had been in the building at the right time and he knew about Helen's work. Ray wasn't sure what he hoped to find in Cecil's possession, though he would have given anything to locate an open box of marine flares, a shortwave radio, or a primer on sabotage. Ray made awkward conversation while he allowed his eyes to drift around Cecil's tidy rented room. It didn't take him long to determine that Hudson didn't even own a radio nor did he appear very knowledgeable about electronics, marine flares, or industrial accidents. He did, however, wax poetically about the charms of Miss Winona Bunce.

Next Ray visited Alfred Smith. Ray tried to convince himself that Smith's unimaginative last name put him high on the potential saboteur list, but he knew that his real reason for suspicioning the man was because of his interest in Helen. Ray reminded himself that jealousy had no place in this investigation. Ray had no luck at Alfred Smith's either. Smith's radio was a common brand and functioned normally. Smith spent most of the time talking about how wonderful Helen was and thanking Ray for preventing any harm from coming to her. The man was so sincere in his appreciation, Ray felt guilty for ever doubting him.

As Ray walked toward William Browning's house, he reviewed what he had learned so far. Both men had been friendly and welcoming though a little perplexed about the reason for his visit. After requesting a refreshing drink, Ray had had no difficulty seeing and to a certain extent searching each man's one-room living quarters for anything resembling marine flares, sabotage tools, or radio components. While they could keep the transmitter parts locked away out of sight, Ray didn't think either of them was capable of such subterfuge. Innocent people leading innocent lives. If only Ray could bring himself to believe that. Something was going on and he was going to find out what.

Right from the start, Ray met resistance from William when he asked to enter the small house located on a shady square. Using the blazing hot day as an excuse, he all but demanded to be allowed to come inside and get a glass of water. Once inside the house, the atmosphere did not improve. Ray nervously glanced around the room, trying hard not to appear as if he were looking for something. When his eyes came to rest, it wasn't on marine flares, sabotage tools or a radio, it was on Helen's neatly prepared productivity, absenteeism, and turnover charts and graphs spread out on the table. The sight of them stopped him in his tracks. Those documents were supposed to have been destroyed in the fire. William must have carried them away with him when he left the meeting. But why hadn't the man come forward when Burt mourned the loss of such important data?

"Pretty nice set up you have here," said Ray in an attempt to make conversation while his mind raced. Ray made a concerted effort not to look at Helen's papers. "With the housing shortage, it's rare to find someone living alone."

Ray sensed that William stiffened at his presumably innocuous words. Ray wondered how he had unintentionally struck a nerve. When William made no comment, Ray continued his rambling monologue. "As you know, I'm staying with the Stevens sisters, though their other sister visits so often, it's like living with all three women." Ray laughed uncomfortably at his own weak joke. Through the open bedroom door, Ray could see an abundance of clothing hanging in a closet. William merely stared at him without saying anything. Ray cast about for something to say.

"Seeing your suits hanging there reminds me of Helen's aunts, Ora and Ida. Since they're twins, they often wear the same clothes. They look so much alike, sometimes I get them confused. Personally, I think they like being mistaken for each other. I know Ora does. She always enjoys relating what people have said and done when someone has mistaken her for her sister." Ray stepped closer to the bedroom, hoping to take a look around.

Browning moved in front of Ray and abruptly slammed the door to the bedroom shut. Realizing that he had startled Ray, William apologized, though somewhat insincerely. "Excuse me; it is rude of me to have left my bedroom door open when I have guests. My apologies."

"No worries," responded Ray amiably. In his head, alarm bells sounded. No doubt about it, William was on guard. What had Ray seen besides clothes hanging in a closet?

Clothes! The man's neatly organized closet contained lots of clothes! Two identical blue suits, two identical brown suits, two white shirts, and two matching blue shirts. On the floor were two identical pairs of brown shoes. Who had such an abundance of clothes in wartime? Ray looked down at the shiny black shoes on William's feet and took in the neatly pressed trousers and crisp white shirt. He thought of his own pants, worn thin with wear. Envy crept through Ray's veins. He remembered with embarrassment Ora Steven's offer of a pair of Richard's pants when she noticed how threadbare his had become. Ray couldn't imagine owning so much clothing. In England, an adult received twenty clothing ration stamps a year with which to buy all the articles of clothing a person needed: pants, suits, underwear, shirts, socks, overcoats, everything. Unfortunately, when it took twenty-six clothing stamps to purchase one suit, most people went without new clothing. Even in the United States, who, in this time of rationing, had more than one suit, let alone two identical ones? Who had three pairs of leather shoes? And who would purchase two identical suits, shirts, and shoes?

Ideas began to come together in Ray's mind. Who would have identical sets of clothes? Two people who wanted to be mistaken for each other, that's who. Ora and Ida. Blue and Beau. Identical twins. William hadn't recognized Ray the other day at the party. Or maybe, just maybe, he hadn't recognized Ray because he hadn't met him yet. Identical twins. Could it be that William had an identical twin?

Startled by the conclusion he had just drawn, Ray peered intently at William. Or was this really William? Suddenly, Ray wasn't so sure. He looked away and then back again. When his eyes met William's, he saw recognition there. The man's expression morphed into something so wicked that the violence in the man became a tangible thing.

"So, now, Captain Birkett, now you know," the man hissed.

"Yes, now, dear brother Heinrich, now he knows. Now that he knows we are twins, he's putting all the pieces together and it won't take him long to figure out our sabotage plans. Nothing can mar our success, not now, when we have accomplished so much with such small efforts."

Ray whirled around to see the real William standing behind him, pointing the barrel of a German Lugar directly at him.

"So now we must take care of this little problem."

Chapter 58

Helen

*H*elen combed Brunswick for Ray. She sensed he was in danger, but she didn't know why or from whom. She felt as if an invisible hand was driving her on to find him. All Helen knew for certain was that Winona Bunce and George White were up to no good. She felt sure the answer lay in the chart she had created. Somehow the parties, the riddle games, the launches, and the U-boat sightings all tied together. Maybe it hadn't been about sabotage at all. Maybe the accidents were just that—accidents. But what should she do with what she'd learned? She simply had to find Ray. He would know what to do.

Helen was struck by the sudden realization that all she wanted in the entire world was Ray. And now, having tried to ignore her feelings for him, she recognized with unexpected clarity that it was not being able to find him that made her understand how much she never wanted to lose him.

Panic dogged her footsteps. Helen felt as if evil walked beside her. Her heart beat faster and she paused to squelch the nauseating fear that threatened to overwhelm her. Helen could still remember of Ray's long ago speech on heroism, on doing what had to be done. She summoned her courage. Like Ray, she chose to ignore her fear and do what she had to do. She always felt it was best to deal with worry by taking action. Helen swore she would find him if she had to search every inch of Brunswick. She located a telephone and called her Aunt Elva.

"Aunt Elva, has Captain Birkett returned?" Helen asked as calmly as possible.

"No honey. At least not that I've seen. Hang on a minute and I'll ask your Aunt Ida." Elva put her hand over the receiver to muffle her shout. "Ida, have you seen Captain Birkett?"

Despite her increasing anxiety, Helen smiled when she overheard her Aunt Ora in the background.

"Elva, when will you ever learn that your mouth is not a megaphone? And even though you didn't ask me, I haven't seen Captain Birkett."

"Did you hear that, honey? Ora hasn't seen him either. Hang on a minute, Helen," said Aunt Elva. "Ida's coming to the telephone."

"Helen, honey, it's me, your Aunt Ida."

"Aunt Ida, have you seen Captain Birkett recently?" Helen asked with more patience than she felt.

"Why yes, honey, I saw him walking with William toward town less than a half an hour ago."

"No Ida, you couldn't have. Give me the phone," said Ora in the background. Sounds of a minor scuffle ensued. "Helen, I've been standing here by the parlor window and I just saw William walking up toward his house. He couldn't have gone to town and come back that quickly."

Helen bit back a burst of irritation. "Aunt Ora, Aunt Ida. This is important. The man can't do both at the same time. Which is it? Was William walking with Captain Birkett into town or was he going toward his house? Please think."

"But, Helen, honey, it doesn't have to be one or the other," said Ora in her usual unfocused way. "William can do both if he's like us—if he's a twin."

Helen stared at the receiver speechless. She wasn't sure how to react to her Aunt's comment. Twins? William? A twin?

"Aunt Ora, please give the phone back to Aunt Elva. Thank you." Helen heard background movements as the phone passed from one sister to the other.

"Helen, honey, it's me, Elva. What's wrong dear?"

"Aunt Elva, I can't locate Captain Birkett and it is tremendously important that I do. If he returns, please tell him to find me at the shipyard in my temporary office."

Since the fire, the Industrial Efficiency department had moved into the same building that housed Ray's office. Helen went there now in search of Burt Dixon. On her way there, she paused outside of Ray's office and knocked softly.

"Enter."

The deep-voiced command startled Helen. Cautiously, she entered the room. A man in an admiral's uniform sat at Ray's desk. Recognizing Admiral Jarabek, she froze in place unsure of what to do next.

"May I help you?" Admiral Jarabek asked politely.

"Admiral Jarabek, sir. I'm sorry sir. I didn't realize you were in here. I'm Helen Stevens. I'm looking for Captain Birkett."

"How do you do, Miss Stevens? I've been waiting for Captain Birkett too. He asked me to meet him here nearly an hour ago."

"He contacted you? When? Have you seen him?" asked Helen in a rush.

"Slow down a minute there, young lady. Why don't you start again?"

"Admiral Jarabek, I'm not sure where I should begin except to say that Captain Birkett is missing."

"It appears that we both have an interest in finding Captain Birkett." Admiral Jarabek flashed her an unexpected smile that warmed his face and made him human. "Perhaps you better sit down and explain why finding him is so important."

Helen perched nervously on the edge of a chair. In preparation for telling the whole story, she gathered her thoughts together. Her fear for Ray compelled her to share everything with the admiral.

She started to speak, but Admiral Jarabek held up his hand.

"There is someone else who should hear what you have to say," the admiral explained. He made a short telephone call and a moment later Helen's brother entered the room.

"Richard!"

"Hi Sis! Pardon me, Admiral Jarabek, sir!" Richard snapped a salute and stood at attention.

"At ease, Lieutenant. When I heard your last name, Miss Stevens, I wondered if you were related to Lieutenant Stevens." The admiral cleared his throat and looked gravely from one to the other. "Miss Stevens, are you aware that Captain Birkett and your brother are working together on a special assignment?"

"Yes sir—I mean—no sir. What I mean to say is that yes, I knew they worked on some project together, but no, sir, I don't know what they are working on."

"Good. '*Loose Lips Sink Ships*'."

"And '*If You See Something, Say Something.*'"

"Pardon me, Miss Stevens. I don't follow you."

"'If You See Something, Say Something'. It is one of our slogans here at the shipyard, Admiral, sir. And sir, I believe I've seen something."

"Go on."

Helen proceeded to relate to her brother and the admiral what she had seen and learned about the accidents in the past few weeks. Worried sick about Ray's continued absence, she tried to be as succinct as possible.

"So you see, Admiral, the type and destructiveness of the accidents have increased significantly since the launch of the Liberty ship in June. And sir, there is something else, something more important."

"Go on, Miss Stevens."

Helen strove to remain business-like, though her anxiety increased with the retelling of the conversation she and Ray had about name changes. She also showed the admiral her diagram linking accidents, parties, launches, radar soundings, and sub-sightings.

"This is all very unusual, Miss Stevens. I'd like to have Captain Birkett's thoughts on this diagram," said Admiral Jarabek after studying the document. He handed the chart to Richard.

"Yes, sir. That's why I'd like to talk to him too. You see, Captain Birkett told me he was going to see you to discuss an idea he had. Since you weren't available, he may have decided to visit the people we talked about, including Alfred Smith, Hank Stine, Cecil Hudson, and William Browning. Maybe he wanted to see what he could learn. I don't know. He didn't share his thoughts with me. After he left, I considered the message on the poster. That's when I came up with the idea of checking the riddle games in the party planning book."

"Party planning book?"

"Yes sir. Winona Bunce and George White have copies of my Aunt Elva's party planning book."

"Miss Stevens, what you're saying is absolute nonsense. What on earth does a party planning book have to do with espionage? Stop wasting my time." The admiral's face turned red with anger.

Helen was seized by the sensation she might fail to make the admiral understand and that that would be very bad for Ray. She marshalled her thoughts and proceeded carefully.

"I assure you, Admiral, I'm not wasting your time. I wondered what riddles from a party planning book meant too. That's why I wanted to see their copies, or at least Winona's copy of the party planning book." Helen pulled Winona's book out of her oversized bag. She flipped it open to one of the marked pages in preparation for handing it to the admiral.

"Miss Stevens, you are trying my patience," growled Admiral Jarabek.

"I'm sorry if it seems that way, Admiral. Truly I am. But, if you'll only give me a moment more, you'll understand how important this is. I've just now figured it out. Look at this." Helen held the book with its marked pages toward him. "Study the riddle games. If you substitute the first letter in each answer with a letter with the number marking its place in the alphabet, you get a number that corresponds to a launch date."

"Miss Stevens, how do you know which riddle to choose?"

"That's a very valid question, Admiral Jarabek. I studied these particular riddles because Winona Bunce always preceded one riddle in each game with—"

Here Richard took the book from his sister and joined in. "Let's see if you can guess this one. What letter is a sheep?"

"'A 'U',' the twenty-first letter in the alphabet," answered Helen. "That's stands for the launch date of June 21st. Winona could have gotten that information from the scheduler, Cecil Hudson. He's quite keen on her and she's always asking him about being a maid of honor for a launch. I just thought of something else. George White always answered the riddles that Winona started with 'Let's see if you can guess this one.' He also has a party planning book. I haven't had time to check the others."

"Winona Bunce and George White," whistled Richard. "White is always trying to get cozy with Winona."

"You are telling me that these people, Bunce and White, communicated launch dates to each other using riddles?" the admiral asked incredulously.

"Yes sir."

"And that they only needed one riddle for each launch?"

"Yes sir. They would only need the day, not the month, because they are only interested in the next launch, not the ones months in the future. They don't need a time either, since the ships are always launched at high tide."

"How could anyone know which riddle game would be played?" asked Admiral Jarabek.

"They wouldn't have to know. The riddle games are written on small slips of paper. Winona always draws one from a big old top hat. It would be easy for her to palm a slip with the riddle game she wanted to play," explained Helen. "Admiral, please take a look at the chart that I created. It shows the correlation between launches, parties, U-boat sightings, accidents, and attendees."

"It also shows the dates we heard radio signals," asked Admiral Jarabek. "Where did you get those dates, Miss Stevens? They are classified information."

Helen felt the heat rising in her cheeks. "I happened to see the list of the dates in Captain Birkett's hand."

"What! Captain Birkett shared confidential information with you?" roared the admiral. "He told you those dates signified the reception of radio signals?"

"No, sir, you did. Just now," protested Helen. "Captain Birkett didn't mean for me to see the dates. He didn't realize I could see over his shoulder. I only saw them for a second and he never told me what they represented. I added them to this chart only because I knew the dates were important to Captain Birkett. I noticed right away that they coincided with the U-boat sightings reported in the paper."

"My sister has a photographic memory. She'd only have to see the list for a second," explained Richard. "Actually, sir, it's a good thing Helen did. Look at her chart, the dates gives credence to her conclusions."

"That may be true," said Admiral Jarabek, only slightly mollified. However, recognizing that it was he who let the cat out of the bag, he moved on with no further admonishment. "So these people sent coded messages to each other about launch dates in order to set up sabotage?"

"No. That's the thing. If you study the chart, the dates of the accidents don't affect the timing of any of the launches except the one on July seventh. That launch had to be rescheduled when Ben McNeely, the rigger, fell to his death. Winona was very nervous at the next party until we played the riddle game. But if sabotage isn't the goal, none of this makes any sense," Helen said almost to herself. "Saboteurs would want to delay the launches." She paused, lost in thought. Picking up her chart, she pointed at the fourth column. "Admiral Jarabek, are the newspaper articles true? Was a U-boat spotted in the area during each Liberty ship's sea trials?"

Admiral Jarabek cleared his throat and took a sip of water. To Helen, he appeared very reluctant to answer those questions, which in a way, was answer enough. He dodged the questions by asking some of his own.

"What about this column, the one with accidents? Are you talking about sabotage or radio transmissions?"

"Admiral Jarabek, I think we're talking about both," answered Helen. "What I mean is, sir, could it be that we are dealing with two different groups with two different goals?"

Again, Admiral Jarabek said nothing. When he didn't answer, Helen suddenly sat very still. She felt a flash of fear at the thought that had popped into her mind. Her brother, Richard, was assigned to the radar training school and he was here with Admiral Jarabek right now. Flashes of memories skittered through Helen's mind. What if it wasn't about sabotage at all? What if it was about something far more evil? "If spies communicating with a U-boat knew the date of a launch several days in advance, they would want it to occur on schedule. They would also want the ship to emit a radar signal that the submarine could track. Richard, what would a radio signal transmitter look like?" Helen asked in a very small voice.

The admiral looked on, clearly perplexed and annoyed. Impatiently, he signaled for Richard to answer her.

"It would resemble a small black box about the size of a loaf of bread." Richard moved his hands in the air to demonstrate the size.

"Richard, the night the rigger fell to his death, I looked up the mast of the Liberty ship and saw a black box just like that on the main mast. When I looked up again, after George White climbed the mast, it wasn't there."

"You did? Why didn't you say anything, Miss Stevens?" asked Admiral Jarabek.

"At the time, I didn't know it was important. I only just thought of it. In the wake of Ben McNeely's death, it didn't seem to matter. Richard, could it have been a radio signal device?"

"It could have been. But we've swept every Liberty ship since the launch in May and have never turned up a signal."

"But what if it was put on after your sweeps but before the launch?" Helen asked breathlessly. "Admiral Jarabek, Richard, George White is a rigger. He has a copy of the party planning book and he's written in it. He climbed the mast the night of Ben McNeely's death."

"What are you saying, Miss Stevens?" asked Admiral Jarabek.

"Sir, according to these dates, the radar operators first picked up signals during the May launch. After that, you sent teams to sweep every Liberty ship launch. The sweep was interrupted by the death of Ben McNeely. When I investigated the accident, I learned three key things. One, due to wear, the harness Ben McNeely used was one that had been marked for disposal. Two, the rigger at the scene at the time of Ben's fall was George White. I spoke with him as he prepared to go up the mast on an unspecified job. Three, I saw a black box on the mast but it wasn't there after George White climbed the mast. I didn't think anything of it at the time. But what if Ben saw the box and knew it wasn't supposed to be there? What if he told White about it? What if he insisted on climbing up to take a look even though George White tried to stop him? Would he have been killed him to prevent him from finding it?"

"Miss Stevens, are you suggesting murder?" asked the admiral gravely.

"Surely it was just another accident," protested Richard.

"Was it an accident? Or did George White intentionally give Ben McNeely a faulty harness?" asked Helen.

"Maybe White didn't mean to give him an old harness," Richard protested again, unwilling to consider the possibility of murder.

"Richard, the harnesses designated for replacement are marked with orange tape. Someone removed all but a small part of that tape," countered Helen.

"Maybe there wasn't another harness around. Using an old harness would make George careless but not a murderer," countered Richard.

"Ben could have used White's harness. He was wearing one when I saw him."

Richard was having a hard time digesting the idea that an acquaintance would be a murderer. "To be a serious suspect, George would need motive, means, and opportunity."

"He had all three." Helen ticked them off on her fingers. "His motive: prevent the black box from being discovered and reported. His means: a faulty safety harness. His opportunity: alone on deck at night. It may not have been the most convenient set up, after all, he couldn't count on the harness failing, but it worked."

"But he would have known the launch would be delayed. He would have known Ben's death would have disrupted their plans," said Richard.

"Perhaps he chose what to him was the lesser of two evils," muttered the admiral.

"Admiral Jarabek, Ben McNeely's death delayed the launch. Winona Bunce insisted on playing the riddle game at my aunts' next party even though there weren't any games planned for that day. She was extremely nervous until she said—"

"'Let's see if you can guess this one. What fish is a royal fish? Yes, a king fish. Now everything is all right,'" furnished Richard.

"Winona gave George the new launch date so that he could reset the transmitter box."

Someone rapped at the door.

"Come in," said the admiral, shaking his head over what he had learned.

"Admiral, sir. Civil defense warden Emmitt Mutterspaw and the Stevens sisters are at the main gate demanding to be let in. With their hunting dogs, sir." The young sergeant looked like he didn't know whether or not to be annoyed or amused by this last statement.

Chapter 59

Ray

 $\mathcal{R}$ ay lifted his aching head and took stock of his surroundings. Heinrich had dealt him quite a blow on the head once they entered the small room that he and Richard had discovered during their sweep of the Liberty ship. Ray didn't know how long he'd been unconscious. The heat was oppressive causing him to wipe his face on his shoulder. In the dim light filtering through a vent in the door, he could make out the outline of a stack of life preservers. He spied his cane lying near them. Angrily, Ray tugged at the bindings holding his arms behind him.

Twins! Heinrich and Wilhelm Bruening were twin brothers. That's why Heinrich didn't recognize him when he saw him at the party. He hadn't met Ray, his brother, Wilhelm, had. Even when confronted with William's closet, the idea of twin brothers had not crossed Ray's mind until it was too late. If it had, William wouldn't have been able to get the drop on him. They anglicized their name when they came to the United States during the 1930s. Once war broke out, they hired on at the shipyard and made their sabotage plans. As twins, they provided each other convenient alibis by being able to be two places at once.

Helen had discovered their intentions when she created her charts and graphs. Like she said, it wasn't the individual acts of sabotage; it was how they added up to affect the productivity in the shipyard. The saboteurs hoped to taint the shipyard's reputation by making the workers feel unsafe. As a result, the shipyard would never be able to build a ship in sixty days or less. If performance got bad enough, it was possible that the yard would be closed. Small actions could lead to a large loss. No wonder William tried to undermine all her investigations. Ray had even said as much the day of the fire. Helen had asked why someone would want to burn their office down and destroy all the records. Until he saw Helen's reports at William's house, Ray had forgotten his answer: "I think someone meant to destroy the office— and you along with it." The importance of his comment had completely slipped his mind, wiped away by his concern for Helen's safety. At least he had made sure that she had stayed home and away from harm.

Ray recognized now that he had handled the entire situation very badly. He cursed his inability to see beyond the concrete evidence in front of him and give thought to how sabotage would affect the big picture. In an effort to determine if inappropriate activities had been taking place, he had been focused on the acts themselves, not on the perpetrators or their end goals. It served him right that he was tied up in the bowels of a Liberty ship hoping to be rescued. Having learned of his assignment to uncover sabotage, the twins must have been watching his movements for some time now, thus the feeling of being followed.

Another thing that amazed Ray was their walk through town. Normally, when he covered the few blocks between his home and the shipyard, Ray would run into several, if not a dozen, people he knew. Today, as Heinrich frog-marched him to the shipyard, not one single acquaintance walked by Ray. Once in the shipyard, no one noticed anything amiss. Of course, Heinrich had his gun hidden in his pocket, but still, Ray knew he looked anything but comfortable.

So here he was, in the small, nearly unnoticeable room deep in the bowels of a Liberty ship, hoping to be rescued before he died of thirst. Surely, a routine inspection of the ship before launch would reveal his hiding place. By that time, though, William and Heinrich would be well on their way to utilizing their destructive skills elsewhere. At least Brunswick ships would be safe. Or would they?

Ray sniffed the air. Though it was barely perceptible, Ray could smell smoke. Fire. Somewhere nearby there was a fire. He stared again at the stack of life preservers, remembering Richard's comment about how the milk-pods used to make life preservers burned easily. Then his eye caught something far more terrifying: an open crate of magnesium marine flares. Next to it sat a package of high explosives. If even one tiny spark were to ignite the magnesium flares, the resulting explosion would be apocalyptic. Given the proximity of the fuel aboard the ship, ensuing explosions would damage the other nearby Liberty ships. This particular ship was sandwiched between two on one side and three on the other. The Browning brothers weren't planning on anyone finding him. Instead, they planned one final horrendous act of sabotage.

Ray spied the source of the flame—a long, slow-burning fuse—long enough to allow Heinrich to get far away from the ship before it exploded. Terror gripped him. He knew what fire could do to a person. He'd seen his comrades jumping into the sea with their clothes aflame. Ray would never forget the smell, the screams, and the fear. The memories made him dizzy. Though seated, he felt the deck tilting and spinning beneath him. He drew a ragged breath and willed himself to be calm. Futilely, he tugged at the ropes that bound him. Heinrich had done a good job securing him to the pipes that ran along the wall. He slid down as far as he could and with his feet took ahold of his cane. Ray pulled it toward him.

After a good deal of twisting and turning, Ray was able to grasp it with his hands. He rotated around as best he could and used the cane to bang against the wall of the room. The clanging reverberated up his arm, bringing no one but causing his head to ache all the more. At the same time Ray shouted for help at the top of his lungs. Richard had been right; this room was truly isolated from the rest of the ship.

Ray paused for a breath and coughed. Smoke from the fire thickened as it reached the life preservers and set them on fire. His time on earth had decreased to minutes. Faintly in the distance, he could hear the sound of hounds baying echoing off the metal sides of the ship. Ray shook his head but the baying continued. Gingerly he touched his temple. The blow to his head must have been harder than he thought.

"Ray?"

"Captain Birkett?"

Voices shouted his name—voices that had no business being on a
Liberty ship. Ray coughed again as smoke filled his lungs. This was it.
Choked with smoke, his mind was no longer his own. He could hear
Beau and Blue baying. He could hear Helen's aunts calling his name. He
could feel Helen shaking him by the collar.

Chapter 60

Helen

"*7*hank heavens we got to you in time," exclaimed Helen as they sat together on the veranda that evening. "Thank heavens my aunts decided to look for you after I phoned them! Using Beau and Blue to track your movements through town and onto the ship was positively brilliant. Without them, we might never have found you. You would have loved seeing Admiral Jarabek's face when the sergeant told him the Stevens sisters were at the gate—with their hunting dogs! It's a good thing they brought Emmitt Mutterspaw along to vouch for them."

"I've always said your aunts are a force of nature." Ray pushed the swing lightly back and forth with his foot. He rested his arm around Helen's shoulders and she leaned into him. In the background, he could hear the radio playing "*A Nightingale Sang in Berkeley Square.*"

"Ray, I am so surprised they decided to look for you. Oh, I know I phoned them and asked about you, but I thought they'd wait there for you. Instead they rounded up a posse and set out to look for you. Apparently, Aunt Ida didn't like the way you looked when you walked by with William. She said you looked remarkably uncomfortable with someone who was supposed to be your friend. Funny that they figured out the twin thing long before we did. All along, I thought William was just acting strange when he wore the wrong color hard hat or seemed to forget our heated discussion. But I never thought of twins."

"I'm very glad you all came searching for me. Wilhelm and Heinrich's plan to set off explosives by setting the Liberty ship on fire could have resulted in the loss or damage of all the Liberty ships under construction. Detonating an explosion so close to the fuel storage area would have been catastrophic. It might have even destroyed the shipyard."

For a few minutes they held each other in silence, lost in their own thoughts.

"Funny how I found the saboteurs and you figured out the radar signals," said Ray.

"We solved each other's puzzles, didn't we?" asked Helen. "Wilhelm, Heinrich, Giorgio, Winola. Ray, why did they do it? Why did William and his twin cause accidents in the shipyard? And why did Winona provide George with information about Liberty ship launches? Why did George signal the dates to waiting German submarines?"

"Helen, it's hard to understand why Wilhelm, Heinrich, and Winola aligned their allegiance with Germany, or why George chose to help the Axis powers. Other American citizens of German or Italian descent have not. I guess people can choose who they are and what they believe. They can choose to be a hero or a coward or a villain. Wilhelm, Heinrich, Winola, and Giorgio all chose to be villains, at least from our point of view they did."

"But why?"

"Helen, darling, I really don't know. Perhaps they felt torn between the home of their forefathers and their adopted land. Maybe they had a grudge against the U.S. government. Either way, losing their moral compass probably started by degrees not with one momentous event. I imagine that for Wilhelm and Heinrich, the acts of sabotage all started small. They probably began by cutting corners and rationalizing their small misdeeds. One small step leads to another and soon they were making excuses for bigger and bigger accidents. What amazes me is that you figured out that what they wanted to do was decrease productivity to the point that the shipyard closed and not draw attention to themselves with major acts of sabotage. It's a very subtle but effective plan, one that allowed them to go virtually unnoticed. Being twins, they consistently provided alibis for each other."

"Thank heavens we were able to figure it all out."

"Until you showed up with those charts, they probably didn't even realize we were aware that something was going on," agreed Ray.

"I'll never understand how they could have hurt innocent people," said Helen.

"I'm sure the money they received from the German government helped lessen their guilt over hurting people they worked with at the shipyard. The sight of all that gold we found under the floorboards in their house would be enough to turn anyone's head." Ray shook his head sadly.

"But you would never allow money to cheapen or dishonor your life."

"Nor would you or any member of your family. We've been able to stay true to our own beliefs. But it's not always easy to put your baser emotions aside. Think about how you felt when you were afraid. How hard was it to put your fear aside to get the work done?"

"You're right, it was hard. But fear is different than greed."

"Is it? Think about it from their point of view. Winona, George, William, and Heinrich are all immigrants. Winola Bunz, Giorgio Bianco, Wilhelm and Heinrich Bruening. Despite their anglicized names, they have strong feelings for their homeland. Those ties were strengthened by having brothers and other family members still in Germany and Italy. Remember, Winona told us her brother is being held in a labor camp. The Germans promised to release him if she cooperated."

"Yes, I remember seeing the Nazi flag behind Winona's brother in the photograph. That's when things really came together for me."

"Giorgio Bianco's family is also being terrorized by the Italian government. Given the difficult position they were placed in, to them their acts of sabotage probably seemed justified."

"I don't know if I will ever agree with that. Oh! Look at the time!" declared Helen. "You need to rest and I have something I need to tell my Momma. Ray, you rest awhile and I'll see you this evening." Helen gave Ray a quick kiss before heading across Hinshaw Square to her own home.

"Marry him!" cried her mother. "You just met him!"

"I love him," Helen responded simply. "I'm going to marry him."

"What do you know about Captain Birkett? What could you have possibly learned in such a short period of time?"

"I know enough. I've known him long enough to know." Not one to be intimidated, Helen straightened her spine and prepared for further battle with her mother.

Seeing her resolve, Helen's mother tried another tack.

"No daughter of mine is going off to England in the middle of a war! Helen, I can't stand the thought of you living so far away from home. You've not even twenty! Fortunately, you won't be able to get to England." Firm in her belief that Helen's plans would be thwarted by the enormity of the Atlantic Ocean, Helen's mother crossed her arms in front of her chest smugly. Therefore, she was unprepared for her daughter's next statement.

"I've already been in contact with the War office in Washington D.C. If I am accepted in the WAVES, I'll ship overseas to England in just a few months. Ray and I can be married here and I'll follow him after basic training."

"No!" shouted her mother suddenly, almost violently. She took a deep breath and then continued, her voice almost pleading. "I won't let you leave Brunswick! I won't let you go to London to be bombed. I won't lose you the same way I lost my two best friends. They died in Zeppelin raids during the Great War. It was all so senseless! I miss them every day of my life. There isn't anything I can do to protect Richard, but at least I can keep you safe from harm. You're staying here! Helen—don't you understand how much I love you?" Enid Stevens began to cry.

Startled by her mother's admission, Helen took a moment to absorb what she had said.

Her mother took a deep breath. "Helen, I understand that you love Ray, really I do. When your Aunt Ida lost her beau, I watched her grieve beyond all consolation. I swore I would never love anyone that much. Then your father returned from Europe and swept me of my feet. Yes, just like Ray did you. Marry Ray if you must. Work at the shipyard if you want. But stay here where you are safe. Ray would want you to be safe. Ask him."

"Helen!" called her Aunt Elva from the front porch. "Helen, you've got to get down to the train station quickly. Captain Birkett is being shipped out on the next train! They came a few minutes ago in a car and didn't even give him time to pack!"

Chapter 61

Ray

*O*n the crowded trackside, Helen launched herself into Ray's awaiting arms. He held her tight, realizing that he loved everything about her: her independent spirit, her intelligence, her unflappable and serenely calm demeanor. How could he leave her behind?

"Thank God they found you in time." Ray cupped her face in his hands and kissed her.

Helen began to cry. "Ray, I don't want you to go!"

"Helen, darling, I must go. I've got my orders." Ray crushed her in his arms, not wanting to lose what he had so recently won. An ache formed in his heart making it difficult for him to breathe. He kissed her again. When they broke apart, he said, "I've got to go, don't you see that?"

"I know! I know and I hate it!" She covered his mouth with her hand. "Please, don't give me that 'a man's got to do what a man's got to do' speech!" Helen cried, tears welling alarmingly in her vivid brown eyes. "I don't want you to go off to war and not come back!"

"I'll be back, you'll see."

"Will you Ray? Will you? I don't want you to become a gold star in someone's window back home."

"I'll be back. Helen, wait for me. Please."

"Oh, Ray!" Helen wrapped her arms around him tightly. "Hold me like you'll never let me go!"

"Darling, I'm sorry that there isn't time for us to be married in South Carolina like we hoped. I'm so sorry Helen. We may be apart for a long, long time. Stay here, Helen. Stay here where you are safe. Let me leave knowing you're safe," Ray said fervently. He kissed the tears on her face. "You won't forget me, will you?"

"Forget you, Ray? I'll remember everything about you. Your blue eyes. Your broad shoulders. The shape of your face." Helen stroked his chin.

"The curve of your lips when you smile." Ray touched her lips with his.

"The way your eyes twinkle when you tease me." She traced his laugh lines with her fingertips.

"What a wondrous feeling it is to kiss you." And he did.

"How your hands feel when you hold me. Ray, I'll love you forever! Please believe that." Helen faltered, her eyes pleading for reassurance. "Ray, please come back to me."

"Helen, I promise I will. My heart is and always will be yours. Take good care of it."

"I will Ray, I will. I love you." Helen pressed half of their postcard, the portion with her name on it, into his hand. "Here, take this with you. It will remind you of me." She tried to smile.

"Darling, I'll whisper your name in my dreams," Ray said into her hair. The train blew its whistle. "Hush. Don't cry. I love you." He held her tight against his chest. "Now kiss me and smile for me. Let me remember you with a smile on your face."

"Ray, I'll wait for you. I love you," Helen said with a watery smile. No longer crying, despite her smile, her eyes were pools of sadness.

Chapter 62

Helen

Spring 1948

"*H*oney, Ray left nearly five years ago. It's been three years since you've received a letter from him. As much as you love him, you must realize that he's not coming back. You worked for the military office of Status, Review, and Determination long enough to know that if Ray were alive, we'd know by now." Tenderly, her mother enfolded Helen in her arms.

"But, Momma, I still love him." Helen's eyes glittered with unshed tears.

"I know you do, but it's time to let go."

Time. Time moved forward slowly and painfully, dragging Helen along with it. Over the years, she had learned just how empty a person could be and still live. Numbly, she carried on, reminding herself each day that Ray would not be coming back. But some wounds never heal, never would heal. Ray was like one of life's scars that ached at unexpected times.

"Helen, honey, the war is over, it's time you moved on," continued her mother. "Oh, I know you went back and finished your Industrial Management degree after working in the Department of Status, Review, and Determination. I know that since then you have been building your career. What I mean is that you've got to move on with your love life.

Ray's not coming back and you're a warm woman who needs to be loved."

"Momma, I try, really I do. I've learned to force a smile when I need to and sometimes I'm all right for a while. But, the truth is, it seems like only yesterday that I danced with Ray." Helen looked over her mother's shoulder and down the wide street. How she longed to hold him tight just one more time. "If I could only see him now."

"Ray's gone, honey. It's a simple as that. It's not like you to stay mired in the mud like this. Where is my little girl with all her get up and go? I never told you this, though you tasked my patience, I admired you for it. Honey, you've got to move on. Alfred is the one you're marrying this weekend. Alfred is a good man. He loves you. He could make you happy if you'd let him. You've said that yourself. Helen—are you listening?" Her mother touched Helen's shoulder gently. "Alfred's been waiting five years for you to say 'I do.' So why don't you?"

"I can't marry Alfred! I thought I could! I know I said I would, but I just can't let go, Momma. I miss Ray every hour of every day. I always have and I always will. I refuse to believe he's gone. I'd know it if he was. I'd know it deep inside myself. Ray promised he would come back and he will. Oh, why didn't I marry Ray when I had the chance? Why is it that by the time you recognize that you're happy and in love, it's too late? Momma, I'm just trying to hang onto hope."

"Oh, honey, you mustn't keep hoping beyond all hope, believing beyond all believing. You don't want to be like your Aunt Ida, grieving her whole life. I don't want my little girl to live like that. That's why I never encouraged you and Captain Birkett. I never wanted you to hurt like this. I know how hard it is, but it's time."

"Momma, don't you understand? In my heart, Ray is always there. I try to let him go, but he occupies a space inside me, deep in my memory. Thoughts of him surface over and over again. It's as if he went away and took my heart with him."

Helen looked past her mother, tears in her eyes. Would anyone ever understand how she felt? Sometimes at dawn, she would hover on the edge of sleep only to have an unbearable wave of sorrow and unshed tears wash over her and remind her of her loss.

Over her mother's shoulder, Helen continued to stare down the street, searching for the man she longed to see again.

Chapter 63

Ray

*R*ay stepped off the train and into the steamy salt air of Brunswick.

Taking a deep breath, he realized he had never forgotten what the air felt like in the Golden Isles. Not even his months of deprivation in the Russian prison camp, his painful recuperation in the hospital, or his stay in England had erased it from his senses. He clutched the worn half of their postcard like a talisman. Somehow he had managed to hang on to it after all he'd been through. Both of them had been battered by their experience. He rubbed it between his thumb and forefinger hoping to wipe out the doubts that plagued him. Would Helen remember him? And after seeing how the years had taken their toll on him, would she even want him?

During the dark times of the past few years when he lost all hope of surviving, Helen occupied a shining space in his memory. Night after lonesome night, in his mind, he'd turn back the hands of time and—just for a moment—pretend she was still his. He'd remember all the little details about her. Sometimes it was all that he had to get him through the days. He had traveled so far and seen so much. Now, after crossing the Atlantic on a refurbished Liberty ship, all he wanted to do was return to where his brightest and happiest memories remained.

Leaving the train station, leaning heavily on his cane, Ray limped slowly toward Hinshaw Square. Downtown Brunswick hadn't changed much structurally, but where were the crowds of people he'd grown to expect? What had once been a bustling, almost hyperactive round-the-clock ship-building city had returned to a sleepy Southern town. He smiled at a dog napping in the shade of a live oak tree. Would Beau and Blue remember him?

After his abrupt departure from Brunswick, he and Helen had exchanged a steady stream of letters, sometimes several each day. Naturally those had stopped with his capture by the Germans when his plane had crashed during a routine flying mission to photograph ships in enemy ports. After a few months in a German POW camp, he and his crew mates had been traded to the Russians. In the endless, disorganized days leading up to and past the end of the war, he and countless others had been overlooked. Much later, while in a hospital recuperating from his ordeal, he had thought about writing her again. Then, he'd look at his injuries and weakened body and decide a vital young woman like Helen didn't need a broken man. So he never wrote as much as a postcard.

Deciding not to contact Helen was the most difficult decision Ray had ever made, one he had regretted for the past few years. He tried to convince himself that perhaps, after all this time, Helen had found another man to make her happy. The thought of Helen with another man made Ray desperately unhappy.

And then, the letter had arrived from Brunswick. How it had found him, he would never know. Based on the postmarks and hand-written forwarding notices, many people had been involved in the effort. Written by the Stevens sisters in the same convoluted manner that they conducted their conversations, it urged him to return to Brunswick as quickly as possible. As quickly as possible—the original postmark was two months old.

On the trip across the Atlantic, to calm himself, he reminded himself of the words she spoke with such conviction at their last meeting: "I will wait for you." His heart continued to tell him that Helen was the one for him, would hers? He had come to find out. He had to know. Resolutely, Ray continued down the Newcastle Street toward her house.

As he neared Hinshaw square, he spotted a young woman in a wedding dress sitting on park bench under the live oak tree named the Lover's Oak. Though he was still at a great distance, there was something achingly familiar in the set of her shoulders and the tilt of her head. Of its own volition, Ray's heart fluttered. He shook his head to dispel his foolish notions. What would Helen be doing in a wedding dress sitting under the live oak tree?

Their eyes met. The woman stared at him, perplexed. Then her face cleared. A warm feeling of relief and joy flooded Ray's body as every fiber of his being recognized Helen. As it had at their first meeting, the sight of her filled Ray with light and hope. He increased his pace, moving toward her as she rose to her feet, gently smoothed the folds of her wedding gown, straightened her shoulders and shook herself like a person awakening from a deep sleep. When her face blossomed into a dazzling smile, all of Ray's doubts disappeared. Reaching her, he swept her into his loving arms.

Epilogue

"I did not come here to tell you 'our merchant marine won the war'—but I will venture the statement that without these ships, the Allies would have lost the war."

Vice Admiral Emory S. Land
Chairman U.S. Maritime Commission
Administrator, War Shipping Administration

During the two years and two days that the shipyard operated, Brunswick's J.A. Jones Construction Company built ninety-nine war supply vessels (85 Liberty ships and 14 smaller vessels) at an average of four per month. All six Liberty ships begun in 1942 were completed in 1943. The first Liberty ship, the James M. Wayne, took 305 days from laying the keel to delivery. The next five ships took 314 days, 320 days, 320 days, 325 days, and 331 days respectively. By early 1943, process improvements had cut that time in half. By the end of 1943, further improvements enabled ships to be built and launched in as little as 51 days. In 1943, twenty-one Liberty ships were built. Throughout 1944, creation of Liberty ships increased dramatically while production rates hovered between 50 and 60 days. Despite a hurricane, in 1944, forty-eight ships were completed. December of 1944 included the record-breaking achievement of producing seven ships in one month. Production continued through the first eight months of 1945, with the construction of twenty-four ships.

The Battle of the Atlantic and the merchant ships that risked the crossings allowed the Allies to supply Britain and Russia. During the war convoys were regularly attacked by German submarines. In the end, approximately 3,500 merchant ships and 175 warships were sunk.

In 1990, the City of Jacksonville, Florida presented U-boat Captain Hardegen with a medal for maneuvering his U-boat between the shore and the damaged tanker. Doing so ensured that the shells he fired to sink the stricken vessel would not over-shoot the tanker and hit the people watching from the beach. Captain Hardegen, while commander of U-123, sank six U.S. vessels off the Southern coast causing the loss of lives of hundreds of U.S. sailors.

In addition to extensive interviews with people who lived during and remember World War II, information and inspiration for this book comes from the following excellent books: *Brunswick: The City by the Sea* by Patricia Barefoot; *St. Simons Island* by Patricia Morris; *Brunswick: A Book of Memories*; *The Marshes of Glynn* by Thora Kimsey and Sonja Kinard; *Operation Drumbeat* by Michael Gannon; and *On the Swing Shift* by Tony Cope.

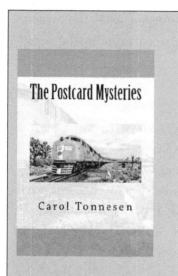

The Postcard Mysteries

By Carol Tonnesen

www.postcardmysteries.com

carol.tonnesen@postcardmysteries.com

Hard Cover

$9.99

eBook

$2.99-$4.99

Availability and Reviews

Would you like to try new mystery series?

The Postcard Mysteries satisfy a reader's craving for mysteries that mix romance and mystery with places and history. In each Postcard Mystery, postcards serve as a catalyst that catapults ordinary people into adventures that change their lives. Written to appeal to people who believe a person can change their life, these books feature strong men and women who throw caution to the wind in order to try something different, opening themselves up to mystery, adventure, and finally, love.

The Red Bus: A Postcard to an Assassin. Two strangers, linked only by a postcard, race across Europe on the Orient Express trying to prevent an assassination.

The Fishing Bridge: A Postcard to a Traitor. British agent Charles Littleton is a man longing to be a cowboy. Trudy Thompson is a nurse drawn into the dangerous world of secrets by a postcard. Only Bandit, a talented Border collie, has all the answers.

The Highlands: A Postcard to Deception. Set against a backdrop of Scotland's Sheep Dog Trials, veterinarian, Iain Fraser copes with deceptions and murder that threaten to destroy his veterinary practice. Can Aylee Duncan and her unexpected Border collie respond to a postcard in time to help him?

Rumrunner's Reef: A Postcard to a Smuggler. The sight of a nearly naked man emerging from the waters of Florida Bay provides an interesting start to Lizette's vacation. But, are the Florida Keys really different from Chicago, speak-easies, and gangsters?

The Golden Isles:

A Postcard to Fear

Book Club Questions

1. What would you do if you experienced the uncertainty of something out of your control?
2. Which character did you like the most? Why?
3. Does Ray make a believable hero?
4. Does Helen make a believable heroine?
5. Were you able to understand why the characters reacted the way that they did to their predicaments (for instance Helen's mother or her aunts)? Would you have done the same?
6. Can you identify with how Helen feels about her life?
7. How would you have reacted if you, like Helen, faced major life changing events beyond your control?
8. Did you take the characters in the book at face value?
9. Do you believe in love? The kind of love that lasts forever?
10. Did the narrative in the book bring up information about the past that was new to you? What?
11. Would you like to meet any of the characters? Which ones?
12. Can people really step out of the mold society creates for them?

Made in the USA
Monee, IL
28 April 2022

94871692R00187